The Undertaker's Daughter

About the Author

Jamaican-born Yvonne Brewster came to England to study drama. During a long and distinguished career, she has worked in films, television and radio, drama schools and universities nationally and internationally as director, lecturer and actor. She founded two theatre companies, The Barn in Jamaica, and Talawa in England. A patron of Rose Bruford College, she has received the USA National Black Theater Festival Living Legend Award, is a Licientiate of the Royal College of Music and a Fellow of the Royal Society of Arts. In 1993 she received the OBE for services to the arts and in 2001 an honorary doctorate from the Open University.

The Undertaker's Daughter

Yvonne Brewster

BLACKAMBER BOOKS

Published in 2004 by BlackAmber Books Limited
3 Queen Square
London WC1N 3AU
www.blackamber.com

First published 2004

1 3 5 7 9 10 8 6 4 2

Typeset 12 on 13pt Horley Old Style by
RefineCatch Limited, Bungay, Suffolk

Printed by WS Bookwell, Finland

ISBN 1–901969–24–X

Acknowledgements

I would like to thank Starr for keeping his humour throughout the process of my writing this book, Michael Abbensetts and Trevor Rhone for knowing it could be done, Joan Deitch, my editor, without whose inspired insight it would have been impossible, Greta Mendez, who was interested, Lisa and Sheldon Decklebaum in whose spectacular home I was allowed to roam free to finish *The Undertaker's Daughter*. Much love to you all.

TO
KATHLEEN VANESSA

Dear Reader

The narrator of this tale is a ninety-year-old Jamaican undertaker. She begins with an account of her early life and gradually intertwines her tale with Yvonne, her eldest daughter's, life journey. The book opens as her ninetieth birthday approaches, and with it the arrival of Yvonne from London. The old lady, matriarch of the family clan, is being threatened with a party to celebrate, as she puts it, her 'descent into uselessness'.

Her recent motto is George Eliot's quip, 'You are never too old to be what you might have been.'

Yvonne Brewster

The Family Shrub

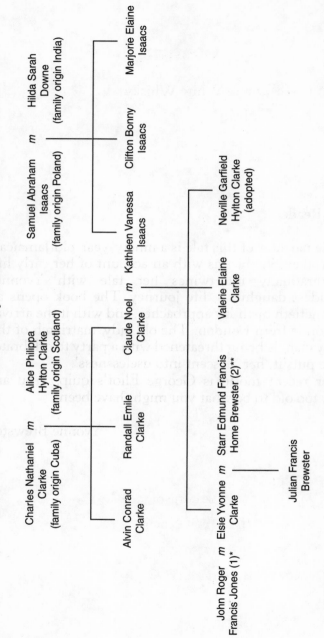

Charles Nathaniel Clarke *m* Alice Philippa Hylton Clarke
(family origin Cuba) (family origin Scotland)

Samuel Abraham Isaacs *m* Hilda Sarah Downe
(family origin Poland) (family origin India)

Alvin Conrad Clarke

Randall Emile Clarke

Claude Noel Clarke *m* Kathleen Vanessa Isaacs

Clifton Bonny Isaacs

Marjorie Elaine Isaacs

Valerie Elaine Clarke

Neville Garfield Hylton Clarke (adopted)

John Roger Francis Jones (1)* *m* Elsie Yvonne Clarke *m* Starr Edmund Francis Home Brewster (2)**

Julian Francis Brewster

* Married in the 1960s; marriage dissolved in the 1960s

** Married in 1971

Contents

ix

Contents

Chapter 1

Black and White Whisky

My eldest daughter is threatening to pay me a visit. I dread these kindnesses with increasing passion and am always hoping something grand will keep her away. She has had a little success in England, where she has chosen to live cut off from her family, flailing around trying to be accepted in that cold and unfathomable country. England. I remember it well. That's where I learned that a smile can mean anything . . . But back to this visit. It is in honour of, or as she says to celebrate, my ninetieth birthday. But do I want to celebrate my descent into uselessness with a lot of senseless noise and bother? *I do not.*

However, once she has made up her mind what is good for you there is little you can do. The woman is a menace. So I shall have to pray for patience to survive it all. St Luke said when you pray for patience you are likely to end up patient. A patient, more like.

The idea of a ninetieth birthday party has made me think about how I got here. Despite everything. Even my childhood.

My father, Sam Isaacs, was a handsome dog, a man of Polish-Jewish stock. His family had fled difficulties in Europe and being people with a bit of money and a lot of culture they headed for America, the Land of the Free, where they prospered. All except his father, who was unsettled, some even say unstable. His training as an attorney-at-law existed but was never used in the Courts. At drunken parties, maybe, but nobody was paying. One day he jumped on a tramp steamer heading for Ernest Hemingway territory. By the time the steamer reached Jamaica he had had enough and jumped off. Permanently.

Eventually his son, who would be my father, came looking for him, but was himself distracted when he met my mother. My parents were both very good-looking. She was in fact a beauty. I mean Pretty. The totally uneducated daughter of Indian cane-field workers, with her flashing eyes and flirty feet she dazzled him. They got married, much to the disgust of his family in the States, who ignored him almost completely for the rest of his life. And to the delight of hers, who felt they had won the Pools.

They were an ill-matched pair, a living example of the folly of thinking you can change people by marrying them. You can't. The change was supposed to happen to her, of course. She was supposed to reap benefit from having nice clothes, good food, a big house, private lessons in reading and table manners. Well, she did learn to read newspaper headlines, write her name and a shopping list, wear the clothes, live in the house and sit at the table – but nothing changed her. She was basically a lonely, suspicious, tight-assed woman.

I, Kathleen Vanessa, was the first child of this handsome couple. My arrival brought home to Papa that he would have to start earning some money, as his reserve was dwindling fast. Should *he* try practising law? This was a non-starter as his foreign accent was too pronounced for Jamaicans to trust him. But money he had to earn, in order to keep his beloved in the style to which she had so swiftly become accustomed, what with his family in the States cutting him off and all.

What wouldn't these black people do for themselves?

2

he asked himself. Not much came to mind until he hit on a brainwave when attending a local funeral. These people spent quite happily a year's earnings on a funeral. The grandeur of these events depended on keeping the body long enough so as to allow members of the family to fly in. All Jamaicans have family abroad. 'In foreign.' Problem was, ice did not last long in the heat. He would introduce embalming. And that's what he did. Went back to the States, did a quick course in Funeral Direction, returned, bought some cheap land in downtown Kingston and opened up shop. He was an instant success. I must admit that the firm still supports me handsomely in this my ninetieth year.

Papa possessed a strange Polish name which the Jamaicans didn't even try to pronounce, much less spell. He had to answer to 'Jewman'. The business had to have a name, preferably his, but 'Lyjinski' did not have the knell of success somehow. Nor did 'Jewman'. He was Jewish, of course, and, although he did not visit the synagogue that regularly, did not want his change of name to disavow or hide his Jewishness. Not a man for half-measures, he changed his name by deed poll to Samuel Abraham Isaac (which mutated to Isaacs eventually). Three pillars of the Jewish faith. The business flourished and became a by-word for the mourning discreet middle- and upper-class clientèle who felt comfortable dealing with a white man. These things mattered in our Island paradise.

Soon a modest palace sprang up in Stony Hill, an exclusive suburb high above hot Kingston. Built into the hillside, taking its shape from the vagaries of the hill, Orange Grove was a delightful folly of a home.

There was some fun to be had but mostly for my brother, who was only one year my junior and by appearing on the scene had seriously diminished my standing. Son and heir it was immediately. The name of

3

the firm was immediately changed to reflect his importance from *Sam Isaacs Undertakers* to *Sam Isaacs & Son
Undertakers* and my brother still in his infant cot.

My mother, having provided the statutory two children, was busy enjoying the status of being Mrs Sam
Isaacs. And it was considerable. After all, Papa did have
one of the first motorcars in Jamaica. Her week was
packed solid with manicures, pedicures, visits to the
dressmaker, the doctor, the chiropodist, the hairdresser
and, always on Fridays, to the Coronation Market in
downtown Kingston – a place she was very familiar with
from her early beginnings. Members of her family had
sold produce there. But now she would arrive chauffeur-
driven in the Model T Ford with two or three maids
running behind the car with baskets ready to be filled
with produce.

My mother would have the man park the car in the
middle of the entrance, blocking the general public's
access. She would then descend like a Mughal Princess
and walk through the market, followed at a discreet distance by the chauffeur and the maids with their baskets,
prodding and discarding tomatoes, yams, plantains,
okra, oranges. Every so often she would forget her new
airs and graces and haggle like the peasant she was. She
never ever paid the asking price for anything.

This royal procession could take up to three hours
before the baskets were filled. Needless to say, these baskets were not allowed in the sacred car and the women
were expected to carry them on their heads the nine
miles back to the home in the hills. Back to the setting
for this perfect rich, handsome couple, with one boy, one
girl.

Behind the mask was a much more nitty-gritty reality.
It wasn't long before the difference in education and
exposure between my mother (child of the cane-field)
and father (son of a highly civilized musical family in

4

exile) was unable to be soothed in the bedroom. The regime of improvement had been a complete failure as far as my mother's sensibility was concerned, in her heart where it really mattered. The hairstyle was modish but cane trash remained in the head. She having been brought up to live only for today, one can't blame her for really not caring greatly about anyone except Hilda, for this was my mother's name.

She dressed in her finery at the least provocation. This was her way of making an effort to keep Sam on side. He, after all, provided her with the trappings she so loved. Being Mrs Sam Isaacs was not something she was about to give up. She was, however, very careful with the housekeeping money as far as we children were concerned. The less she spent on us, the more there would be for her daily self-improvement appointments. She fed us top of the milk with a bit of jam, bread pudding, occasional treats of curried goat and runny egg custard. To this day egg custard brings me out in hives. Sam's dinners were a different matter. They were substantial and properly served on linen in the dining room with help hovering in the shadows. During this daily ceremony we children were banished to the care of the nurse with strict instructions not to let us roam free.

The house was, however, big enough to allow for several individual pursuits of happiness. There was a junior study room, Papa's den, bedrooms for us all, no shortage of reception rooms and of course the cool veranda and garden. We should have been able to be happy there.

The junior study room was intended for homework. My mother decreed that this was for Bonny, my brother, as he was the boy. I would have to find somewhere else to study, if I must, but please remember no books allowed in the bedroom or the living room or on the dining table. I found a comfortable crook halfway up a tree and made it my personal junior study room.

Bonny was never bright. Handsome, he was a lover of cricket and girls from an early age, but not of books. My whole world was the printed page. So he fiddled and fumed in his junior study room, carving his name in the posh desk whilst I did my homework and read my books in the crook of my junior study room tree. Can't have harmed me as I got a scholarship to Wolmers Girls' School and eventually matriculated with honours.

I have never needed people much, preferring the companionship of dogs. My first puppy was called Pup-Pups, a small stray who had taken up residence in the grounds. Mother had little time for animals but disliked dogs particularly. I managed to keep the existence of Pup-Pups a secret for quite a few weeks before I got careless. One day on coming home from school my little dog was nowhere to be seen. I searched everywhere in vain until Benjamin the gardener took pity on me and said, 'Him gone, Miss Neesa.' (Neesa is my pet name. Not many people call me that these days.)

'Gone where?'

'To Heaven.'

'What happened?'

After quite a few 'What happened?s' he finally told me that the poor little dog had ventured too close to Mrs Sam Isaacs's house. When she saw it all hell broke loose:

'Benjamin, wey dis dawg come from?'

'Ah don't know, Miss Hilda.'

'If I find out is lie you telling me you going pee pee yu pants.'

And so on until Benjamin spilled the beans.

'What! That little wretch keeping a dawg when she knows how much I hate them? Bring him come. Now!'

Poor Benjamin. There was no gainsaying Mrs Sam Isaacs when she had made up her mind. A bit like my daughter Yvonne. He was instructed to hold the small dog's mouth open while she put the garden hose down

6

its throat, turned on the tap full throttle and drowned Pup-Pups.

Nowadays, I have as many dogs as I can afford, and then some.

Even at the early age of nine I realised I would have to be clever if I was to survive my mother. I intended to survive my mother. The recurring nightmare of the hose down the small dog's throat didn't leave me for many a year. In fact, telling you about it now has got me going again.

I was able to survive the nine-mile walk to school every day while Bonny got taken in the car. There was not enough room for me, you understand, and he was delicate. So delicate that one afternoon when he was supposed to be doing his homework in his junior study room, he ate an entire loaf of hot bread which had been smuggled in to him as a study aid and promptly choked. I heard the gasping sounds and so did Mother. She ordered me to put him on my back and carry him up to the doctor. It was not too far away but the hill was steep. I survived this, too. Luckily the doctor, who was appalled, drove us back to Orange Grove.

I have to be grateful that I was bright, that I could even then read unspoken signals between man and wife in time to absent myself from the coming fray. The awful memories of the taunting! My father taunting my mother about her lack of class, her lack of friends, her lack of everything. My earliest recollection of this time is of when Sam, thinking that we children were both safely snuggled in bed, was working his way through a bottle of Black & White whisky. In came his wife to complain about some slight she felt she had received at the hands of one of his 'ugly black employees' as she put it.

Unfortunately Benjamin had told him earlier about the incident with my little dog Pup-Pups. This must have been still rumbling around in my father's head. To treat a dumb animal like this was unforgivable. Uncivilised.

He listened to her moans and groans for a while but eventually he banged the thick green bottle on the table, then forced the label with the two Scots Terriers into her complaining face.

'You see these two dogs? Well, that's us. One white and one black – and that's you. You are nothing but a black dawg in truth. You think I don't know that you killed Kathleen's little puppy? Hilda, you old black dawg.'

I must explain here that my mother's family had been brought from India to Jamaica as indentured labourers not many generations ago, destined to work in the cane-fields when the supply of African slaves was curtailed. My father, when he was in a good mood, would call his wife his Indian Queen. That went by without too much trouble, but calling her a black dawg was a very, very different affair which only the very brave would attempt. The fisticuffs were verbal and physical and they lasted a while. I don't know who was the victor. Probably Mother.

My father and I were close. I was Papa's girl. In his study, lovingly carved out of the hillside, he would read Dickens to me, and I would read it back to him, 'with expression', as he put it. Got through most of Dickens's novels that way and as a result learned the joys of the English language. He gave me *The Mysteries of Paris*, a very large book, to read at the age of twelve. It was indeed a very big book but I managed to finish it, some-times reading in bed with a candle under the sheets. I had to. Papa expected it of me.

My mother did her best to cramp our enjoyable tutor-ials, for that is what they were really. She would inter-rupt on the flimsiest of excuses with as much noise and bluster as she could manage.

Similarly, years later when Papa acquired a top-of-the-range gramophone, one of the His Master's Voice editions with the dog guarding the large lily-looking amplifier, he was able to play the music of his youth, especially Chopin, and Ella Fitzgerald, whom he loved. But the audience had changed. Taking my place then was Yvonne. He now played his music and read his Dickens and his Shakespeare to her. They would listen to Ella's records over and over again and Papa would say, 'Listen to that riff – now repeat it. Listen to that scatting – do it, do it,' and so on until she could sing 'Lullaby of Broadway' with the best.

One evening when the volume was up to maximum and Grandfather Sam and Granddaughter Yvonne were happily scatting along with Ella, the door burst open and there was Mrs Sam Isaacs in one of her rages. She spied a likeness of Ella on the dust jacket of the record and, recognising that it was a black woman's voice giving her husband such joy, she took the record off the turntable and smashed it to pieces with the parting shot: 'You, Sam, can lower yourself but don't you ever expose Yvonne to this kind of black rubbish again.'

The result was that Yvonne learned to love Ella and American jazz. To love Dickens. To love Shakespeare. Never say never. It backfires. My mother's aim was to destroy anything she couldn't understand. She succeeded only in strengthening my resolve and later Yvonne's to be educated, independent-minded women who always questioned motives.

Parents steel you when they least expect to. As do grandparents. To get me out of the clutches of my father's superior intellect I was sent to visit my maternal grandfather, whose job it was to oversee the big house, in fact two houses on the same plantation property, in the parish of St Catherine. There were a lot of fowls and a lot of dogs.

Thieves have always been the bane of Jamaican society and his job was to protect the property. He therefore trained the dogs to do his work. They would lie low, silent, watching, allowing the thieves to climb in over the fence. When they had caught their fill of fowls, crowded them into the baskets they had brought for the purpose and were about to escape over the fence, then the dogs would hold them fast by the ankles. Human alarm. No barking, ever. Worked every time.

His method of stock control of the mangoes was less sophisticated. In those days people used to regard a mango tree as public property. They used to say it was impossible for anyone to starve in Jamaica. My grandfather had ingenious ways of protecting the fruit. Even from me. He would mark his initials on every fruit and then number them to make sure he could easily identify any missing fruit. With my temperament, you can imagine, I wouldn't put up with that. I would announce, 'Mango number twenty three was ready, ripe and delicious.' He would go ballistic and chase me with intent to harm. Having his foolproof system proved not so foolproof so frequently was too much to bear and I was soon on my way back to the delights of Orange Grove with a note to say I would not be welcome ever again.

When I was with my grandfather he did talk to me quite a lot. He was a lonely old thing. One conversation I remember unearthed this revelation: 'Your mother, Hilda, she has got too big for her boots. She thinks she is Lady Muck now, but I wonder if she remembers how much her husband paid me for her. Mek her stay deh form di fool. T'ink she is any Queen.' Oooh, what lovely ammunition for a rainy day, thought I, and into my memory bank it went.

Chapter 2

Speak British

All of a sudden, when I was eleven there arrived on the scene a new sister called Marjorie Elaine. Very pale, very delicate, she managed to get pneumonia within months of her birth. I had to supervise the bath of ice into which she was plunged. Strange, but it saved her life. Very unpromising, this sister who turned out to like dolls, make-up, clothes but not books or arithmetic. It was no fun whatsoever and too much responsibility as I was expected to act the big sister role. The gulf widened as the years rolled by. To tell the truth I thought she was a waste of space. I suppose age allows you to tell the truth in the end.

Marjorie fell madly in love early in life but not to the liking of her mother. Eddie Ferguson was a handsome man, a mechanical engineer. A whiz with motors. He was, however, 'a little on the dark side'. As Mother would not speak to him, even recognise his existence, this acted as an even greater spur to Marjorie's love and they planned their marriage with help from Papa, my husband Claude and myself.

The wedding day dawned and Marjorie was a picture in satin and lilies. Her mother sat in the left-hand pew of the church, no emotion on her rock-solid face. When the priest finally arrived at the bit where he asks if anyone has just cause or knows of any impediment why these two may not be joined together, on the word joined, up

stood Mrs Sam Isaacs and walked down the nave, her
high heels clicking on the stone until she arrived at the
font, turned round, took one look at the astonished con-
gregation and exited.

It took a good few seconds before the priest gathered
his brain, coughed and continued. Imagine, if you will,
the reception. Our house in Oxford Road has seen some
dramas, but this one takes the biscuit. Mrs Isaacs
attended the reception but spoke to no one, an avenging
angel in green. The happy pair departed for the United
States of America forthwith and 'for good' as we say.

Eddie drove trucks at first but climbed an impressive
ladder of swift Uncle Sam success, ending his career as a
vice-president of the Florida triple A (American Auto-
mobile Association). Marjorie was air hostess and hostess. They never faltered in their love during a marriage
which lasted half a century and ended only with her
death. Romantic, isn't it? But Yvonne tells a different
story. Doesn't she always?

When my daughter was a student in London, we
thought Yvonne would benefit from a visit home mid-
way through her studies. In those days a straight-
through flight from London to Kingston, Jamaica,
wasn't possible so we suggested she pass through New
York, spend a couple of days with Aunt Marjorie and
Uncle Eddie, and then head for the sun. The plan was
actioned. Arriving at Idlewild Airport she was whisked
away to their apartment.

In the car: 'Now, honey, I want you to listen carefully.
There are no coloured folk where we live and we have to
be very careful about who visits. We're very happy to
have you, but this is Uncle Sam's country. We think we
can get away with you, if you speak with a British accent
to anyone who talks to you. Only if they talk to you.
Don't make conversation. Understand?'

'British accent?'

'Yes, as strong as you can manage. If they realise that you are not American but foreign and visiting, it should be OK.'

'So what about Eddie? He's the same colour as me.'

'Oh, I always say he comes from the Yemen. Is a Yemeni Jew. That works.'

'Why Yemen?'

'They don't know where it is.'

'Does he know?'

'Here we are. Remember, now. Speak British.'

Yvonne thought the apartment was fine. She says she was silent, not that I can imagine this, admired everything and asked about the neighbourhood. How to shop. How to get taxis. How to use the phone. When the coast was clear and everybody else had retired for the night, she phoned a cab which took her to the airport, from where she phoned us in Jamaica to say she was on her way down. Three days early. Then she hung up. Marjorie and Eddie realised the bird had flown only when it was too late to do anything about it. We got the story when she arrived. She said she did them a favour. She had considered affecting a loud Nigerian accent and the body language to go with it . . .

I did well at school, and anxious to get out of that house in Stony Hill decided to get a qualification. I wanted to become a nurse. To this day I am at my best when nursing the sick, but this was thought by my mother to be work for lesser humans. I was to be an accountant. So that's what I became officially. In reality, at first I was nothing but a glorified bookkeeper in the service of Sam Isaacs & Son. I never objected to Sam Isaacs but I objected to the Son.

In those days, a single woman didn't set up home alone in an apartment. The only sure way out of Orange Grove was to marry. Now I have never been a romantic sort of person. All that lovey-dovey business leaves me a bit cold. There were suitors, many of them, mostly after the hefty dowry I promised. Very boring, mostly thick as two planks and as predictable, so you can imagine my joy when Claude came into my life. Bliss. He looked just like me. He was newly qualified as a commissioned land surveyor. He was intelligent. What's more, he did not seem too hell-bent on the sweet nothings.

Our courtship was wonderful. He would present himself on the veranda of Orange Grove and sit, hat in hand, on the cane sofa while I sat opposite him. We made polite conversation about the news, the weather, the lack of transport up the hill, the latest books. Always remember I had, as they say, a head for figures so I could understand the intricacies of the theodolite equipment used in surveying and even the co-ordinates, so he too was lucky in finding me. We couldn't, however, move from our positions on the veranda as Mother always set one of the maids behind the door to raise the alarm if Claude got within three feet of me.

Anyone having the temerity to approach Old Man Sam for the hand of his daughter had, of course, to be extensively vetted. I did not know it at the time, but a small industry of prodding and poking into Claude Noel Clarke's family background had sprung to life.

It was simpler to begin with his mother, Alice Philippa Clarke née Cook-Hylton, the only daughter of a well-heeled Scottish plantation family. Her antics had been for years the fuel of many an expatriate veranda gossip. The Cook-Hyltons migrated to rule over the cane-fields in western Jamaica many generations before. For decades they put about the idea that they were descended from the seafaring Captain Cook. It made them feel special and forever expatriate. People like them could get away with these vague claims in Jamaica of the late nineteenth century as the great majority of Jamaicans didn't think to question white people – or perhaps knew better than to threaten their livelihoods by challenging this kind of insecurity.

So young Alice of the lily-white skin, bright green-blue eyes and an abundance of long, perfectly straight hair, was considered beyond most Jamaican male dreams. Tomboy, great on horses and guns, under-educated she may have been, but what did that matter when they could always clean her up when the suitors arrived from 'Home' to bid for her hand? Unfortunately for her parents and for the purity of the clan, Alice Philippa Cook-Hylton had other ideas.

Riding out to one of the far boundaries of the plantation one hot morning, she came upon a handsome man, black, tall. This man did not behave in the manner she had grown to expect from the lower orders. He didn't cower, nor did he look away into the middle distance; he greeted her simply in his strange accent, all the while giving her an appraising eye. It was clear he liked what he saw. It was clearer still she liked what *she* saw. Over many weeks of meeting at the edge of the plantation Alice discovered that Charles Nathaniel Clarke was the son of a runaway slave, who had left Cuba to find a new life in Jamaica. He had been the maker of soft kid shoes for the ruling class in Santiago de Cuba, but the ninety-mile stretch of water between Cuba and Jamaica had proved too beguiling, so here he was, attempting to start a new life after his hazardous journey across that choppy sea.

Charlie was thinking of farming, that's why he was in Westmoreland. Land in western Jamaica was cheaper than in the garden parishes of the Island. However, farming soon took a back seat to more romantic pursuits and before long the son of the runaway slave decided to runaway with Alice.

You must remember that if the family had even suspected that this liaison was taking place Charles

15

Nathaniel would have been 'disappeared'. Running away was the only option, but how far could they run in an island 144 by 72 miles? The only answer was to get someone to marry them before they were caught. As it turned out, they were caught before the ceremony but the public display of physical affection which Alice managed to exhibit put all respectability to flight. This unusual couple were left well alone, to go it alone, which they did.

Alice had a number of really handsome brothers but only one supported her, Reuben. I got to know him quite well. He also had, as it happened, an enduring influence on my daughter Yvonne's approach to life and maybe death. Reuben was tall, great-looking in a poetic way. Lanky and lovely, with hair worn in the Oscar Wilde style. Always impeccably dressed in white linen, with a floppy bow tie, Panama hat and ivory-topped walking stick, he sang beautifully, flirted outrageously and was one of nature's gifted but idle creatures. How he earned his living is anyone's guess. He could charm the monkeys from the trees so he probably charmed himself a living too.

Reuben used to serenade the objects of his affection by singing 'Ramona', a popular song of the time. He was always a favourite with my children, especially Yvonne. She tells the story of his demise ad nauseum as the model for her departure when the time comes.

Reuben the Beautiful arranged a large luncheon-party at a family house in Outlook Avenue which was very close to a jetty in a bywater of Kingston Harbour where a few small craft were often tied up. Everyone had been encouraged to wear white, linen preferably, and the place was smothered with white blooms. At the height of the festivities no one noticed Reuben as he slipped quietly away dressed in his white linen, his floppy bow tie, his Panama and his brogues and strolled into the Caribbean

Sea singing, 'Ramona, I'll meet you at the garden gate
. . .' as he disappeared from view, walking away to his
watery solution.

Somehow the revelry had quietened in time for the
assembled guests to hear the last refrain of the song and
they watched speechless from the shore as only the Panama hat was left bobbing on the waves. No one moved.
No one. There was a sort of instinctive cultural understanding. Maybe he simply didn't want a Sam Isaacs
funeral.

We would probably all be charged with assisted sui-
cide in these insensitive days. Some say he was inebri-
ated but I know he was terminally ill, and he must have
decided to end life in the same way he lived it. With
style and flamboyance. 'Ramona'. I can't hear that song
without Reuben appearing before me, laughing as only
he could. Yvonne's hero.

Of course the Cook-Hyltons had long ago cut Alice
off, as they say, without a penny. Not that it seemed to
bother her. She had always been happy with her 'African Prince Maas Charlie' and didn't care who knew or
objected. Quite a spirited set of in-laws I would
inherit. Luckily they met with approval from Papa,
who liked a bit of spirit. He and Miss Alice hit it off
particularly well. Mother didn't too much approve of
Maas Charlie. Him too black. By this time everything
she said was ignored. Must have been some life, knowing that you were totally irrelevant. Did she realise
this? I wonder.

The wedding date was set. The cake was a marvel.
Claude and I looked very cool. Nice man, my husband.
He was a good man. That's why he probably died over
forty years ago and left me to contend with life without
him. But in 1937 we were not thinking of death except
that the Europeans were busy killing themselves and
had involved us in Jamaica in being cannon-fodder. In

fact, Claude's youngest brother Alvin had quite a successful war, flying sorties for the Royal Air Force. He came back alive, that's the important fact.

Chapter 3

Elsie

—◦◉◦—

Yes, as I was saying, in 1937 we were thinking about life. The first of our two daughters arrived in October 1938. That's the one who is now threatening me with a visit.

She caused confusion from the word go. Claude, whose second name was Noel, was partial to a bit of French in a girl's name so it was to be Elise Yvonne. My father, who found this pretentious, offered to register the birth and he promptly swapped about the order of the letters and instead of Elise she was registered as Elsie. Some thought this was funny – after all, both her godmothers were called Elsie. I don't think Claude ever forgave Papa for this caper. To him, it was undermining and not at all funny. Nevertheless, the name Elsie stuck until one day when she was about four years old and we were sitting around the dining table.

'Elsie, did you draw any nice pictures today?'

Silence.

'Elsie . . . Elsie?'

'You don't hear your father talking to you?'

Still silence, and so it went on till the end of the meal. I had much less patience with this than Claude, who finally got to the root of the problem. This four-year-old madam had decided never again to answer to the name of Elsie, as that was the name of a big brown cow with a daisy stuck in its mouth. She had seen it on the jar of Borden's malted milk.

'So what are we going to do?' I asked.

'Call me Yvonne.'

Call me Madam! It was agreed. I told you she was difficult and she is due here to change my furniture around to suit her London tastes and give me all the trouble of putting it back after she has gone.

I did sometimes ask my mother to babysit her first grandchild. I thought she might like to do what most grandmothers regard as a joy and a right. Occasionally she turned up and used the occasion as an opportunity to show off her lovely voice, usually only heard in the choir on Sundays. As it happened, one day when Mother was babysitting, my grandmother Caroline, Mother's mother, was brutally assaulted and murdered. Mrs Sam Isaacs proceeded to blame her infant grandchild for her mother's untimely death.

'If I wasn't looking after that child those men would never have been able to end my mother's life. I would have been able to save her.' Huh. This from her who kept her mother at arms length and made her sleep in a maid's room.

My grandmother's murder was the first of the murders which were to haunt my life. But more of that anon. Mother was very superstitious, always wearing a trifle of red about her person to guard against evil. I always saw these fragments of red pinned to her underclothes and thought it quite a natural thing, as one does. It was some years before I realised that real sophisticates wouldn't dream of wearing hidden fetishes. Or at least they would be clued up enough not to let them show. In keeping with her superstition Hilda insisted that Yvonne, as the youngest member of the family, should be passed over her great-grandmother Caroline's coffin at the funeral.

Passing a baby over the coffin is a Jamaican ritual which is said to ward off the spirits of evil from the child. I did not approve of this rigmarole, especially as

20

part of it included slapping the baby until it cried, but it couldn't harm, could it? Claude, the Anglican church warden, pillar of St Michael's Church and dedicated Mason, was incensed but powerless in the face of Mother's determination.

My other daughter, Valerie, never ever gave any kind of hassle. True, I can never quite understand what on God's earth she is talking about, but at least she doesn't impose herself so much on me. And at least she stayed where she belonged in Jamaica, not running off to live so far away where they don't care. Yes, our second daughter arrived three years after Yvonne. Born on Peacemakers Day, she can't take the war of argument, which is really hard for her in a place like Jamaica where noise and war are king. Poor thing, she could never really make up her mind about anything. She was Claude's favourite as she was pretty, musically talented, good at ballet, loved baking, sewing, knitting, crochet, was obedient and didn't rock the boat. And she hasn't changed. Anything for a quiet life. My two daughters are as different as rice and peas.

Our family home in Kingston was a lovely house, which Claude was lucky to be able to buy. Designed and built for some white Jamaicans called the Harts in the 1930s, Donsyville was solid but not ugly. Claude set his sights on it mainly because of the way in which the air passed through it. In hot, humid Kingston the air currents passing through a house make all the difference, and this Oxford Road house was cool. Large windows in large rooms, lovely wooden floors, bathrooms for all the bedrooms and, most important, a wide veranda which wrapped two sides of the house. A fancy circular gazebo-like protrusion was the showpiece of the veranda. I sometimes imagined the English folk sipping cups of tea in the afternoons. We never did. We used it for serving drinks of the alcoholic variety.

21

The house was surrounded by roads on three sides, enveloping the full-sized tennis court, the orchid house and the garage large enough to house four cars which would in the fullness of time become the Barn Theatre. In those days this abundance of access gave a feeling of welcome openness; nowadays it gives robbers more opportunity. We were living higher on the hog than was discreet but Claude was not a man for half-measures. Anyway, he felt he had to continue proving to my mother that he was good enough for me. Daft. I mean, she didn't walk out of *our* wedding, did she?

There were always lots of children in our house – the more the merrier. I loved small children but it was much too much to go to all the trouble of actually giving birth to them. As I said, I am not one for the lovely-dovey business. The solution was not hard to find in Jamaica, where so many parents were willing to give away their children to the better off so that they might have better lives. Funnily enough, the first candidate for adoption was a distant relative of Claude's. He was only a few weeks younger than Valerie, our second daughter, so when the unfortunate unmarried mother offered him to Claude I was all right with it. Might as well look after two children simultaneously. Better use of resources. Neville Garfield Hylton became Neville Garfield Hylton Clarke. For those who did not know better, I had been delivered of twins. Heaven forbid.

Little did I know that this was the beginning of a rash of adoptions – some legal, others social. During the years of our marriage I think we 'adopted' twenty-one children. Most of them remember me occasionally. At Christmas it's quite lovely to read all the cards which are inscribed to 'Mummy'. Strange how I never heard from my lovely Neville, not once in years. He married badly and was corrupted. He died the other day, I believe. I wasn't even told of his death by his extraordinarily bitter blinkered wife. This woman prevented me from attending her son (my grandson) Nicholas's wedding. 'She'll steal the day,' she said, 'and I'm not having that woman' (that's me!) 'there.'

Her loss. Their loss. I do hope, Dear Neville, you rest in peace.

Chapter 4

Strong Back Soup

—◦◦◦—

Sometime in 1945, Claude's youngest brother, Alvin, came home unscathed after the war, looking delicious in his blue Royal Air Force uniform. This homecoming was a great excuse for a celebration. First on the agenda, our three children had to plant three mango trees, one each, in the garden in honour of Alvin's safe return. (One of these is still alive, which is more than Alvin is. His is the second of my murders. More of this later.) Second on the welcome agenda was the small feast luncheon ending up in the Glass Bucket, a hot, very exclusive nightclub in Half Way Tree where champagne flowed like water. Third on the agenda, on the Sunday we all went off to Ardsheal where Mr and Mrs Clarke, proud parents of the returning hero, had laid on what can only be described as the killing of the fatted calf. In Jamaica, it's more the fatted ram whose every particular is used to its best culinary advantage.

Ardsheal was set on a hill high above Morant Bay in the Parish of St Thomas. The view from the veranda was magnificent. An unrestricted vista of the Caribbean Sea with the odd freighter meandering towards Kingston Harbour or Port Antonio, miles of surrounding coconut and pimento plantations, with not a building in sight except far away to the left the low structure which was the Princess Margaret Hospital down on the coast in Morant Bay. The place left nothing to be desired. Magnificent. Cool. Private. It had been built by Scottish landowners in the late nineteenth century and Miss Alice liked the irony of buying the Scots out. 'Putting a finger in my family's Scottish eye' was how she put it.

The house was approached by a long driveway which culminated in a circle of magnificent old cotton trees. This was a party house extraordinaire with an enormous kitchen, a really large reception room with great mahogany pillars and polished floors, encircled by a wide veranda on which Miss Alice used to sit in the evenings, shotgun in lap, just in case anyone thought they might steal up on her and her beloved Maas Charlie with dishonourable intentions. She had no intention of letting them get away with it. The children on the property used to have a very healthy respect for her as they knew she was a good shot and wouldn't hesitate to prove it. Some children are taught to be scared of the bogey man; these knew to be scared, very scared, of Miss Alice's shotgun.

There were hundreds of people present at Alvin's war-end Victory Feast. On arrival there was rum and coconut water, cold Red Stripe beer, hot Red Stripe beer known as 'hataps' (hot hops, for the uninitiated), rum punch and Solomon Gundy – a fiery delicacy made from preserved salted shad and mackerel served with dry crackers for ballast. As children we learned the rhyme to beware stale Solomon Gundy:

> *Solomon Gundy born on a Monday,*
> *Christened on a Tuesday,*
> *Married on a Wednesday,*
> *Sick on a Thursday,*
> *Worse on a Friday,*
> *Dead on a Saturday,*
> *Buried on a Sunday.*
> *That is the end of Solomon Gundy*

Small cups of Mannish water followed. Some, I think, call this 'strong back' soup, a sort of old-time Jamaican Viagra, but whatever the name the ram's very private parts are the essential ingredient, along with green bananas boiled in their skins in the biggest kerosene pan to be found.

The main meal did not stray from the traditional: jerk chicken and pork like the Arawaks used to cook – buried underground wrapped in pimento leaves and pepper and spices, fry plantain, rice and peas, escovietch fish, curry ram goat, roast yam, macaroni and cheese and mixed green salads, followed by fruit baskets of sweet sop, june plum, oathethi apple, naseberry, rose apple, ripe banana, pineapple and star apple, finished off with big juicy rumcakes, coconut drops and coconut 'gizzada' cookies, the Jamaican brownie.

My daughter Valerie has always been a stickler for the correct way of speaking what she calls the Queen's English. She objects strongly to the way in which Jamaicans insist in turning adjectives into verbs – to wit fry plantain instead of fried, curry goat, roast yam, jerk pork. What can I tell you? She has a point.

All this food took a good week to prepare. Everything was grown right here in Jamaica and cooked to the old-time recipes. There were no hot dogs, no pizzas or hamburgers on offer. We'd never heard of them, then.

Many long speeches, sometimes witty, were made during the course of the day and even more toasts to His Majesty the King of England and Winston Churchill, to Anansi, Bustamante and the hills of Jamaica. Some of the throng went on horseback to check out the property, others reminisced, a few of the die-hards set up a serious poker game, others drank themselves into a happy stupor, many sang 'Rule Britannia', 'Slide Mongoose' and ad nauseam:

Strong Back Soup

Sammy plant piece a corn down a gully oh ho
And it bear till it kill poor Sammy oh ho
Sammy dead Sammy dead Sammy dead oh oh ho

This chorus was to tease my father, Old Man Sam Isaacs, who was the life and soul of the party. As always. Much mainly good-humoured ribaldry whiled away the hours until it was time for the dozens of cars to begin the thirty-mile journey back to Kingston before it got too dark. But not before having selected their choice of the bunches of bananas and hundreds of coconuts which had been prepared for the guests to take back with them to the barren capital.

The heavily laden cars were apt to fall prey to punctures and other delights, as they made their precarious way down the deeply rutted ravine-clinging road. So everyone travelled in convoy. In fact, the journey back was another kind of party, and more rum was dispensed at every puncture stop. In those days when cars were few and far between and driven only by the more privileged, the horrors of driving under the influence did not register on the Richter scale of Jamaican society.

27

Chapter 5

A Funeral for Doll

From early on in their lives the alliances between the three major junior players of the family, Valerie, Yvonne and Neville, panned out in an interesting way. As cute 'butter wouldn't melt in her mouth' Valerie was her father's favourite, a fact which he took little trouble in disguising, the other two, one ugly (Yvonne) and one adopted (Neville), formed an unbreakable allegiance. Their motto was Get Valerie. And they did, poor sod. She had a lovely doll with bright pink cheeks and long blond hair, which could speak and wet itself. Very expensive. Very top of the range. Doll was pushed in her expensive carriage around the veranda ad nauseam.

Eventually this got to the other two, who could stomach it no longer. They managed to find enough very fine fishing line which they tied around Doll's neck, slinging the end over one of the beams on the veranda. They held firmly onto the loose end, waiting for little Miss Val to take Doll for yet another stroll in her fine carriage. They didn't have to wait long. As the carriage set off, rounding the gazebo, they pulled on the fishing line and Doll obligingly flew out of her carriage through the air, lodging in the rafters. She had been effectively garrotted.

Being children who considered funereal procedures a part of everyday existence, they knew what to do. It was swiftly decided to hold a burial service for Doll. That little devil Yvonne was the producer of this spectacle.

28

A Funeral for Doll

Dead Doll was embalmed (injected with slimy water making sure it would never grace the carriage again), dressed in a pillowcase shroud, placed in a shoebox coffin. A hole was dug in the garden.

A child called Curtis had become one of my adoptees when both his parents were reported to have died in a car crash somewhere in America. The truth, when it filtered out after some years, was more dramatic: Mr had shot Mrs, then himself. Anyway Curtis, who had a flare for intonation, took the service and duly committed Doll ashes-to-ashes to the earth. All the neighbourhood children attended and were given their parts to perform by the Boss Producer – who else but Yvonne? The ceremony concluded, there was a drum roll and out came Cookie preceded by a dancer, with loads of fried fish and hard-dough bread and jugs of cool lemonade. Cookie had been bribed by you know who to prepare this repast without my knowledge or permission.

Nine days after Doll's burial, a Nine Night ceremony was held in good Jamaican tradition, which holds to the belief that the Spirit passes over to the other side nine days after the burial. A choir consisting of all the long-suffering children of the neighbourhood were drilled during the nine-day interval to sing the Sankey hymn 'A Little More Oil in My Lamp Keep it Burning' in real revival style, employing the high-pitched nasal tones of the country parts. Parents were beginning to get a little worried at the length and intensity of the long rehearsals. However, the Nine Night ceremony went off without a hitch; the singing was perfect and the fry fish, bammy, lemonade and now the music attracted quite an appreciative crowd. I always said that was Madam's first production. Claude was convinced no good would come of her. I secretly thought she had some bottle. I had to hide my giggles at the whole affair.

I had no trouble in banishing the giggles, however,

when one day I was phoned to come home immediately to witness the driving lesson. I did not appreciate being summoned away from the office, where by now I had become essential to the operation of the firm.

Parked at the back of the house was an old hearse licensed U2, in fact the first hearse the business ever bought. In those days each parish of the country had a different letter to indicate where the vehicle was registered. So Papa queued up to wait for the car tax office in the parish of St Mary to open for business. This caused quite a sensation among the locals, who were determined that a man from St Mary should have the first registration U1 and not this Kingston white man. This is exactly what Papa had foreseen would happen. Eventually, much haggling later he had sold his first place in the queue to the man in the second place, thereby getting the licence plate U2 (how droll for a hearse) and making a profit. That's the sort of thing that appealed to my father's sense of humour.

So, old U2 could still be driven but was rather the worse for wear. Papa wanted it kept for a rainy day – which incidentally turned out to be a thunderstorm when they were filming the James Bond movie *Dr No* on the Island and wanted a hearse to use for that spectacular crash into the gully. He drove a hard bargain and got loads of money for it, only to recover it and use it as a tourist attraction for a while.

But I digress. The driving lesson I witnessed had Neville laid out flat on his stomach operating the pedals, clutch with left hand, brake and accelerator with the right, while Yvonne knelt on the front seat firmly gripping the steering wheel in one hand and the gear lever in the other, yelling 'Clutch now', 'Accelerator now', but never 'Brake now'. Sitting terrified in the back where a coffin ought to be was Valerie. They were achieving a decent speed, too, and no one could stop them. That's why I was called. The only one to show any remorse was Valerie.

Then there was the small matter of using the Sunday-School collection money for purposes other than the starving children in Africa. With the Jewish, Hindu, Scottish-Presbyterian, Animist combination of grandparents we plumped for the faith with the fewest rules. Church of England won hands down. It demanded your money, not your life. Anyway, as we lived next door to the Anglican Deputy Bishop of Kingston, known to us as 'Priest', it seemed the right and proper thing to do.

Sunday School every week at three o'clock was a foregone conclusion for the children. There were nine little souls in the crocodile headed up by Nursie which wound its way down to St Luke's: our six resident children at the time Yvonne, Valerie, Neville, Curtis, Beverley and Shelia, joined by Roberts' neighbours Christopher, Bryanna and Richard Walcott. Not many of them liked this weekly oasis of quiet, well-behaved contemplation, but they had no choice. Bishop Gibson expected every Clarke and Roberts child to attend Sunday School and there was an end to it. Everyone was given a shilling to throw for the collection. To Yvonne, this seemed a lot of money. So unimaginative to give away the whole shilling when a sixpence would surely be enough for the starving children in Africa.

Yvonne had quickly thought up a way of making a profit on the nine shillings. As the party walked down Ripon Road she would collect the nine shillings and take the individual orders for four shillings and sixpence worth of sweets divided into ten packets. The tenth packet was the bribe for Nursie, who accompanied them to keep order. Ha! Time was limited and the man at Kong's sweetshop in Cross Roads was always ready for them.

They munched happily through Sunday School and

31

on the way back home. Four shillings and sixpence bought a lot of sweets in those days. This went on for months until they got a bit lax. On arrival back from Sunday School one afternoon, everybody was chewing away. Sweets were officially forbidden.

'Where did you get those sweets?' Silence reigned. Nursie burst into tears and everybody else looked straight ahead. The question was repeated a few times, with Claude, who had a short fuse on his temper, getting more and more irate. In the end Yvonne offered up some elaborate lie about a stranger in a hat buying them the sweets and how they had to eat them so as not to hurt his feelings. This was too much for Valerie, who blurted out the truth and got off scot-free. Yvonne was comprehensively beaten in the back bathroom with the sash cord from the window. With every stroke she was reminded that the beating was not for being an underhand thief of the collection-plate dues but for telling the lie. I must remind her of this when she arrives to change round my furniture. Might calm her down a bit. Maybe.

Living at 'Donsyville', 5 Oxford Road was challenging. I had no intention of staying home to be a housewife. A wife, yes, but not a housewife. The prospect of being at home all day would have surely driven me mad. Accordingly, the small army of servants now called helpers needed to keep the home afloat numbered at the very least five. This number swelled with need.

A lot of entertaining went on as Claude was a much more social creature than yours truly his wife. He had a sort of latter-day Sophoclean approach to life. He quite liked the idea of him sitting on the stool and eager minds questioning and discussing the human condition, which I suppose is all right for some. In the early evenings around dusk, he would be host to a wide variety of people who had come to chat. He held, you might say, Open Veranda. Those who came included his Phoenix

Lodge Masonic brothers who I found usually rather dull fish, his surveying colleagues who at least had some life about them, youngsters like Andrew DePass and Paul Fitchett who would bring him their problems to be sorted, and really interesting folk such as our neighbour at number 3 Oxford Road, Percival Gibson, Suffragan Bishop of Kingston, pioneer educator and founder of Kingston College. Conversations would begin across the fence and speak their way onto the veranda.

Jamaica had a number of enlightened governors-general in the 1950s Hugh Foot, later Lord Cadogan, and Sir Kenneth Blackburn being two of them. Both these men took advantage of the rum punch, the whisky, the easy living and the lively debate which Claude encouraged. The ancient Austin Princess with its silver royal coat-of-arms would glide into our driveway under cover of darkness. Wouldn't do for the word to get out, as what would Kitty Kingston in the *Gleaner*'s society columns make of this?

'The big English Governor seen talking! Debating! Not entertaining at Kings House! Sitting on this jumped-up pleb's veranda! What is the world coming to?'

I sometimes think a lot of Yvonne's education or exposure to thought derived from her eavesdropping on these early evening soirées. There were large double doors leading from the living room onto the veranda. She would crouch behind them for hours and listen to the big men talk. For instance, when Aldous Huxley dismissed Jamaica with a sweep of his imperceptive pen in *Beyond the Mexique Bay*, comparing our Island home to 'the Clapham Junction of the West', the argument got heated, with one side accusing Huxley of English arrogance and the other rebutting with the fact that Huxley *never* found anything to his liking. Take his description of British Honduras for instance: *If the*

33

world had any ends, British Honduras would certainly be one of them.

Yvonne would store these discussions, realign them for reproduction whenever the situation demanded. I knew she was eavesdropping, Claude didn't. I thought it could only do good to open up her eyes to the ways of the world, seeing how, with her personality, she was always going to be in the eye of the storm.

Another eye-opening ritual for her was the Sunday afternoon ice-cream and cake parties at Busta's Tucker Avenue residence. Busta, incidentally, is the affectionate name for Sir Alexander Bustamante, the first Prime Minister of independent Jamaica, flamboyant Jamaican hero who fought for universal adult suffrage for the workers of Jamaica. Busta and Old Man Sam were close, and the children were among a chosen few invited for the Sunday treat at Tucker Avenue when Busta made ice cream from mango, coconut and soursop which he would churn himself in a hand-driven machine surrounded with coarse ice and salt.

'Mummy, is Busta really important? How come he serves us ice cream?'

'Suffer the little children. Always remember that.'

Chapter 6

Halfway up the Tree

If our children were lucky with their father, they did all right with grandfathers, too. Claude's dad Maas Charlie was probably the more creative man, as shown by his beautiful hands with their tapering fingertips and his long elegant body which never ran to fat. After his early days of making those delicate kid slippers, he turned to working with wood.

One Christmas we all packed into the car to deliver the Christmas presents to his cattle farm in the country. The kids really loved to visit this set of grandparents who made them so welcome. No top of the milk and prunes here. It was fun running around barefoot in the fields, terrifying the cows and climbing the coconut trees. What greeted them on this occasion was a beautiful handmade merry-go-round with carved Picasso-like horses. It even had a music box which worked as the horses revolved slowly on the hand-carved axis. I almost fell in love with Maas Charlie at that moment. The children certainly did.

The major hurricane of 1951, which almost destroyed Jamaica, blew up suddenly when the children were holidaying with the Clarke grandparents. Yvonne's school essay on this adventure is maybe worth reproducing here. Got her a good mark anyway, in spite of the punctuation.

My Holiday

6th September 1951

*I usually like to spend my Summer holidays in King-
ston as I have to spend most of my life at Boarding
school in St Ann but my Father thought I was spending
too much time playing tennis in the sun listening to
records and fooling around Ba's horses at Knutsford
Park (Ba is my Grandfather my Mother's Father) so
he sent us to Grandma and Grandpa his Mummy and
Daddy, which was nice but not as nice as being in
Kingston where you could go to Carib and see movies.*

*Everything was OK as Grandpa is OK and shows
us lots of tricks with the cows and how to roast yellow
yam and climb coconut trees he used to listen to the
radio every morning and one morning he got scared
and started penning up the animals and nailing boards
up at the windows and bringing a lot of food into the
house he said a hurricane was coming. Boy we got
really excited with the grown ups looking so scared.
Then the rain started it was so heavy up there on the
mountain that it sounded like hammers on the roof
then we began to get scared too the wind was making a
duppy sound and we were all hugging up each other.
The roof began to leak and we had to keep moving
from one spot to another. There were really strange
sounds and every time GrandPa and GrandMa would
say I'ts just the outhouse door banging or something
like that.*

*We wanted to peep outside so he found a place
where one person could see out at a time. I saw something fly through the air so fast that it cut off the head
of a coconut tree like a helicopter spinning. GrandPa
said come away from the window but I wanted to see it
happen again.*

Then there was no rain, no wind no helicopter coco-

36

nut trees. It was very quiet and we were quiet too. GrandPa said not to go outside because the hurricane wasn't finished it was only the eye passing over, and the rain and wind would soon start again but from the other side. We didn't believe him but he looked very serious so we shut up.

Whoosh the other side of the hurricane came louder than the first one. Some of our roof blew off and Uncle and Aunt Dor who were with us were sort of crying. It went on for a long time GrandPa and GrandMa told stories about Cuba and Captain Cook and horse and buggy days.

When it finished and we went outside everything was flat, except the coconut trees which didn't have any heads some cows were dead, the chickens were gone and the outhouse kitchen didn't have any roof or walls. It was very quiet.

Uncle Alvin said he had to get us children to Kingston. GranPa said the car couldn't make it but he packed us all in anyway after he had started it and he drove over all the bad washed-away roads with fallen trees and rocks and got to Oxford Road in about twelve hours. Mummy and Daddy were OK but this house had lost its roof too. They were cooking soup for lots of people and we got some.

I'm glad I didn't spend my holidays in Kingston.

Yvonne Clarke.

My father, Old Man Sam (Ba to them) loved his grandchildren too and arranged for the most perfect doll's house to be built for them. Actually, you say doll's house but I have been in something they call a studio apartment in Kingston the other day, and if I remember aright the doll's house at Oxford Road was bigger, better equipped and furnished than that rabbit hutch but I kept quiet and pretended to be amazed by the view.

Yvonne was never one for playing with dolls but Valerie was in her element. Papa also used to give them all rides in his fancy motorcars. He had a special way to blow the horn to announce his arrival (Ba Ba Ba Cart played to sound like the first four notes of Beethoven's 'Ode to Joy'), which always heralded treats and sweets. They also got taken to the racetrack at Knutsford Park and to the stables to get acquainted with the racehorses he owned. He taught them how to bet – which is not to. I remember Kostalanitz as his best winner. For many years there were photos in the *Gleaner* of him leading in this horse. He made some money on that horse.

Nowadays I am told you don't beat children, and you don't show favouritism as the little darlings might suffer in later life. Well, my father knew nothing of this and he showed his preference for his granddaughter Yvonne very clearly. Just as well, as she was not a favourite of many. I suppose she did rather well out of this, being exposed to the intricacies of African-American jazz and the Victorian novel.

Yet another favourite pastime for these two was polishing the jewellery. This jewellery was kept in the drawer of his desk and didn't belong to him except when the owners failed to pay back the loan they had received on the surety of the 'jewellery'. The desk drawer was always full to overflowing as he drove a hard bargain, and often the pathetic bits of gold and glitter remained unclaimed. My father didn't make any exceptions; in fact, when he heard that Marcus Garvey was planning to leave Kingston, he made sure his loan to him was not in danger of going the way of the world. He appeared on the docks with his henchmen and Marcus saw the light. Papa would probably not have done so nowadays with the change in Marcus Garvey's status as a National Hero, but you never know.

He did give Yvonne a diamond ring once from the drawer in his desk. She says she has it still: it reminds her not to live above her means.

I have always worked for my father's firm. In fact, housekeeping was not my strong point but as we lived in Jamaica this was not a problem as there were always people willing, indeed happy, to wash and cook and clean. Our house was always well-staffed so I didn't have to put on any pretence about liking the role of Earth Mother. I don't cook, OK? I was much happier at work. I did all the dogsbody jobs – accounts, stock control, chasing bad debts, apologising for mistakes. I suppose that today you would call it PR. Papa marketed the business and dear sainted Brother Bonny did little or nothing except comb his hair. He was thought to be handsome. Decoration indeed. Sam Isaacs & Son. That's life.

The name never reflected the fact that for many years I ran it single-handed. I suppose it was too early for equal opportunity as a concept to have had much influence. But the business did amazingly well, allowing Claude and myself to send the children to boarding school as soon as it was decent.

St Hilda's Diocesan High School, set on a hill above Brown's Town in the garden parish of St Ann, was *the* boarding school to get the girls into. Rather as with fancy establishments in England, you were best advised to put names down at birth and then be prepared to pull strings. I am proud (or ashamed) to say that both Valerie and Yvonne are St Hilda's girls. Isn't it strange how ungrateful the young can be? To this day they both complain about the school.

As far as Valerie was concerned, she hated the place because of the cold showers with no doors, the ghastly food, and the fact that Yvonne was such an embarrassment to her. This latter reason I can understand as she really does test the patience of Job. Claude was forever being summoned up to the school to help in the chastisement of his elder daughter. He was not a happy man as the school was seventy miles from Kingston. Driving on the country roads in Jamaica today in the new millennium is no picnic, much less so in the 1950s. He was determined never to bring her back with him to Kingston. The holidays were quite long enough to endure, so he perfected the art of riposte.

On one occasion he excelled himself. He had been summoned as his eldest daughter was, in the headmistress's view, presenting a danger to the morals of the entire school and should be removed forthwith.

St Hilda's had a Latin motto, *Res severa verum gaudeum*. This motto formed an important climax to the school hymn, which was sung on very special occasions. This tickled Yvonne's imagination and she secretly trained members of her form to replace the Latin line with its English translation: 'And a hard hard thing is a true true true joy.' Sung to a heavy Jamaican blue-beat. Not funny. Miss Norman, the ancient headmistress and native of Yorkshire, went so red in the face she choked. Laughter vying with apoplexy. Soon the culprit was identified and the phone call to Claude made.

When he met with all the ancient virgin teachers, he asked to be told in detail what Yvonne had done this time. It took them a little while to get the words out.

'Ah!' he pounced. 'I think instead of attempting to expel her, you should be happy that she is now paying attention to her Latin translation. Remember, last term you were worried about that, weren't you? And anyway, ladies, do you not find this to be true? Is not a hard thing a true joy?' Before they could recover he was gone, leaving Yvonne on the quad, bags packed and all.

Yet another of these unscheduled drives up to Brown's Town was the result of a schoolgirl prank to which the teachers accorded the status of gross misdemeanour. St Hilda's was affiliated to St Mark's Church in the town – a ten-minute walk in crocodile. The poor unfortunate boarders had to attend four different church services every Sunday, two in the school chapel and two at St Mark's. Down they would go in a perfect crocodile, dressed in impeccable white, hymn books and Bibles in hand, not looking left or right at the townspeople who stared and laughed sometimes, then across the market square to the rear of the church to take up their appointed seats.

The sermons preached by the Reverend Horace Bedlow (known as Bedbug) were unimaginative, predictable and just what intelligent young persons didn't need. Yvonne, always a bookworm, having discovered Daphne du Maurier's *Frenchman's Creek* was loath to waste the whole Sunday without getting on with the exciting tale. She proceeded to cover the novel with brown paper and inscribe THE BIBLE on it. She was not famed for her attention span in church, but on this Sunday the suspicions of the teacher in charge were tickled during the first service and by the last she had been rumbled. The heavens shook with righteous indignation.

'Such blasphemy! Not enough to pretend the disgusting novel was the Bible, but to be reading it as well!'

Claude was summoned once again and didn't manage to wriggle out of the suspension this time. He was Not Amused.

No wonder Valerie found her time at St Hilda's embarrassing. Give the school credit where credit is due. They realised they were stuck with my elder daughter and sensibly made the best of a bad job. Soon she was encouraged to organise anything that was vaguely in need of staging, even the dramatisation of 'Linstead

41

Market', that hoary old folksong. They drew the line at
the school hymn.

Claude mentioned once that he thought there was
some sort of tension between the girls. Dear sweet man.
Of course he couldn't see that he was a major cause of it.
Could his treatment of Valerie as his Little Princess be
responsible – his adoration of her many talents, her singing, her piano-playing, her angelic ways? No? So I
reminded him of the incident of the end-of-term report.

At the end of each St Hilda's term a report on their
progress and achievement over the past twelve weeks
was written up for every student. As the proud parents
arrived on the quad to collect their girl children, the
reports were handed over, together with the invoice for
the fees for the next term. None of the girls were party
to what was inside. On one occasion Claude, sitting in
the back of the car with Valerie while Yvonne sat in front
with the chauffeur, had both envelopes in his hand. As
soon as they hit the road he opened Valerie's and oooed
and aaaed and promised unending treats. Apparently
Yvonne's envelope had fallen unopened to the floor and
remained there for the journey.

I know about this as when the happy family arrived in
Kingston I was bombarded with Valerie's success.
Seemed quite natural to ask about Yvonne's. There was a
terrible silence as Claude realised that not only had he
not opened the thing but also he couldn't put his hand
on it.

The car was searched. No envelope. Eventually
Yvonne presented it to me. She had retrieved it from the
floor of the car. I don't think she has ever forgotten this
incident. Maybe it made her what she has become.
Independent. And annoying with it!

All good things must come to an end and with the
Senior Cambridge Board exams duly passed – and very
well so – it was time for Yvonne to leave St Hilda's.

What to do with her? I think we finally got round to asking her and of course we needn't have worried. She knew exactly what she wanted to do. She had done all the research secretly with the help of the British Council representative in Jamaica, a Mr Murray. Together they set out to find a drama school in England which would agree to take her without a live audition and which, more importantly, would provide a piece of paper at the end. The Rose Bruford College of Speech and Drama fitted the bill and the brochure had arrived. No sooner had we asked the question than she was ready with her prepared presentation.

Lights. Action. Brochure. The ornamental lakes with swans swimming around and some very posh-looking white people practising archery in the background, together with the promise of a Teaching Diploma at the end, won Claude's approval immediately. I don't think he paid any attention to what was on offer to the students or the College's level of academic achievement. It looked safe, and well he knew that once Yvonne had made up her mind it was useless arguing with her. We both thought it would be some sort of finishing school. She often says she was nearly finished there, for true. My husband paid for the three years' tuition in one go. I expect his experiences with St Hilda's keenness to be rid of Yvonne on every pretext made him anticipate trouble. The College's probable reluctance to return money might help to keep our daughter there for the full three years, in spite of the havoc or mischief she might create.

Everything happened so quickly one might be forgiven for thinking we were anxious to see the back of Yvonne. Perhaps. However, once she had been accepted she was on a British Overseas Airways Corporation (then known locally as Better On A Camel) flight to New York to get the SS *Queen Mary* to Southampton. We were lucky enough to have Marjorie Kirlew to chaperone our dearly beloved. I keep two letters from that time. One from Marjorie and the other from Yvonne.

Dear Kathleen,

Here I am in England having crossed the Atlantic with Yvonne. Did you know that the voyage we were booked on was going to be the last before the Queen Mary *had stabilizers fitted? Well, it was.*

I suffered a lot from headaches and seasickness and although I tried my best to shield dear Yvonne from the temptations of the voyage I fear I did not succeed as well as I might have done. She is young and energetic and such a voyage is understandably exciting, but I think she may have taken her enjoyment too far. In fact, it appears that one night she locked me in the stateroom when I thought I had hidden the key very well under my pillow. I believe this to be the case as next morning she was being congratulated on winning the fancy-dress parade of the evening before. There were photographs of her. I have copies if you would like to see them. When I gave her a good look she admitted to having locked me in.

I tell you this in case you hear it from anybody and think that I was not doing all I could to keep her safe.

Anyway I can tell you she is now in Sidcup in agreeable lodgings with the Alexanders in Hurst Road. Nice people. He is a policeman, I believe.

I hope she enjoys herself.

I am staying on a bit longer in England but will call to see you on my return.

With good wishes,
Marjorie.

This letter was never shown to Claude as he would have blown his top and it would have been too late anyhow.

Waste of good breath. The second letter is from none other than student Yvonne.

Dearest Mummy and Daddy,
   I don't know how much I can get to hold on this air letter. The flight to New York was OK but there was no time to see New York. Aunt Marjorie likes to be early for everything. The Queen Mary is super. I had a really lovely time. I expect Aunt Marjorie will tell you I locked her in and went to a party. She is so boring. On the train coming up from Southampton I asked a man if everybody baked their own bread in England, as there were so many chimneys. When he laughed at me Aunt Marjorie put on one of her faces and looked out of the window. By the way, Aunt Marjorie wasn't talking to me.
   The Cumberland Hotel was super, especially as you could see the whole park from the window. Sidcup is horrible and my room is called a boxroom. I can't have more than one bath a week and they wanted to see my National Costume. No space for that now. Can I please leave this place? In fact, I have had to. I am at the Lumbers' but I won't give you the address as I won't be here long. The lake in the College brochure is actually here in front of the College and there are swans but no archers. O yes, Miss Bruford called me into her office. She was dressed all in green with tiny tight curls on her head. A perm, they call it. Anyway another woman was there – a Lady Henniker Heaton who breathed like a dragon with hiccoughs. You should know that Miss Bruford asked me if I was the girl whose father had paid in full for her. Then she said she would take the money but wanted to let me know that I would never work. Because I was Jamaican. I think they will probably want me to leave as all I said was 'Watch me and see.' In my best Jamaican accent.

45

These people are really weird, but the students are
super. Tobi Weinberg a Canadian student is also hav-
ing problems with the bath rationing at her digs. We
have found a flat to rent which we could share but we
need permission from parents. Can you please phone
the college – please? As soon as you can.
    Love,
    Yvonne

I didn't show Claude this letter, either. Just crossed my
fingers. I had no intention of going back to England ever
and it looked like we might have to. In the end I needn't
have worried as Yvonne soon got swept up in the excitement of being a rarity. If and when letters arrived from
Sidcup they were reasonably upbeat if somewhat lacking
in the niceties of punctuation and grammar. Seems
people on the buses and on the Underground trains
either wouldn't sit next to her or made a beeline for her,
depending on their turn of mind. The ones who made
the beeline usually touched her skin or pulled her hair
surreptitiously in order to find out if her colour would
come off or if her hair was real. Yvonne enjoyed these
outings and was ready with a scream whenever she felt
the errant hand at its business. Apparently this caused a
lot of confusion and embarrassment. People don't
scream at the top of their lungs on London buses and
most certainly not on Underground trains. Most of the
time the culprits were male so there were a few even
redder faces around.

She often pretended not to be able to speak English
and that made it even more uncomfortable. I suggested
she remember that most of these people had probably
never been outside of England's green and pleasant, so
she should be patient with them, but she was never one
for the quiet life.

There was one meeting on the Northern Line platform at Tottenham Court Road which haunts her even now. She made the mistake of mentioning it to an American professor at Harvard, Skip Gates, who was doing an article for the *New Yorker* April 28 and May 5 1997 on successful Blacks in Britain. And there it was for all to see a few months later:

> . . . *that situation can lead to some cultural contortions. Yvonne Brewster, the artistic director of the black theater company Talawa and a recent OBE (for services to the arts), tells me about what she dubs "the raffia ceiling." She says, "Linford Christie will say to you, 'I cannot drive my Porsche.' The man is a millionaire, but could get arrested for stealing the car. That's why someone like the boxer Chris Eubank dresses up like a kind of antediluvian English toff, with plus fours and a monocle, so he is easily identifiable. You know, there's method to his madness. Even if they stop him with his Mercedes-Benz, they say, 'Ah, it's Chris Eubank — drive on.' In this country, there's absolutely no chance of burning that raffia ceiling. If you put your head above the parapet, you're likely to get it cut off."*
>
> *For Yvonne Brewster, a member of Jamaica's "mulatto élite," there was never anything abstract about the vagaries of race and class in her new country. "My father had two farms, one in Portland and one in St. Thomas, and there was a man who used to do the horses in St. Thomas," she recalls. "He used to call me Miss Yvonne. Anyway, he came over here as a migrant, because there was no future for him and he didn't have any education. I was over here studying and I was at Tottenham Court Road underground station and he saw me and came up and hugged and kissed me." That the laborer should have presumed the solidarity of color and acquaintance horrified her,*

and, in her vulnerable state, she recoiled. "I suppose what flashed through my mind was that in Jamaica this man wouldn't even come within six feet of me," she says. "Anyway, I never saw the man again." She breaks off, and I notice there are tears in her eyes.

When I read this I thought, there she goes, exposing herself again. Will she ever learn that feet do not belong in mouths? What she says is true, although there are many who might not admit the truth. One can maybe now imagine more precisely her reaction to living at a respectable two-bedroomed and a one-boxroomed house in Sidcup. Not a bag of fun, really, especially with the one-a-week limit on baths. She was nevertheless kindly invited to spend her first Christmas Day with her landlords the Alexanders, on condition that she would dress in her national costume after Christmas 'dinner' and before the Queen's Speech at three o'clock. The Christmas meal was delicious and plentiful. Both Alexander children were beautifully behaved in the presence of two sets of grandparents. His father was a retired police constable with all the brash assurance of his breed. At 2.30 Mrs Alexander politely suggested that Yvonne might like to get ready. Taking the heavy hint she disappeared into her boxroom and put on what she had planned.

It was 1956, remember, when a style called the New Look was in. This consisted of a generously frilled mid-calf-length skirt teamed with a peasant-style blouse worn 'off the shoulder'. In Jamaica we had adapted it to our sensibilities by adding some colourful appliqués and local 'john crow' beads in red and black. She put on this finery, adding a head tie of colourful bandana plaid material and Carmen Miranda large hoop earrings. Da dah!

There was no applause on her dramatic entrance.

Instead a great anger exploded, especially from the ex-policeman who, reverting to form, chased her out of the room.

'Did you think we invited you to our Christmas dinner for you to take the piss? Get back and put on your grass skirt! I know you have it hidden in your room. Out! Out into the garden with you until you put on your grass skirt.'

My daughter never did hear the Queen's speech that year. She was homeless, thrown out of the digs on the grounds of being grass-skirtless. These were the same people who, on hearing that her home in Kingston was near Half Way Tree, were very impressed. Middle-class, they thought. You know, halfway up the tree . . . Unfortunately, Yvonne's natural reaction to this kind of insularity and sheer 'cor-blimey' was to take it to another level of the ridiculous.

'Oh yes, you are quite right. The Half Way Tree is halfway between Kingston, the town of the King, and the Constant Spring, home of his wife, for she is a mermaid. Half Way Tree is a special watering hole for the people as they travel to pay homage to the royal couple. You know, the middle classes will always find ways of making money. From way up in the middle branches of the tree they sold the water of the coconut to the pilgrims.'

They believed her.

I have no idea why she could not have simply said, 'No, we don't live in trees. Our house in Kingston is rather larger than your Sidcup semi-detached. It has four full bathrooms and no restriction on how many times you shower.'

She was forced to find digs at another house after the National Dress Christmas episode with the Alexanders. Her new landlords lived in a much smaller house, and he was a peg lower in class as he rode a motorcycle to

unskilled work at the Ford Motor car plant at Dagen-
ham. Here she had yet another, this time much smaller,
boxroom in the house, the size of a cupboard. A small
bed and a chair were possible if you entered backwards,
threw yourself on the bed and closed the door with your
feet. The signal for tea was when the radio in the kitchen
downstairs was turned up to full volume just before it
was time for *The Archers*, that everyday story of country
folk. Yvonne had to fly down the stairs to get to the table
before the theme tune was played out. No speech was
allowed for the next fifteen minutes as tea was taken with
The Archers. It consisted of sausages or tinned spaghetti
or thin slices of boiled ham, egg and cress salad or something equally disgusting.

Her new landlord would be in his vest with his lady
wife in her pinafore, and Yvonne in her winter woollies.
The place was seriously damp. After about a week of
this she was already anxious to move out with her friend
Tobi, when one evening after *The Archers* when she had
retired to the boxroom, there he was knocking on the
door, telling her in an unnecessarily aggressive tone to
turn down her radio, which was strange because it
wasn't on. Once the door was open he threw himself
on the bed, taking her with him and kicking the door
shut.

No flies on my girl. Her reaction was to set up an
almighty row for which there had been a lot of
rehearsals. In public transport. This brought an out-of-
breath spouse up the stairs. Upon forcing the door ever
so slightly ajar, she spied her husband prostrate upon the
bed with Yvonne standing screaming on the window-
ledge. In her agitation, for she was not slim, Mrs managed to get stuck (remember there was no room for
manoeuvre) and she too began screaming for help.

Obviously Yvonne, having to make another quick
exit, called us reverse charges on the phone, and we

immediately approved the move to the flat with Tobi. Digs are dangerous.

That reminds me, I must phone Valerie to find out exactly when Madam is arriving, as I must make sure I have my nails and my hair done. Oh yes, it's not only my furniture that she messes about, she messes about with me. This colour is wrong and those shoes are out. Actually I don't really mind as she does have an eye for these things, but on no account will I let her know how I really feel.

When she's here the house is full of life. People I haven't seen for ages pop in and out and there are parties and laughter. Hey ho.

Chapter 7

The Little Black Boy

—◦●◦—

While Yvonne was at Rose Bruford College of Drama learning to speak the Queen's English, to fence, to teach recalcitrant children in Kentish suburbs to dance around as fairies and obey her teaching-practice tutor Miss Allchin's preferred way of keeping order in the classroom – softly cooing, 'Tinklebell wants you to be quiet,' there were many moments of real-life drama. For example, I had to leave Jamaica and travel to London with my father when all of a sudden she announced her engagement. At the age of eighteen. Her fiancé was 'Someone who works in refrigeration,' she said. As a matter of fact he drove one of those frozen food lorries which were quite rare in those days, but still a truck driver, no? I know when to leap into action and in no time there we were in the Strand. Papa came with me as he was an avid stamp collector and the famous Stanley Gibbons shop was situated near the Savoy.

When I remember this incident I am not proud of myself but there was no time for niceties, and after all our investment in the girl, I couldn't stand idly by and watch her throw herself away on someone who quite simply wouldn't do. Mike was his name and they, this Mike and Yvonne, were invited to dinner. Wasn't long before it was the poor lad's turn to flee: in confusion at the supercilious waiters and their menus. Not nice but effective. Sometimes, I wonder if we did the right thing, as I don't think she has ever forgiven us. My argument is that if this Mike was worth his salt, he would have stood up to white linen, polite conversation and a heavy silver setting, but he fled in fear. Wouldn't do. Backbone missing.

It was three years before she scared us once again with wedding bells. Which rang this time.

You do have to have bottle to survive in this world, especially if you come from Jamaica. Apparently, today being a Jamaican is not a great thing to be in the eyes of the international media. In fact, these days Jamaica is only in the crime news. I keep hearing Jamaica being accused of producing shoe bombers, Muslim clerics preaching death and destruction and drug-smuggling mules taking over Pentonville Women's Prison. I can only say they should add some of those noisy musicians to the list. You should live where I do here in Kingston, and have to listen to the dancehall music which bombards us at decibel levels which no civilised society should allow. It booms out from the environs of the Priory School, the Ranny Williams Centre and the Police Officers Club. *Yes*. To whom then, does one complain? I wonder if the Prime Minister hears this people's music at Jamaica House?

But back to having bottle. Yvonne's time at College was not a bed of roses. I expected her to throw in the towel at any moment but no, she persisted. There was a crunch time when the teacher of Voice and Speech, a Greta Stevens who dressed in blue with red tights, insisted that my daughter recited William Blake's poem 'The Little Black Boy' in which there hides the line *And I am black, but O! my soul is white*.

She wouldn't say the line. She decreed the poem racist. Why did the poor little boy have to excuse the colour of his skin, and in the next breath decide his soul was white which made it all right? 'I'm not reciting this

poem,' she said. (Reminds me of a similar refusal round
the dining table when she suddenly wouldn't answer to
the name of Elsie.) Miss Stevens, poor woman, had
never come across this kind of Jamaican insubordination
before and tried the calm soft voice of reason. William
Blake should not be taken literally. 'It is usual for the
devil to be portrayed in Europe as black. Souls are usually white.' To no avail. Yvonne failed verse-speaking
that term.

Another problem had also reared its head. This had to
do with Received Pronunciation or RP, as it was known.
One of the tasks of Rose Bruford was to iron out all
traces of regional and foreign accents. The phonetics
class was an essential part of every student's life. Having
quite a good ear Yvonne did all right with the regional
accents, especially Yorkshire of course, and was very
good with the RP. In fact, to this day when she wants to
make a point she sometimes reverts to this awful manner
of speech. However, she had read somewhere that Lang-
ston Hughes the African-American poet who died in
1967, had said that poetry was a personal thing and
should be spoken in one's natural voice and accent. So
the, anonymous I think, 'Your love is a flower in which I
am a bee' was fertile ground to try out this theory. Gone
were the lilting tones of Received Pronunciation and the
rather more pronounced beat of Jamaican rhythm took
its place. Frankly I see her point because that could be a
very sexy concept, given the right treatment. All she got
was GET OUT.

As for acting, she was never cast in anything spectacular. The height of her achievement in the end-of-year
production was to play a troll in *Peer Gynt*. She did
almost play the lead once in all her time there, as the
Maid in Thornton Wilder's *The Skin of Our Teeth*. It
was clear to see that Miss Bruford and her earnest band
of lecturers were quite convinced that it was a waste of

time paying any attention to her progress in acting classes. They were all quite sure that she would never get a part, for reasons already mentioned.

A term I hear used constantly on BBC World Television programmes these days is 'joined-up thinking'. This seemed to be missing from the College staff at that time. Yvonne was there in the late 1950s. Did they not notice that Jamaican playwright Barry Reckord was at the height of his powers and at one moment had three plays simultaneously on in London? One of these, *Skyvers*, had to be cast with white actors as enough black actors could not be found to do these six parts. Errol John's *Moon on a Rainbow Shawl* won the Observer Prize in 1956 and casting it was very problematic. Most of the actors had to be brought over from the Caribbean. American plays like *Raisin in the Sun* and *Anna Christie* came fully cast from New York. So where was the imagination which should lead a drama school to changing this state of things? Certainly not in Sidcup, where it was a case of finding something harmless to interest my daughter.

Everyone wanted to act but very few saw the attraction of directing. Surreptitiously, this niche was filled by Yvonne. She says it is the problem-solving aspect of theatre directing which fascinated her from the beginning. For instance, in the first play they let her loose on, Bernard Shaw's *Saint Joan*, she asked herself how to convince the audience that the wind had *really* changed direction, sending Joan on to victory? The actress playing the part was too mannered when absolute simplicity was called for. How to persuade this debutante to really believe in her voices? How to conjure up original technical miracles with no resources? How to? How to? How to? Nearly half a century later she is still at it, sometimes managing to make molehills out of mountains, but striving to identify the moments of truth within a play with the actors, giving it everything she has, often collapsing after opening night.

And above all, learning *never* to read the English reviews. It's a hard row to hoe when the majority of critics working in the English press prefer black work to be either jolly and community in spirit, the more people on stage, the more colourful the mixture the better, and if they are singing and dancing – preferably smiling – much, much better. Failing this, a detailed examination of the woeful plight of the under-privileged black single mother in a coldwater flat will do nicely, better still if garnished with a generous dollop of social engineering. The critics wield an enormous amount of power, disproportionate, if you let them. It took some time for Yvonne to realise that if one wants to please the critics, one must hide one's intelligence, act grateful and 'jig' nicely.

Back to Rose Bruford College. In spite of all the hassle I think Yvonne enjoyed her years in Sidcup, although from what I remember everything was a struggle. For instance, she used to leave her digs in enough time to allow for a stroll through Lamorbey Park on her way to College. She would do her voice exercises during this stroll and arrive in time for the first class. She was never late. Unlike many Jamaicans, she is punctual. Her father, who wasn't always, used to warn her that she would be perpetually lonely if she kept up this habit of being early for appointments. So vulgar to appear anxious. However, this habit served her not at all well. The other students would ask, 'Why do you leave home so early? You could get ten more minutes in bed!' While the teachers suggested, 'To walk so slowly is the sign of an under-active brain.' Rock and a hard place?

Most of the students in her year, the ones with the large, active brains, failed to enter the profession after

College or to stay with it if they did, with the following notable exceptions: Nerys Hughes, Laurie Taylor, Brian Hewlett in *The Archers* and Norman Bennett. I believe the College did ask Yvonne to be a Patron some years ago. This is one offer she took up immediately. I think she liked the irony.

Reality struck home forcefully yet again sometime during her second year. These people were going to let her continue attending classes at the College, probably because, we suspect, they were loath to return the fees Claude had paid in advance, but they had absolutely no intention of allowing her to graduate with an RBTC Diploma in Speech and Drama. Knowing that there was no likelihood of her remaining alive if she returned to Jamaica without that piece of paper, my daughter set about finding a way around this dilemma.

At that time, the Royal Academy of Music in Euston Road near Baker Street tube station held extra-mural courses in a number of subjects not strictly musical. Yvonne enrolled for Voice and Speech and Mime. For about fifteen months she attended Rose Bruford and the Royal Academy. Neither knew about the other. Burning the candle at both ends was the only way to go.

If this wasn't enough of a strain she wanted to (and I quote) 'Do some real work in a real theatre for real.' How elegant. Students were not allowed to take professional jobs without permission from the College and as Yvonne knew that she was highly unlikely to be given such a thing, she secretly went up for, and got, a job in the pantomime called *Aladdin*, at Colchester Repertory Theatre for four weeks during her final Christmas holidays. *Without permission*. The letters I keep help me with the details so I'll just try to find the one letter she wrote then, and put it in here.

December, 1958

Dearest Mummy and Daddy,

Guess what? I am in Colchester, Essex playing the Fairy of the Ring in a pantomime called Aladdin. *I am doing this to get my Provisional Equity card. I want to be the first to get it just to show them! But you must promise not to tell. Anyway no one's at College as it's the hols so you can't.*

It was fun getting digs as if the landlady saw me it was no go, so as there were three other white girls looking to share digs they hid me and we got this room with two arm-chairs and a double bed. We take it in turns and there is a roster up on the wall to tell you what nights you get the bed and what nights the chair.

<u>Daddy don't read this</u>: *Mummy, do you know every night just as the girls in the chorus are doing what we call a quick change, Mr Digby the producer always finds a reason to come into the dressing-room. He thinks we don't twig what's going on so some girls put on a show for him one night and he hasn't been back since.*

It's a load of fun. Actually one night, you know I wear this tutu thing and appear in a puff of smoke, well a spark from the box caught my tutu and in a moment there were flames. Anyway I wasn't hurt but there was something to talk about. I was the centre of attention for a couple of days. I didn't get a Christmas pudding from Aunt Elsie this year. You did send one didn't you? Next Christmas I'll be at home.

Lots of love
Yvonne the pantomime star!

Back at College with her Provisional Equity card, which she flashed whenever the occasion demanded, Yvonne continued the rushing back and forth from Sidcup to

Baker Street, sitting exams in both establishments. During the final term she was on tenterhooks, waiting for the results from the Royal Academy. I remember her telling me what a fright she had when at the viva for her Mime exam at the Academy who should be sitting on the other side of the desk but Thea Tucker, who taught Greek Dancing at Bruford!

Remember, no one was supposed to know that she was taking the LRAM exams. Luckily, Thea Tucker winked at her to put her mind at rest. Just as well, as 'the dolly house nearly mash up', as we say in Jamaica.

One afternoon a month or so later, Yvonne was sent for by Miss Bruford, still in green and still with Lady Henniker Heaton still hiccoughing by her side. As soon as Yvonne was summoned into the presence, the Bruford woman forgot her cool and shouted at my daughter:

'How dare you? How dare you? And again, *how dare you*? I have just had a phone call from the Royal Academy of Music in which they informed me that my student had passed her Mime examination with Distinction. How did they know it was my student? They recognised my hand movements in your performance. How dare you? How dare you?' And so on and on and on.

By this time Yvonne had recovered and was doing a sort of Red Indian war dance (they liked those things in those days), whooping and chanting, 'I don't need your stupid RBTC Dip now, do I?'

As it happened Miss Bruford was an Honorary LRAM. Yvonne had just got hers, not one but two, by sheer hard work and a bushel of luck. No wonder she hooped and swooped. I don't think she minds not being liked by people like that. Just as well.

Of course the College was constrained to award her its Final Diploma. It would have seemed too petty, even for them, to deny her it when she had collected two from the Royal Academy. Also, I believe Claude had a word with Benson Greenall, a friend of his in London, who made a discreet call to the College pointing out certain inequities which might be embarrassing if brought to the attention of the Minister of Education.

So home she sailed not with one piece of paper but with three. Always falls on her feet, that one. I found it all very trying. Still do.

Chapter 8

Pieces of Paper

———•◦◯◦•———

In the meantime life went on in Jamaica. Valerie was pushed into making up her mind about her career and she too was off to London to study. Poor child, she didn't really want to go. She wanted to knit, crochet, read the Gospel of St John and be a nun, but that really wasn't on. She had to be packed off to Tooting in deepest south-west London, in order to become a Company Secretary. Her letters home were short and breezy, not complaining and alarming as Yvonne's were. Later, Claude and I realised just how miserable our younger daughter had been during her three years in South London. She never fully used the Company Secretary qualification, as she has always preferred being helpful to people – with disastrous results on her finances. Too trusting and much too kind, is our Miss Val. Should have been a social worker.

Yvonne returned to Jamaica with her pieces of paper, only to be told by the Jamaican Ministry of Education that they had never heard of her qualifications and that they would only pay her at the lowest rate going as a Pupil Teacher. Of course, this set Claude on the warpath and luckily the Headmaster of Excelsior School where Yvonne worked, Wesley Powell (relative, I believe, of Colin Powell, the one who's very important these days), was game to challenge this decision by the Government. He felt the Government needed to realise that the Arts were just as important as the Sciences and that Music, Art, Drama, Dance and Physical Education should not be relegated to the status of leisure pursuits and regarded simply as pastimes.

The plan was that Claude should support Yvonne for the time it would take for Wesley to make his stand. This was to refuse to pay his Drama staff (Yvonne) at a rate so much below what her pieces of paper demanded. Claude's rationale was that, as he had supported her up to this point, six months more were unlikely to make that much difference.

For six months Wesley Powell stood his ground, until the decision was made to recognise Drama as a proper subject; it has remained as such to this day. Of course, when the six months' back pay arrived there was a great celebration. This family is a sucker for celebration. Good party, though.

It was a good time she spent at Excelsior working under the benevolent eye of her mentor WAP (Wesley A. Powell, educator extraordinaire). We were quite worried at her having to teach boys in the sixth form who were her age and in some instances a little older but it all worked out just fine. Some of her ex-students from that time have done well for themselves. I wonder if Radcliffe Butler and Willard White remember those days? Yvonne always spoke of Alma Mock Yen as a bit of a star colleague.

In the late 1950s amateur theatre was in its heyday in Jamaica. This was one way of keeping the expatriate community amused during the long dark tropical evenings. *South Pacific* was to be the musical of the year and auditions were called.

Yvonne, full of her brand-new qualifications, felt sure she would get a good part – if not the lead. After all, she could sing, she could act and she was a picture of Jamaican womanhood. She duly auditioned, only to be told by the Director of the Jamaican Operatic Society, Billy Pilgrim, that she could have a non-speaking part in the chorus. You see, all the leading parts had already been shared out among the many expatriate wives who had little to recommend them but their skin colour. I think of this whispered ditty:

> *If you're white you're all right.*
> *If you're brown you can hang around*
> *But if you're black just stay at the back.*

Yvonne was patently *not* all right. Hang around or stay at the back she did not do. The inequity and frustration of it all served as a spur to create her own possibilities. This is the political truth upon which the Barn Theatre was founded, similarly the Talawa Theatre Company: *Expect no favours.*

Luckily, however, not all the local thespians were so caught up in the colonial past. Orford St John, an escapee from Oxford University, who was a brilliant director, decided to produce a double bill using Carol Morrison and Yvonne as his leading ladies. For them he unearthed Strindberg's *The Stronger*, a two-hander with one nonspeaking part, thought to be very cutting-edge, dealing as it does with infidelity. Tasty for Jamaica. The second half of this double bill was Tennessee Williams's *Suddenly Last Summer*. Carol played Mrs Venables and Yvonne Catherine. Filled the Ward Theatre's 900 seats on many a night.

A letter arrived from Rose Bruford. The College had received an application from someone in Jamaica for a place in the first year. It was a man called Trevor Rhone. Did she know him? Would she be good enough to interview him and report on his suitability? No problem. Trevor Rhone arrived for the interview on the capacious Oxford Road veranda. Claude heard his boisterous

63

rendition of 'Friends, Romans, countrymen', and thought it pretty appalling, but then he never liked the man. Yvonne was not too enthusiastic about his Shakespeare, but the delivery of a Robert Frost lyric won the day.

She informed Miss Bruford that, although Rhone's Shakespeare shook the rafters rather, his voice was an untapped, untrained and quite beautiful instrument which would benefit greatly from three years at Rose Bruford's. He got in. And the voice is still with us. Selah! as Yvonne would say.

After only a year back here in Jamaica, off she went again to England. Wedding bells summoned Claude, Neville and Valerie to London to see Yvonne become Mrs Roger Francis-Jones. I didn't stir myself as ceremonies full of fuss, especially weddings, never did interest me and I didn't think the marriage would last long. It didn't.

I grew to like Jennie Jones, the mother-in-law, who was a bundle of energy and lively to the point of exhaustion. I miss her visits to Jamaica now she's dead. As is her son Roger, my one-time son-in-law. It was a timely and lucky release for one of God's likeable rascals. Tall, good-looking but weak, he gave up a promising job managing some of London's finest hotels, for the bottle. As soon as he discovered Jamaican rum, that was it. Nowhere but down. Soon the bailiffs arrived at their London apartment.

Yvonne, resourceful as ever, pretended to be the maid, who didn't speak English. 'What, sah? Mi no speak di Hinglish.' However, as soon as the big black van drove off, promising to return the next day, she was away to London airport and on the first flight to Jamaica. Seems to make a habit of this. When in doubt, hit the airport.

Roger followed her out to Jamaica. Claude, always one to stick up for the men, managed to get him a job as Manager at one of Montego Bay's hotels where it was even easier for him to hit the rum bottle. Yvonne would not speak to him. (She has this habit of enforced silences.) He went from bad to worse when finally, one night around four in the morning, the telephone rang.

'Kathleen, this is Roger. I need a hearse.'

'You do? Where? Why?'

'At Long Bay in Portland. You see, I took this young thing out for a swim but she got into difficulty and drowned. Kathleen, you must hurry as I think they are looking for me. Please. They will kill me.'

'Who will kill you, Roger?'

'She says – sorry, said – she was the Cuban Ambassador's daughter.'

'I see. Don't go anywhere.'

This 'young thing' was due to be married that weekend, I believe. Exactly what was she doing on the other side of the island with this married man? you may wonder.

I did say Yvonne's marriage wouldn't work. Didn't I?

I am, after all, in the business of funerals. Finding a hearse was the least of my troubles. The more important matter was to get John Roger Francis-Jones out of Jamaica, never to return. I just couldn't deal with the scandal when it broke. I arranged for Roger to be spirited away in a hearse and hidden in a sleazy small hotel in Half Way Tree, the haunt of many local expatriates, while I booked him on a plane out of our life with a one-way ticket in the name of John Francis. He made it out, in spite of Cuban vigilance, knocked around in London for a bit but dropped down dead one afternoon in Knightsbridge, before his fortieth birthday. Cirrhosis. Charming rascal.

It was round about this time that Yvonne started using some of the expensive education we had paid for. Free from the fear of the haunting Roger, she blossomed in the sun and took up teaching again at Kingston

College Junior School at the old Melbourne Park cricket ground. The pieces of paper were coming in handy. It was a special time at KC during those years, as just for a year or two the staff was particularly talented. I am speaking of Trevor Rhone, who had successfully completed his Rose Bruford stint, Rachel Manley, one of Michael's many offspring, Maud Fuller – perhaps the brightest actress Jamaica has produced – Trevor Parchment, athlete extraordinaire, Marjorie Whylie, musician of the first order, and my daughter Yvonne, who, it must be said, wasn't that rusty.

Many of the students who benefited from that short period of staff creativity, like John Jones, Teddy Price, Raymond Watson, Lovindeer and Mickey Smith, went on to become important poets, sportsmen, artists, musicians and Jamaican citizens of note.

Claude and Bishop Gibson (Bishop of Kingston and Headmaster of the school) could be overheard discussing this renaissance in whispers as they sipped whisky and water and listened to the nine o'clock BBC news on the shortwave radio. Apparently they both hoped Yvonne had finally settled down to be a respectable girlchild.

Not a chance.

Chapter 9

Sun and Rum

Before long my daughter had taken up with Trevor Rhone. They were inseparable – 'batty and bench' as we say – much to the disgust of Claude, who thought poor Trevor was pompous, sly, and 'over-ripe', whatever that meant. I didn't mind the lad as he worked hard. The difference in his background was a plus in my eyes, however beyond the pale it was in most others'. I always tried to support their efforts to activate and politicise the local theatre scene, which was dominated at the time by some 'big no dough' white people who thought that their tastes were, by some heavenly ordinance, superlative.

I encouraged the small troupe of thespians Yvonne, Trevor, Munair Zacca and so on to experiment with the form, and after all these years it's quite lovely to know that, although they exiled our four cars from their rightful shelter in the garage and concocted a theatre out of the space, costing us an arm and a leg in the process, the Barn is still going strong nearly forty years on. Claude was secretly quite pleased that his money spent on Yvonne's education had not been entirely wasted.

Without my knowledge, he subdivided the land on which his late lamented garage, now the Barn Theatre, stands and put it in Yvonne's name. Never told her. He was funny that way. He was always enraged when, later on, he would read articles which seemed to give all the credit for the Barn to Trevor. I guess that was why he gave it to Yvonne. 'Time longer than rope,' he would say. But I didn't care who claimed what about anything. The important matter was the work. And work they did.

Theatre in Jamaica has had a long history which, until relatively recently, had very little to do with the majority of the citizens. In fact, it is the subject of the entertaining book *Revels in Jamaica 1682–1838* by Richardson Wright, one-time editor of *Homes and Gardens*, first published in 1937, the year of my marriage The revels he reports on include *Plays and Players, Tumblers and Conjurers, Musical Refugees and Solitary Showmen, Dinners, Balls, Cockfights, Darky Mummers and other Memories of High Times and Merry Hearts.* From the mid-1700s here in Jamaica there have been performances of plays for the entertainment of the expatriate community. Touring actors on their way to the new colony America would sensibly take a detour here for some sun and rum.

Theatres to house these extravagancies were built. In fact, today in Kingston we have one of the finest examples of a Victorian theatre in the Third World (for this is how we are expected to refer to ourselves). The Ward Theatre is exactly twice the size of the Frank Matcham Theatre Royal at Stratford East in London's East End. That reminds me, I met Philip Hedley of Stratford East once when he visited Jamaica with strict instructions from Madam, who had directed at his theatre, to look me up. Kept me entertained with theatre stories which had me in stitches. Anyway, our Ward Theatre is built to the TRSE design: red plush, gilt cherubs, the Stalls, Dress Circle and the glorious Gods or 'penny section' as we used to call those lovely seats where you could make your honest opinion known. Full many an unfunny comic has bowed to pressure and missiles from the Gods.

It wasn't until around the middle of the twentieth

century that theatre in Jamaica began to be relevant, or even accessible, to the people of the country. When George Bernard Shaw visited Jamaica in 1911 he said this about theatre in Jamaica: *The next thing you want is a theatre, with all the ordinary travelling companies from England and America sternly kept out of it, for unless you do your own acting, write your own plays, your theatre will be of no use. It will in fact vulgarise and degrade you.* I saw this written up in Errol Hill's *The Jamaican Stage 1655–1900*, which Yvonne brought home with her on one of her fleeting visits.

Well, not being a wordsmith I couldn't have put it better but those were the sentiments I used to drum into Yvonne's head, not only about theatre but about *all* the Arts. So in some way I guess I am partly responsible for how she tackled the opportunity which clearing out our garage provided. Those kids were addressing the gaps in theatre provision. 'People have to see themselves on the stage or else what's the point?' is how she put it, and how she continues to put it.

For a while I too was struck with the acting bug. My style was a little over the top, declamatory even, but who cared. Keith Binns, a lovely young man, no relation to the English Binns, a member of the Drama Club at St Michael's Church, always reminds me of the time when we were presenting *Sunday Costs Two Pesos* and Norman Rae, who was Drama Critic at the *Gleaner*, turned up. As he had the reputation of being a little too rigorous in his criticism for my liking, I had him removed from the auditorium. I wasn't having my cast upset by him, you understand. Apparently he was *forcibly* removed. I remember threatening him at the Barn once, so this could just be true.

Keith, raconteur to the end, also delights in recalling the night when, being given a lift home from rehearsals in a large station wagon which was a 'service vehicle' down at the Funeral Home, and thinking that his companion in the back was a bit silent, asked what was the matter only to be told that it was a corpse. He says he leaped out of the moving vehicle and ran for his life. This is true. He did do this once.

When the children were at prep school I used to arrange to have them collected by the driver at the end of the day. Some days the only vehicle available was a hearse, so off it would go up to Blake Prep in Glenmore Road and they would climb aboard. Well, many of the other children wanted to hitch a ride in the hearse. So boring to go home in a car. The passenger numbers grew with each passing day. On a particularly popular day the hearse set off with six cars following it as it did its rounds to the various residences (the six cars belonged to the six extra tiny passengers). Unfortunately, one of the mothers had a nervous disposition, and upon seeing the hearse pull up outside her front gate got the palpitations. Then, seeing her son jump out of the back of it, she fainted clean away.

The practice was discontinued.

It's quite usual for heightened tales about Undertaking to do the rounds. Something to do with a perfectly natural human fear of death. Papa always used to say you were a hundred times safer with the dead than the living. Certainly safer than working in the theatre . . .

But I digress. By working at Kingston College as teachers Trevor and Yvonne had the afternoons and evenings free for the Barn. The really exciting times to the onlooker were when they were devising the work they had to put on. As far as they were concerned, there were no plays dealing with the everyday life and times of the ordinary common or garden Jamaican, and the challenge was to find them or to make them. In the meantime they had to put something on, starting with classics (Strindberg's *Miss Julie*), difficult plays (Edward Albee's

70

Zoo Story), English semi-political plays (Joe Orton's *What the Butler Saw*).

Finding the right plays was always difficult. Yvonne used to spend her summers in London on the pretence of researching plays for the Barn. One lunchtime she found herself in a tiny, sparsely populated theatre, the Ambiance, in the basement of a restaurant at the Bayswater end of Queensway, West London, run by a Trinidadian, Junior Telfor: *The Electronic Nigger* was being presented. I think the title was the attraction. However, at the end of the performance she turned to one of the few members of the audience and said: 'I wish I could get hold of the rights to this play. It's really what we need to see in Jamaica.' The man looked at her long and hard and said, 'They're yours if you wish. I'm Ed Bullins, the playwright.' An Yvonne trademark 'leap before you look'.

The play was produced at the Barn but not before the theatre had been picketed by the then young Robert Hill, now a grand academic and professor in the United States of America. His grouse? The title. He had no idea what the play was about, nor that it was one of the most revolutionary black plays of that era. I think his father, Stephen Hill, had to rescue him from his embarrassment.

There was also the time when the eccentric Ken Maxwell wrote a revue for the Barn called *Soon Come Please* in which an earnest graduate of the London School of Economics, now head honcho of one of the two local trade unions, was portrayed promising his workforce his undying loyalty and dedication to their interests before going in to see the bosses for a negotiation lunch which consisted of delicacies beyond the dreams of the workers, only to emerge with the promise of free piped music. Rather tame undergraduate stuff really, but not to Michael Manley, who sent one

71

of his followers down to the Barn to put the frighteners on.

Trevor's brother Neville Rhone being a good Party man was aware of this and Trevor had been warned of 'Joshua' Michael's rage, but Yvonne had not. When duly summoned into the presence of the great man himself and ordered to take the revue off or risk having an injunction taken out, my daughter's usual response of the leap then look variety was: 'Mr Manley, your name is not mentioned in this revue, but if the cap fits, please do feel free to wear it.'

Explosion all around as MM leaped to his feet, as did all those around him, including Eric Bell and trade unionist Hopeton Caven (recently retired, I believe, after thirty-four years working for the Shipping Association of Jamaica). This resulted in Beverley Anderson running out from the office to pacify the raging leader. He didn't touch Yvonne but it was a dramatic moment. I think the assembled company all felt a bit silly.

No injunction was taken out and the play had a long and interesting run. In the Jamaica of those days, censorship was not as subtle as it might have been. There was a fondness for the rule of the heavy stick. Pity all that fuss wasn't about something really important like corruption or the proliferation of firearms, instead of one large political bruised ego.

Meanwhile, in the Barn, the devising of plays went on. I remember a large Grundig reel-to-reel tape recorder on which the devised work of the acting company was recorded. The talent roll-call is impressive. Janet Bartley, later to woo us in the film *The Harder They Come*, Paul Issa, Melba Bennett, Pat Priestly, Leonie Forbes, Billy Woung, Sidney Hibbert, Joanna Hart and of course Munair Zacca again. The genesis of many of the early plays at the Barn was from the sturdy Grundig. *It's Not My Fault, Baby* was the first such. To this day I can still see Janet Bartley devising the Coca-Cola bottle scene in that play.

You may well wonder how I came to know all these things. Well, Claude and I used to eavesdrop on rehearsals now they were no longer on our veranda but in our garage. Moving with the times. He to make sure there was nothing too near the knuckle going on, me for the excitement. I mean, spending all day with the dead and all night with the birth of plays. Not bad.

At one moment the Fowlers of the Little Theatre Movement, together with the University of the West Indies, brought out English theatre director Sam Walters to do some work in Jamaica. Apparently, however, Sam and his wife Auriol were seriously under-employed. They were quickly poached, and ended up doing some splendid work with the Barn. Together they assembled a tour intended for Jamaican secondary schools of three three-quarter-hour excerpts from *Hamlet*, *A Midsummer Night's Dream* and *Julius Caesar*. Trevor got to do his speech properly at last. It was all considered very cutting-edge at the time, the six actors dressed all in black with nothing but a prop table for support. Minimalist, they called it.

The most successful excerpt was *A Midsummer Night's Dream*. One of the actors was Bim Lewis, known and loved by the public as a stand-up comedian working in the vernacular. It was Sam's stroke of genius to have him play Bottom in the *Dream*. It brought the play alive for Jamaican children, who quite honestly had difficulty seeing, hearing or believing Shakespeare had anything to do with them. This little tour was successful, although it caused one or two ripples – especially at stylish and expensive boys' boarding school Monroe College, where the teacher in charge was highly dubious of the educational value of having Bim Lewis 'ruin Shakespeare's play'. Bim didn't ruin anything except the teacher's image. In fact, judging from the comments after the performances, he had elucidated the text.

Sam, Auriol and their two baby girls finally went back to England, where Sam opened the Orange Tree in Richmond, Surrey, one of the first pub theatres in London.

The early Barn rehearsals used to attract a small band of devotees, including Karl Parboosingh, a gifted, wonderfully impressionistic painter whose work I have always liked. I would love to own an original painting of his. I have Gonzales, I have Dorothy Wells but I need a Parboo. We would see him steal down the driveway and in at the back of the theatre sometimes with Douglas Manley.

One afternoon Karl turned up at the Barn and asked to be allowed in. He proceeded to measure up the triangle-shaped lintel. About two months later he turned up again, this time in his famous long-back station wagon, and offloaded six panels of the most dynamic figurative art depicting all the stages of performance. 'A gift for the theatre,' he told Yvonne. I may be wrong but I think this is the largest piece of Parboosingh's, work in existence. I remember when there was some talk about having a mural of his at Kingston's Palisadoes Airport, but I don't think that ever happened. I do like to remember this old-time Jamaican story of love, talent and generosity among artists. It still is in the Barn nearly forty years on, so have a look next time you visit.

Chapter 10

The Harder They Come

———•◦◉◦•———

Teaching pubescent boys at Kingston College eventually began to pall. Unsurprising after the excitement of the Barn. Yvonne has always had a short attention span when it came to teaching. Bright, challenging students were one thing, but she did not excel at the everyday routine – the marking of registers and the patience needed for work with the less gifted.

When a job came up with Radio Jamaica as a duty announcer and newsreader, she took it. I laughed aloud when the raunchy gossip columnist Stella (who was really Barbara Gloudon in an early mutation), complained in Kingston's evening newspaper the *Star* about this new radio announcer who had discovered a new sea, the Bibby Sea. It's so easy to be bitchy. Yes, there were, as one would expect, some snide remarks. Worry when they ignore you, I say.

Yvonne had been trained in radio technique at Rose Bruford. This training was necessarily quite different from the training many of the other Jamaican radio announcers had received at a North American establishment called Ryerson. She sounded nothing like Charlie Babcock the cool fool with the live jive, or El Número Uno Don Toppin, Del Weller or the late lamented Desmond Chambers – a favourite of mine. She sounded English. Which was uncool.

However, Englishman Graham Binns, who was

General Manager at Radio Jamaica, took a special interest in her and tried to make sure that she continued to
pronounce words in a manner satisfactory to his ears.
Every now and then, the red light in the announcer's
booth would flash on and there would be GB the GM
reminding her of the silent w in Keswick, or that
Guantánamo Bay had its stress on the second syllable.
He and John Colly, another BBC-trained man, taught
her how to introduce the Queen properly for the annual
Royal Christmas Broadcast.

'There are thirteen introductory pips which you will
hear in your earphones. Begin speaking on the third.
Ladies and Gentlemen, pause for two pips, *Her Majesty*,
pause for three pips, *The Queen*. After three more pips
HM's voice will be heard. On no account must you
crash her voice.' Again. And again. The other day I
heard someone on the radio turn 'compromise' into
two words, 'come promise'. I wonder if they still have
pronunciation classes?

I came into my own as Mother of Yvonne Jones. 'You
could get your daughter to read out a greeting for me on
Open House on RJR? Please!' I was supposed to put
these requests on her pillow. In those days it was a big
thing to have a greeting read out over the radio. She did
have a favourite listener called Delores Harriott from
Manchester, who got a greeting read out nearly every
afternoon and a Jim Reeves record dedicated to her.

While working at RJR one Christmas Yvonne was
sent a live turkey, quarts of gungo peas, much yam and
ham and sorrel – all gifts from admiring listeners. The
live turkey strutting up and down was from Delores
Harriott, the Jim Reeves fan from Manchester. Or so
said the card hanging from the gobbler's scrawny neck.

When Graham Binns saw the reception area of
Jamaica's poshest radio station transformed into a back
yard complete with a turkey on the hoof, he was so

enraged he took on the appearance of the strutting beast himself as he ordered the area to be cleared. *Immediately.*

I was persuaded to send a pickup van for the goodies. We had an excellent Christmas that year. Bigger parties than ever.

There were more serious aspects of the job. When His Imperial Majesty, King of Kings, Lord of Lords, Lion of Judah, Emperor Haile Selassie paid Jamaica a state visit in 1966, Yvonne got the peachy job of reporting, mike in hand, from the red carpet on which HIM and his royal daughter, the Princess Mouna, were to walk when they arrived at the National Stadium for the official national welcome. Always a perfectionist, she was there early, having driven us all mad by reciting the Emperor's proper mode of address and practising her curtsy. In position at the edge of the red carpet at the stadium, she was a little nervous, as reports by Dotty Dean at the airport were worrying.

So many Rastafarians had gathered on the tarmac smoking the sacred weed that there was a palpable risk of explosion of the Imperial aircraft. However, it was said that Mortimer Planno, Rastafari Elder, had saved the day by persuading the Brethren to stand back and 'out the weed' momentarily.

Eventually HIM was driven away to attend the many functions planned, including the affair at the National Stadium where Yvonne stood on the red carpet awaiting the official motorcade. Looking nervously behind her, she saw a sea of people dressed in red, green and gold who were quietly awaiting the arrival of the person who meant most to them on earth. Ras Tafari Makonnen. When the limousine drove up and the tiny figure in much-medalled military dress appeared it was an electric moment.

Here was an Imperial man of colour – a man who meant so much to an important section of Jamaican society, the Rastafarians, who were often either ignored or ridiculed as a matter of course. One can understand why, in their excitement, they broke ranks and made a beeline to touch HIM. The archives at Radio Jamaica kept the broadcast for some time. I wonder if they have it still, as in Jamaica we have little sense of occasion. After all, we wiped all Miss Lou's *Ring Ding* tapes, didn't we? Trevor Rhone calls it: 'The ritual erasing of ourselves by ourselves, Mrs Clarke. We don't need others to do it for us, we are so good at it ourselves.'

Listening to the broadcast from the Stadium on Claude's fancy radio, we heard Yvonne begin as she had rehearsed. The long title was perfect, as was the shorter name of His Imperial Majesty's daughter, the Princess Mouna, and then noises off began to take over the air-waves. Yvonne kept on as best she could with her rehearsed speech but as she was dragged to the ground (at least she kept the mike in hand) all we could hear were yells and screams punctuated with odd bits of the rehearsed commentary until Control finally cut the channel.

Our daughter was brought home by a worried RJR executive who looked gravely on her damaged thigh and talked of doctors and hospitals. About an hour after the ceremony had ended, an official outrider came roaring into the Oxford Road driveway with a note from His Imperial Majesty's entourage inviting Yvonne to a private reception at the Sheraton, now the Hilton. Apparently HIM had seen her fall, had made enquiries, found out who she was and the invitation was in some way a recompense. The bruises faded but the memory lingers on. Claude insisted on accompanying her, of course.

'I'm her father and I have to accompany her, you know. You take this thing for poppy show?'

Another yarn for cronies at the Phoenix Lodge. 'He can understand English, you know, but converses in

Amharic and French in public, so he won't have to get into any debates. He was interested in the Rasta locks. I don't think he has ever seen anything like them before. He asked for them to come closer so he could see and hear better . . .' and so on. My dear husband dined out on that for ages.

Soon television beckoned. The Jamaica Information Service wanted to produce a half-hour magazine programme to be shown at peak time on Saturday evenings. They were keen to capitalise on the increasing numbers of famous faces – I think they are now called celebrities – who were visiting Jamaica for a variety of reasons including sand, sea, sex and sensation.

Yvonne was to join veteran presenter Easton Lee, now Father Easton, as his sidekick. One must remember that television was still in relative infancy and locally produced programmes were at a premium, so this was stardom of a kind. She couldn't refuse. I must say, it was gratifying to see her holding her own with the likes of Jim Brown, Andrew Young, Eartha Kitt and home-grown heroes like Ranny Williams and Louise Bennett.

Speaking of Louise, sometime in 1976 Yvonne took Maxine – one of my adopted daughters – with her up the hill to Gordon Town to visit Ms Lou. As it happened Ms Lou was watching a recording of the *Ring Ding* programme she had done earlier in the day. Colour television had not yet reached our shores; the set she was watching was black and white, but she had 'colourised' it by taping a large sheet of reddish-purple lighting gel to the screen. Maxine and Yvonne joined her on the enormous four-poster until the recording came to an end.

Maxine was a tiny five-year-old who had grown up watching Ms Lou's *Ring Ding*. It took a few minutes before the grown-ups realised the confusion the child was experiencing. There she was, lying in that great bed beside the very person who was on the screen. She kept looking at the screen, then looking at Ms Lou, then the screen, then Ms Lou, with tears streaming down her cheeks. She didn't know which Ms Lou was real. Louise came into her own and put her at her ease by singing to her.

Maxine says she remembers the coloured gel over the screen but not her confusion or the comforting song from Ms Lou. Privileged young woman.

I think presenting this Saturday evening TV programme gave Y the confidence she now pretends she has, and served her well when she returned to live in England once again in 1971. But not before she dabbled in the making of *The Harder They Come*. There is no keeping Yvonne quiet. She turns up in the most unexpected places.

The story of *The Harder They Come* is worth repeating here. Life was full as she was free, single and enjoying the unfolding of the Barn, being seen on television every week, going to too many parties and still doing some teaching.

Perry Henzell, who came from a rich white Jamaican family, decided he wanted to produce, write, direct and generally be the main man in a film based on a flamboyant Jamaican criminal called Rhygin, whose cult status was based on his ability to elude the law. *Rhygin was here but him disappear* was a familiar slogan daubed on downtown walls. Perry's access to the wealthy in Jamaica meant that money was not a problem, but getting the creative team together was not such an easy ride. For a start, Perry's writing skills left a lot to be desired. I mean the script was stilted and long-winded. This wasn't dialogue, it was attitude.

Perry was persuaded to seek help from Trevor Rhone, who by now was an accomplished writer, having cut his teeth at the Barn. Trevor produced something much more alive, but the working relationship between the

80

men was not good. How do I know this? Yvonne, who was living with me, had also been persuaded by Perry to join his team to help with casting and managing the production. Her daily reports on the tension between Perry and Trevor were hysterically funny, as she would act out the scenes of one-upmanship between the two men. The black man speaking perfect Queen's English and the white man coming on heavy as he could with his whiney Jamaican middle-class accent. In fact, Trevor never once visited the set of *The Harder They Come* — that's why he had no say in how his words were interpreted and in some instances changed altogether.

As cameraman, Perry found David McDonald, who had established himself as a proficient cameraman with Ridley Scott when he was shooting commercials. David had never done a feature film but gave off the right vibes. Perry's inspired idea was to persuade Jimmy Cliff that there was an actor waiting to get out from the singer. How right he was. Jimmy had a natural love for the lens and it loved him, too. Although he had never really acted before, his understanding of the human condition and his essential humility made him amazing to watch as he made Rhygin come alive. He, above all others, understood society from the sufferer's point of view.

Here was the heart of the film. Here was the man who lived life to the lees. Getting him up for the early-morning calls was problematic, as one never knew where to find him. Jimmy was a very popular man and didn't want any- and everybody knowing his business. Something had to be worked out so Yvonne, along with Sugar, one of the sparks, would be told on the QT where he might be and they would have to rouse him for the day's toil.

One story I remember exactly. Jimmy was expected to compose a song for the film and although he would sit in the hammock on the veranda at 10A West Kings House

Road with his guitar looking beautiful, not many words were forthcoming. The location day in the recording studio loomed. There were snatches of lyrics but no real song. Yvonne said what she really feared was that Perry might offer to write the song. Stranger things have happened.

However, one early-morning trip to the studio, Jimmy was sitting in front with his guitar and out popped 'The Harder They Fall' in all its glory. That was the title of the song, as his intention was to see 'Babylon' fall, not to glorify the means. However, the film was called at first *A Hard Road to Travel* and ultimately changed to *The Harder They Come*. This, the moneymen said, had the edge needed for a film title. Those were heady days. I used to feel so much a part of the action.

The casting of the other parts was not easy. Take the Janet Bartley story. Most of the young actresses around at the time were up for the part of the young girl, but most of them had never known poverty, never known hunger, never even been to downtown Kingston. Perry's new toy was a video camera (very oo-la-la in 1970) and he would delight in putting these young women through their paces in front of his new toy.

Yvonne had been working with Janet Bartley and thought her the ideal person for the part, but Janet didn't have the Upper St Andrew polish which would get her through an audition with Perry pointing a strange object which made a funny whirring noise in her face. However, my daughter is a determined woman. She groomed Janet, who didn't want any part of it at first: 'All dem St Andrew people. I can't take dem at all.' She was so stunning on tape, though, that Perry, to give him his due, began to seriously consider her for the part. The rest is history.

Sadly, Janet died in London of an aneurysm when she was only forty. A great talent cut off in its prime.

Let us consider next the case of the casting of Karl Bradshaw. Yvonne was doing some Drama classes at Excelsior where Karl was the Physical Education Instructor. And a beautiful specimen he was, too. He had never really acted before but there was something about his body in space, his way of fixing you with his always bloodshot eyes which made her suggest to him that he audition for the part of Jose. He's never stopped playing it since. I just love the shot of him on the small motorbike and wonder if Jamaica will ever produce a film of such truth again. Many have tried. Perry's *Countryman* lacked the fibre, while *Smile Orange* did not leave the play far enough behind, especially in the kitchen scenes. It should have had a screenplay writer as Trevor was too close to it to write the screenplay and then direct it. It's done OK but it will never be *The Harder They Come*. Yvonne and Starr were involved with it but there was nothing like the excitement of November 1970.

There have always been films made in Jamaica and I don't suppose things will change. The current emphasis on the dancehall phenomenon might give way to something more durable. Who knows? Trevor never stops. Maybe he will produce the next truly international hit film of creative quality from Jamaica. He is working on something called *One Love* which sounds promising. I hope so. I like the man.

Chapter 11

Clan Brewster

In 1971 Yvonne went back to England and married her second husband. When I first met Starr I couldn't for the life of me see what she saw in him. Something must have worked, though, since they have been married for over thirty years now. He was monosyllabic except when grilling you about your life. Nothing about him ever slipped out. He was pale, had terrible dress sense, but he grew on you. After ten days of him as a guest in my home I was truly won over. Starr: no show, just substance.

Over the years bits and bobs have slipped out about him and his family – very interesting people and for me more than a little intimidating. Especially his mother. Elizabeth Home Brewster Beatson was quite a gal. Elegant, urbane, sophisticated and a source of all knowledge. She was a professor at Princeton, I believe, working in the Index of Christian Art, and spoke at least five languages fluently in a horsy upper-class English accent. I have never been a wimp but in this lady's presence that is exactly what I became.

Her father had been a Brigadier. Born in India, she was a perfect product of the Raj. Yvonne once showed me a photograph of her family's servants in India all lined up with the tools of their special calling held aloft. Grooms had brushes, cooks saucepans, maids feather-dusters and so on. Scary.

Elizabeth was generosity itself to Yvonne, on whom she lavished jewellery, offering her never-ending lessons on how to dress properly in Europe. Never did succeed there.

When Starr announced his intention to marry my daughter, polite hell broke loose within his family. You must remember these people are very 'civilised' (a favourite word), so ranting and raving were out of the question. However, Elizabeth flew all the way from Princeton to Paris and took the Paris Express to London so as to appear calm about the announcement. Princeton/London looked like panic. Paris/London was everyday business.

Starr and Yvonne met her at Victoria. At first they didn't see her, then Yvonne spied this elegant woman looking like a million dollars in silk and cashmere and a hat to stop Ascot. My God, she thought, this is it. So she pointed out the divine outline to Starr, who sauntered over. 'Hello, Elizabeth, darling. Come on. Let's go. Oh yes, this is Yvonne.' And he was halfway down the platform.

I think things went reasonably well as soon as Elizabeth realised that Yvonne worked in theatre. She, Elizabeth, had attended the Royal Academy of Dramatic Art and had 'trod the boards'. This made up for the fact that Yvonne was on the plump side. In one of her less guarded moments Elizabeth told Yvonne how surprised she was that her darling Starr had chosen such a fat person, as he had always, to her knowledge, preferred slim women. At least Jamaican quick wit saved the day. 'It's the thin Yvonne inside me that he fancies. But he'll have to work hard to get at her.'

Family friends were dispatched from all over Europe to give Yvonne the once-over. We – Yvonne, Starr and I – have laughed over one particular visit many times. Starr and Yvonne were living in the family pied-à-terre in Villiers Street, Charing Cross, in Rudyard Kipling's old rooms. How he must have turned in his grave.

One Saturday afternoon around three, there was an insistent ringing on the bell, which heralded a visit from Reynald, Le Comte de Simoney, dressed in all his finery and swathed in his cloak of the Order of the Knights of Malta. One must remember that Flat 2, Kipling House, was a tiny affair. Spectacular, perched as it was at the top of the building with one of the best views of the river, but minute. This personage took up much of the space, especially his cloak. After clicking his heels he offered his hand for Yvonne to kiss, which she declined to. Embarrassment number one. Tea was offered but declined. Embarrassment number two. Starr sat calmly reading the *Guardian*. Yvonne, never a French-speaker at the best of times, was completely tongue-tied as Reynald the Count examined her in detail through his pince-nez. Rum punch saved the day. Reynald, the very aristocratic snooty château-living fossil, was fascinated/repelled by the idea of the tropical drink, lime and rum and syrup . . . ugh! Once tasted, however, he loosened up a bit. Sugar-cane does have its uses.

Starr's father I never met but he wrote me a number of charming letters. He seemed very interested in visiting Jamaica as he had never really been in the tropics. Kenya, yes, but not the tropics. His letters were fascinating. They told of his journeys to places I could only vaguely imagine. He would set off sometime in July, driving an ancient Volkswagen piled high with camping stuff. Some company was always required on these long treks, female and preferably much younger than him. Difficult but not impossible. Although he would be away from July till late September he never had to travel alone. He persuaded Yvonne to go with him once and she kept me up to date with her journey.

Clan Brewster

San Francesco di Paola, Florence, Italy

Dear Mummy

Harry was looking for someone to travel with him on this year's annual trek. I sort of said yes and couldn't get out of it. I flew to Florence with my usual suitcase of summer things – fancy sandals, light cotton tops – you know the drill.

Harry took one look and said I could take one small bag of clothing if I had to. Not too delicate, he said, as I'd probably be washing them in rivers. Then he looked at my sandals – remember those pretty pink and brown affairs? By the way, he said, we will have to get you some decent sandals. Those things won't last a day. I took a look at his sandals and thought, I'm certainly not wearing anything looking like that. Famous last words.

We spent a whole day packing all the stuff into the back of the car. No way does this car look like something which can drive all the miles Harry plans. Oh yes, maps take up much of the room, alongside cooking pots and pans, primus stove, groundsheets and rusty tins of rice, sugar and coffee. Mummy, what have I got myself into? It's too late to back out now.

I'm posting this in Florence as at least I know they deliver mail in Italy.

Lots of love,

PS: I'll try sending postcards as I know you like getting mail although you don't write any letters. Ha Ha.

Postcard one, posted at Brindisi, Italy.

Mummy

This might be the last time you hear from me alive. Harry drives like the devil is on his case and other

87

drivers are always honking their horns at him. In Florence he cut up two young bloods in the latest Maserati who were not amused and swerved their car in front of his ancient Volkswagen which promptly stalled. Out they strode and proceeded to kick both Harry's headlights in.

I am told we are to catch a ferry to Corfu. Apparently we sleep on the deck. I managed to take along most of my clothes. I wore them. It's hotter than in Jamaica so you can imagine the game was up pretty soon. But too late. Hope I find a post box. It's quite exciting really.
Yvonne

Postcard two:

Corfu is a bit like Surrey. Imagine – there are English people playing cricket on the green. Harry the traveller is quite different from Harry the sort of English gent. Here we sit under some arches outside a café eating lovely yoghurt and honey, great bread and awful muddy coffee. Harry seems to know everybody and they all greet him in various languages. In about half an hour there was French, Italian, English, and Greek.

Actually I am amazed. I didn't think Europe could be so right on. I hope you can read this. Small space.
XOX

Postcard three:

Lots of ferries and many boats later I need a manicure badly but am beginning to realise the greater importance of mosquito repellent. Must tell you this: Harry knows I'm into theatre so he drove to a site just before sundown, told me to close my eyes, spun me round twice and when I opened my eyes, there we were in the most beautiful ancient theatre of Dodona. There were goats on what were once the seats but the shape was awesome. Go on, he said, don't you know any speeches from the Greeks? I did not let the side down. Miss Bruford would have been proud.

> The same blood flows in both our veins,
>   doesn't it, my sister,
> The blood of Oedipus. And suffering,
> Which was his destiny, is our punishment, too,
> The sentence passed on all his children.

The sound was amazing. Always wanted to play Antigone. Look, I have to continue this on some of the notepaper I found the other day. There is so much to write about. Anyway, I haven't seen a post office for days.

On notepaper:

Last night we spent our first night under the stars. I mean it. I thought Harry was joking when he said he didn't approve of tents, but he was quite serious. What happens is when the day looks like it has about another half an hour before it calls it a day then the search is on for somewhere to bed down for the night. As he's done this so many times he always has some possibilities up his sleeve but the challenge is to find a new place. Last night after the excitement of the theatre (I think he was quite pleased with my reaction) he left it a bit late so he chose a quite open space on a ridge of a hill. The groundsheet was spread, the flashlights found, the bread torn, the olives unwrapped, the wine opened and the cheese hacked – then sleep. At around four in the morning, the sound of bells.

Thought I'd died and gone to Heaven but it was the sheep being driven to their pasture, and we lay directly in their path. And you know what they say about sheep. Stupid. They weren't diverting from the accustomed path.

Never known Harry move so fast. What he was most worried about in the chaos was his radio. You see, at eight o'clock every morning he almost stands to attention. Beep beep beep beep. Tam to to tam tam, tam to to tam, tam to to tam tam, tam to to tam. 'This is the BBC World Service and here is the news read by Alexander Moyes.' Not a word dare be spoken for the next ten minutes. Actually although I take the piss you do need that fleeting contact with the world you have left behind. We went down into a market today to get some provisions – simple stuff, courgettes, aubergines, bread, cheese and whoopee retsina. This is a very good drink. I could become addicted. I was hoping to be able to post this off but no sign of a post office. Anyway I don't know if this would ever get to you as I am in what Harry calls Asia Minor (Turkey to most people). The natives seem never to have heard of the West Indies much less Jamaica. There's a problem with the J. I don't think they have one.

Walking and viewing ancient sites was what the journey was all about. These were always Greek, as the Romans are thought not old enough: 'Really rather a touch too ornate to be taken seriously. You will soon appreciate that after the 4th Century BC it all goes downhill . . . ' Poor me – all I could say was 'Just so.' He is a good teacher and I did become less intimidated but never quite comfortable with it all. The sandals Harry was so disparaging about have all but fallen to pieces, especially because when we were taking a short cut through some very picturesque fields, the mad guard dogs took great exception to this trespass and attacked us. I sprinted off and left Harry to do battle. I know you love dogs but you have never seen fangs like those. That's when the sandals gave out altogether. From a safe distance I was able to see Harry fight an almost choreographed battle with the dogs, wielding his fearsome stick and yelling for all he was worth. He prevailed. The saga of the useless sandals meant having to return to civilisation again to buy another pair. You should see the thickness of the leather and as for the soles, I think our Rastafarian brethren do a better job with old car tyres. Still no post office. I think I'll give these observations a break for a while. I'll post it when I can.

Love.

PS: You thought I couldn't cook, eh? Well you should see me with the portable gas ring boiling courgettes and aubergines, making salads of cheese, olives and tomatoes with olive oil (yes, they eat it here, it's not just for rubbing on the skin) and cooling the retsina in the same stream you bathe in. I could get to like this life. For a while. Well, the English keep telling me how primitive, how charming, how sweet, how simple I am so why not subscribe to this for a while at least. It's less bother. A post office! The stamps are cute.

Postcard from the Vale of Lethe:

Harry found the place where fancy beauty product companies get the green mud which is so fashionable and essential for a sparkling complexion. We took photos of one another covered from head to toe in this green muck. 'Think what it would cost on Fifth Avenue,' Harry said. My feet are disgusting, but I have lost weight. My kingdom for a bath in a bathroom. One more week to go. Love, the traveller.

Yvonne survived the test of a summer with Harry. Because that was what it was. He could now approve of the match. He showed his approval by digging out some lovely Georgian silver vases from the bowels of San Francesco as a marriage present, together with a ruby and diamond ring for her. Elizabeth supplied the champagne and hoovered the flat, housekeeping not being my daughter's strongest point. I think she has managed to stay sane because she lives in the moment and sees the funny side of things. Later on, the anger takes over, but usually when it's too late to be effective. At least she's still alive.

The Brewster family is actually very interesting. Elder William Brewster (1566–1644) was the pastor on the *Mayflower* which took the Pilgrim Fathers to the New World. He had three sons, Faith, Love and Wrestling. Names have always been startling in this family. There are Seaburys, Kingmans, Havelocks and yes, Starrs. Our Starr's direct ancestor was Love, the second son of Elder William, who travelled with his father on the *Mayflower*. My daughter's husband is the eleventh generation of these God-fearing people. They can't be that bad – I mean, way back in the late sixteenth to seventeenth century they were naming children Love. I drink to that, especially to Christopher Starr, who was the Brewster to bring the family back to Europe in 1830 at the age of thirty-one. He was a dentist with newfangled American ways of treating the teeth and had a great success first at the Russian court of Tsar Nicholas I and some years later in France, first serving Louis-Philippe, and then his successor Charles-Louis Napoléon at the Elysée Palace.

Christopher Starr re-ignited the Brewster dynasty in Europe, which is now centred in the lovely old monastery of San Francesco di Paola in Florence where the family has lived now for over a hundred years. The old three-storey sixteenth-century monastery used to house the Brothers of Good Rest (I Frati di Bel Riposa), an order of monks founded by St Francis di Paola in the 1500s.

Christopher Starr's grandson, called – yes – Christopher, married Lisl Hildebrand. They were a familiar Florentine couple who entertained the likes of Henry James and Ethel Smythe at home in the Villa San Francesco di Paola, walked the dogs in the Campo, painted, philosophised and praised God.

Lisl (our Starr's grandmother) was definitely a character in her own right. During the Second World War she hid many Jews from the Nazis at great risk to herself and her family. A favourite hiding-place was the cellar of the ex-monastery. She was able to get away with this because to the Germans she was above reproach, being the daughter of a famous German sculptor and architect, Adolf von Hildebrand. She entertained the occupying German officers to tea while in the cellar below lay hidden a large number of Jews of all nationalities. Some lady.

Yvonne is devoted to San Francesco di Paola. 'The place is the most peaceful spot on earth.' Always one to exaggerate. Truth is, it sounds amazing. When the money ran out, the main villa was converted into six apartments, ranging from the very grand four-postered to the very broom-cupboard. The outbuildings got similar treatment. It's not as elite as it once was but it's still pretty astonishing that in the middle of Florence this unspoiled oasis of calm and beauty should exist seemingly unaware of the passage of time.

The current Brewster/Peploes, some of them anyway, keep up the tradition of knowing what's going on internationally in the world of film, the Decorative and Fine Arts, and in the Arts generally – which now apparently include Cooking and Criticism!

Harry brought out some four or five books in as many years, most of which he sent to me. I found them difficult to get into as they dealt with so rarefied a society and what's more took themselves a trifle too seriously for my liking. I do admire his determination and application. In fact, one book of his about San Francesco and the Brewster dynasty was published posthumously just after what would have been his ninetieth birthday. And this one's quite readable.

I don't write letters. Never had the patience so phone calls have to do. They are expensive but immediate. I'm at my best on the phone so I used to make notes before my conversations with Yvonne, and Starr. That way I'd be kept up to date.

It was during this time that the teaching certificates which Yvonne had accumulated during her student years came in handy when she needed money in London. She did something called supply teaching. This she gave up after an encounter in a rough secondary modern school in Footscray, Kent.

Her job on this occasion was to teach poetry to a group of fifteen-year-old boys who were in school only because they had to be, who were wasting out the time until their sixteenth birthdays, when by law they could legally escape from school. In walked Yvonne with her folder of *Poems Ancient and Modern*. The class took one look at her and thought almost aloud, 'Oh yes! We can have some fun today.' The leader of the pack produced a large penknife and began cleaning his nails. Many of the others followed until there were almost as many knives in the room as people. When it comes down to it, poor girl, she has had to make so many knife-edge decisions (no pun intended) in her life. It's either put up or shut up. So she recited without opening her folder of Poems Ancient and Modern:

94

Is this a dagger that I see before me,
The handle toward my hand? (moving toward the leader)
Come, let me clutch thee:
I have thee not, and yet I see thee still.

'Do my eyes deceive me? I still see knives . . . '

Silence reigned for a moment. The knives went back from whence they came.

'Gentlemen, that was from *Macbeth* by William Shakespeare. Shall we get out the knives again? We can use them as daggers. Let us see how we could use them in this speech, which you will have to learn. Ready?'

Supply teaching came to an abrupt halt after that. Once bitten twice shy. Perhaps she is not cut out to be a martyr after all.

Yvonne had a happier time at Fulham Grammar School with the S-level girls, one of whom she still talks about – Maureen. It was easier altogether in refined Fulham, but teachers are born not made, and Yvonne was certainly not born one. She always and only ever wanted to work in theatre.

One day in 1972, there came a cry for help from Jillian Binns, wife of her Radio Jamaica ex-boss Graham Binns. The Binnses had lived most of their lives abroad, teaching the natives in Malta and Jamaica how to run decent radio stations. They had returned to England, he to head up the new Capital Radio and she to work in theatre. Jillian was directing *Lippo the New Noah*, a play written by yet another expatriate, Sally Durie, ex-wife of Times Store's Alex Durie, and loosely based on the life of Jamaica's finest intuitive painter, Kapo.

It was a strange play. It tried to draw some analogy between this revivalist priest-painter and the Biblical flood expert and ark-builder Noah. Apparently, the cast of experienced black actors had arrived at an impasse with the director and production team. Would Yvonne be willing to pass by the ICA (the Institute of Contemporary Arts) in the Mall to see whether she had any ideas which might take the thing forward?

The Mall is only a spit away from Kipling House in Villiers Street and off she went. She crept in at the back, and who should she see but Mona Hammond, rehearsing her song in the piece which to this day she still sings.

> *Dust in the gutter,*
> *Dust in my eye,*
> *Dust come down*
> *Make the angels dem cry.*

Mona Hammond. Yvonne had last seen her acting in *Huis Clos* by Jean-Paul Sartre at the Ward Theatre in Kingston, when she persuaded her father to take her into the stinking Rum Lane behind the theatre, leaping over open gutters to get the actress's autograph. There was no stage door to speak of as autograph hunting was not a major pastime in downtown Kingston, especially at night.

This was when she decided that she would work in theatre. Never changed her mind. Seeing Mona Hammond nearly twenty years later was just so exciting for her. It was a moment of real catharsis.

Mona took Yvonne aside and explained that 'The production needs a cultural kick up the bum, especially the music and movement. The cast have agreed to continue if you will help out.' She did. The show did well and many lasting friendships were made.

Trying to carve out a career in theatre in England is hard enough but when you are exotic/different/black/minority/non-traditional, you name it, it is a job for the brave or the foolhardy. Yvonne brave? I don't know but she did work against the odds. Of course I would never tell her just how proud I am of her as her head is big enough already, but she took chances.

I recently came upon the programme for something called *Black Feet in the Snow* by Jamal Ali, which she directed using music, rhythm and poetry in a multi-disciplined production. Doesn't sound much now but then it was state of the art, so much so the BBC filmed it – a black show in the early 1970s, which was quite something.

Then playwright Louis Marriott wanted to produce a play in 1972 to celebrate the tenth anniversary of Jamaica's Independence and somehow got the money together for a tour round London venues of Trevor Rhone's *Smile Orange*, which Yvonne directed with her precious Mona Hammond, Charles Hyatt, Trevor Thomas, Stefan Kalipha and Louis Marriott as a very good Bus Boy.

Turns out this was the first all-London tour of a black play ever, and what a success it eventually had! After a first night in Acton Town Hall with four people in the audience and dear George Carter, who happened to be in London, helping with last-minute adjustments to the few lights they had, the tour finished six weeks later in Anson Hall, Cricklewood, with hundreds of black people noisily queuing up outside.

This got even noisier when some had to be turned away. Full House! That same night, when everyone had gone home again and the streets were quiet, the Hall mysteriously burned down. Spontaneous combustion?

Often fire is a good solution to knotty problems in Britain. The television soaps rely on the occasional sensational blaze to keep the viewers happy. Birthday parties in New Cross end in ashes. Why indeed, then, should this quiet neighbourhood in north-west London be the scene of such raucous behaviour? Was this heralding a new noisy trend?

The word was that the fire started mysteriously in the basement kitchen of the hall. Arson was officially ruled out.

Pantomime is a word which Jamaican thespians have made their own. In Jamaica it no longer means cross-dressing and 'Look who's behind you', it describes a Christmas musical in which Anansi is often the anti-hero. Socio and socio-political matters are a fundamental aspect but are heavily disguised under a thick layer of farce, song and dance.

In 1972 Frank Cousins, a Jamaican actor living in London, Artistic Director of The Dark and Light Theatre in Brixton, asked Yvonne to direct *Anansi and Brer Englishman*, the first Jamaican pantomime to be produced in England, at his venue. Gloria Cameron played the part Louise Bennett would have taken, had it been in Jamaica. The production caught the imagination, and even the mighty Royal Shakespeare Company loaned them one of their actors, Jason Rose. Manley Young wrote the script and Gloria's son Chris Cameron composed the music. He was all of twelve years old, I think (he's now a big-time musical director and composer for the stars).

At that time, people Yvonne had never met were going out of their way to assure her of the success of this production as the homesick, lonely new Londoners queued round the block that Christmas. They wanted it every year like sorrel and Christmas pudding.

Chapter 12

Cool Breeze

England is a damp, inhospitable place, as I remember well. In 1974 Yvonne's knee started to swell up. 'Arthritis,' said the Brewster family quack, threatening to pump cortisone all over her, so she escaped to sunny Jamaica. I think Starr was quite glad to accompany her. That's when I began actually listening to her, even talking to her, and making notes of our conversations which are coming in so useful now. Frankly, she was more interesting than most of the people around me at the time.

At least she appreciated my little ruse to get the office telephone repaired. I have always kept the clipping from the *Star* newspaper 27 October 1975, with the banner headline:

Funeral for dead telephone

A funeral service for a dead telephone was conducted on Saturday afternoon in the chapel of Sam Isaacs & Son Ltd undertakers and outside the Jamaica Telephone Company Headquarters on Half Way Tree Road.

Inside a coffin topped with wreaths were the remains of the deceased telephone, 922 2896, which resided at

99

Sam Isaacs & Son 4 Hanover Street Kingston. It died two months ago. At 4.30 pm on Saturday organist Mrs Kathleen Clarke led a small group of mourners in the chapel in the singing of 'Abide with Me'.

Funeral rites were conducted by the Rev J. Scarlett.

The casket was then borne to the hearse by 6 pall bearers. A six car procession then proceeded to the Half Way Tree office of the JTC, where outside another funeral service was conducted by Rev Scarlett.

The services seem to have had some life-giving powers for when the mourners went back to the funeral home there was a dramatic resurrection of the dead: the phone was back in service. But by morning it suffered a relapse. Its condition was described as extremely weak to the point that it could barely transmit the voice of a caller.

The front-page report was illuminated with photographs of Rev Scarlett, who was a real sport, Bonny and other assorted mourners. Of course, I was nowhere to be seen. I like pulling strings behind the scenes. You have to have an occasional laugh when you are an undertaker, not so?

Starr and Yvonne settled into a new townhouse, which was then very new on the Jamaican scene, and spent a busy couple of years. They had no idea what they would do for money, but these things have a way of working out. No sooner had they arrived than a telephone call came from Bernardo Bertolucci to say that an Italian film company was coming to the Island to film a comedy starring the popular Renato Pozzetto called *Honeymoon for Three (Luna di miele in tre)*. It was to be now-famous director Carlo Vanzina's first film. They were looking for some local help with employing, interpreting and managing the Jamaican end of the production. Perfect. Starr speaks fluent Italian and gets on well with Jamaicans, whom he understands most of the time, and Yvonne had all the contacts necessary in the local film and theatre world to make them an effective double act.

Starr had started a personal dictionary of Jamaican words and sayings to help while away the tropical hours. I saw it once and wish I could remember more of what it had. This only sticks in the brain: *Nyam, verb, Pronounced knee-am. Origin probably Ghanian (Twe) meaning to eat voraciously. Impolite.*

Early in 1975 the Brewsters adopted Julian at the age of four months. A beautiful baby in need of a home. They offered him one and he thrived. Starr had made one or two friends who would turn up usually unannounced for a session of reasoning and Red Stripe. One was a particularly witty Nyahbingi Rasta broom-seller. Julian's sudden arrival prompted this spontaneous quip. 'Hail to thee, Ras Twinkle. A Little Starr.'

Starr's mother Elizabeth was soon on the scene, flying down from her perch in The Index of Christian Art at Princeton. Initially, she came only for a short visit but she fell in love with her new grandson Julian and it was weeks before she returned home. She set herself the task of finding a suitably docile nurse who had a soft musical voice. There was little chance of her leaving before this had been achieved. Interviews – or shall we call them auditions? –were hysterical. Can you imagine these buxom women from the country being asked to sing Jamaican folk songs as part of the interview as a child's nurse? Mothers sent daughters who sent cousins who sent friends just to get a look at this white lady with the broad jippi jappa hat and the funny accent who wanted them to sing. Myrtle got the job. She was pronounced 'docile as a lovely heifer.' I hope she doesn't read this. Myrtle, that is.

Yet another film project presented itself. There had been talk of filming *Smile Orange* for a while and this quite suddenly became a reality as some forward-thinking Jamaican property developers and businessmen put up the money. The directors of Bryad Engineering had no great monetary expectations from the enterprise but wanted to invest in Jamaican talent. I admired their sense of irony in calling the production company Knuts.

The double act got going again with Yvonne assisting Trevor and Starr as Production Manager. They brought in the thing under budget. Amazing! And the film is still being shown late night on television stations around the world. It's not *Gone with the Wind* but it was honest, reasonably funny, and more than made its money back.

Lucien Chen, one of Jamaica's more flamboyant Chinese entrepreneurs, decided to get on the bandwagon of the fledgling Jamaican film industry by producing *The Marijuana Affair*. Things were not going well. His stars were living high on the hog, and champagne flowed at the Pegasus. Calvin Lockhart looked every inch the movie star as he paraded around town but in fact shooting was slow, the acting uninspired, the story dull, managing skilfully to avoid the ingredients Lucien needed so badly for the project to work: sensation and sex. The footage at the end of each day was a producer's nightmare. It was clear, with just over a week left of the time scheduled and not enough useable footage for a decent trailer let alone a full-length film, that serious action needed to be taken if Lucien was ever to see any of his backers' money.

One morning, Yvonne got a phone call from Lucien. The distraught producer offered her a very respectable fee if she would help get enough images in the can to allow him to draw down his investors' money.

She did it. To this day it's one of the very few pieces of work my daughter has done which give her night-mares just to think about. Her job was to be brutal, to tread heavily on the sensibilities of the director, the actor and the cameraman, who was now expected to set only for the wide shot, with no reverses, no close-ups, moving quickly on to the next scene and so on until the entire script was in the can. No Cannes do. So sorry.

The premiere night audience's reaction to the finished version of *The Marijuana Affair* in Kingston's Carib Cinema was more dramatic and entertaining than any-thing on the screen. The punters soon started shouting abuse at the flickering figures on the screen, and the odd missile whizzing through the air provided the sensation if not the sex. I don't think *The Marijuana Affair* ever saw the light of day again. Appalling stuff.

By this time Julian was twenty months old and Starr was getting a bit anxious to return to England. I think he missed the bigger European environment, the choice of films, books, concerts and exhibitions which are meat and drink to him. He says he saw the expatriates around him and was terrified of becoming one of them. I think it was getting on his nerves, living in a country where he was in the minority. Don't get me wrong, he fitted so effortlessly into Jamaican society that most people forgot he was a foreigner. But he *was* foreign, not only foreign but a white Englishman to boot. Every now and then the old mistrust of the English, the question of slavery, would leap into the foreground. One incident sums up the difficulty of overcoming this history.

The University of the West Indies appeared to be an admirable seat of learning. Starr fancied doing some

post-graduate work and filled in his application. He was
rapidly invited for interview with almost the promise of
a place. Different matter when he turned up. They took
one look at him and immediately lost interest, and the
place on the course evaporated. You see, he had given his
place of birth as Mombasa, Kenya, which is quite accur-
ate because that is where he was born. According to him,
the interviewing committee was expecting a 'proper
African', i.e. a black man. He even got the impression
that they felt he had misled them. It's a droll story but
this helped send him back to England. Starr felt that he
was being asked to answer for the actions of people of
many centuries ago for whom he felt nothing but dis-
taste. This sort of thing wears one down. Well, dear
Starr, welcome to the club. That's what happens to
minorities.

So off he went to pick up the threads of life in
England. Yvonne and Julian were to follow when he had
sorted out a job and so on. During this time Wycliffe
Bennett, chairman of Carifesta 76, suggested Yvonne
help him with the drama programme, which included
the ambitious Gala. Better say what Carifesta is. In 1972
when Forbes Burnham was the all-powerful Prime Minister in Guyana he instigated the first Carifesta. Simply,
it was an opportunity for the people of the West Indies
to learn more about each other by coming together to
share their art. Great idea. She's often in the right place
at the right time, my daughter, as this job turned out to
be a delicious adventure.

First of all she was to travel around the West Indies
evaluating the various plays up for inclusion in the festival. This meant visiting many of the participating
twenty-three nation states. What an opportunity to see
the countries of the Caribbean, not only the British
West Indies but the Dutch, the American, the French
and the Spanish as well. I encouraged her like mad not to

miss this opportunity. Often Jamaicans prefer to go to desultory Miami rather than explore other Caribbean islands. Talk about 'Great Britain' mentality – this is the itsy bitsy Island mentality.

She came back with so many tales we called her Dr Livingstone for a while. Some stand the test of time. For instance, in Trinidad after being kept waiting in a dusty hot room in an even dustier museum, when he finally showed up a Mr Alladin told her that 'Yes, the Republic of Trinidad and Tobago will be sending something, but what right do you, a nonentity from Jamaica, have to stand in judgement on work from Trinidad, the centre of all Caribbean creativity?'

Island pride has been handed down to us. This myopia is responsible for the continuing economic stagnation of the Caribbean. It aborted the Confederation of the West Indies and will continue to keep it fractured. Sensing the need for diplomacy she played the 'I am very honoured to be insulted by you' card, instead of the 'Get lost, you relic!' She was at least then told what play they intended to take to the festival, which, as it happens, was (St Lucian) Derek Walcott's *O Babylon!*.

'Isn't that about Jamaican Rastafarians?'

'Yes. So?'

'Do you think this might prove difficult in Jamaica?'

'No.'

'Rastas with Trinidad accents is very creative and forward-looking, but I suspect the audience may not be quite ready for that yet.'

'Too bad. Good day.'

It was too bad. The whole exercise was doomed from the outset. The cast and crew of Trinnies arrived with Derek Walcott in his playwright mode. He has a poet mode for other occasions, of course. Derek Walcott – Yvonne's long-time pin-up. She was so excited at the thought of meeting him but this was short-lived. After

105

her first ever encounter with the great man she was devastated.

'Why have we been given this dreadful theatre?' he had demanded.

'This is the Little Theatre – Kingston's pride and joy. I fought to get it for you, especially considering we had no idea whether you would show up or not.'

'Let me speak with your boss.'

'I *am* the boss. Look, the Little Theatre is the best equipped venue in Kingston, seating over four hundred souls.'

'But you haven't sold many tickets. Forgive the pun.'

'Miracles take longer, sir. We are doing our best.'

'Well, do better.'

Ho hum.

The play itself was wonderful. However, as had been feared, the audience regarded Rastas with Trinidad accents as travesties and there was no way round their often quite vocal opposition to what they regarded as ridiculous. The more sophisticated among you might pooh-pooh this as backward and insular. I know in England nowadays it doesn't matter what you look like, you can play most parts, but I believe even there you are expected to *sound* right. Here in Jamaica in 1976 there was a lot of nationalistic angst, and not too many people showed up. Derek Walcott was absolutely furious and let it be known. However, apart from kidnapping people off the street there was nothing to be done.

The highlight of Carifesta for me was the Carifesta Gala. This man called Wycliffe Bennett I had always found a little pompous and patronising, but after his success with managing Carifesta as a whole and the Gala in particular I can forgive him for anything. It was his larger-than-life approach to life which allowed his special brand of creativity to flourish in this arena. He had a plan which lesser men could not even imagine, much less deliver. Many of these timid souls thought the idea of staging a pageant with thirty thousand people in the large National Stadium was 'foolishness, you know, one of Wycliffe's over-the-top grandiose ideas. No way that can work, man.'

They were wrong. The Gala was dedicated to the Heroes of the Caribbean. I remember noting at the time that they were all men, but that was par for the course then. Bit better now. Enormous papier-mâché effigies of Toussaint L'Ouverture, Simón Bolívar, Benito Juárez, José Julián Martí and Marcus Mosiah Garvey paraded round the Stadium to excited cheers. The ranks of police, soldiers, schoolchildren, cadets, nurses, voluntary organisation workers, dancers, singers, athletes and flag wavers, all thirty thousand of them singing, parading, performing to an overflowing audience including numerous Heads of State, were disciplined and entertaining.

A particularly high point was the phalanx of forty Rastafarian drummers who entered the stadium and silenced the tongue so the heart could feel. Good. And of course the sight of beloved Jimmy Cliff as a lone figure dressed in white singing 'Many Rivers to Cross' brought tears even to my cynical eye. Whew. Never seen anything of this sort in Jamaica before or since. We couldn't do it now.

Yvonne was enjoying her job in charge of Theatre for Carifesta but she really grew in confidence as Wycliffe's assistant for the Gala. This meant her assisting him with the non-stop rehearsals in the broiling sun. 'All you have to do is follow my lead and love the participants.' Wycliffe had a phrase which he used to calm the ruffled feathers when the sun was too hot or the standing too long: 'Cool Breeze – let me hear you all say "*Cooooool Breeeeeeze*".' It worked every time.

On the day of the Gala when the dignitaries all

showed up in force Wycliffe turned to Yvonne in the control box and said, 'There's Michael Manley, I must go and meet him. It's all yours.' She was on her own to 'call' this mammoth show with over thirty thousand participants and a similar number of spectators. But she had been well trained by Wycliffe and the affair went off without a hitch. Cool Breeze. Simply wonderful to see so many Jamaicans in one place without rancour, without gunshots, with talent, with love, just existing for a couple of hours of excellence.

Chapter 13

Town Crying

—◦◉◦—

Yvonne's arthritis having disappeared, it was back to London and Kipling House for herself and Julian. On a banana boat actually. I remember from my time in England how smart alecks would refer to unsophisticated people of colour as having just arrived on a banana boat. One must always remember that the arrogant often presume greater knowledge of the world than they in fact have.

The real fact of travel on the banana boats that plied between the West Indies and England (white goods, machinery and cars out; bananas and sugar back to Blighty) was that they were much too expensive for the ordinary immigrant to afford. They were twelve-passenger floating luxury hotels on which one had to dress for dinner, and a place at the Captain's table was a sign of even greater arrival. To the under-exposed in Britain, the image of immigrants sharing space with the bananas in the hold of the ship was easier to imagine. Halfway up the tree? The grass skirt?

Off they went, back to England on a banana boat. I thought I wouldn't be seeing them again for a while. I had no intention of ever going back myself to London. Too many painful memories lurked there. I was afraid that if anyone pulled my hair to see if it was real, wiped hands on my skin to see if the colour would come off, or called me nasty names, I might end my visit in a police

109

cell. Back then, I used to grin and bear it but not any more, no sir. Not this gal.

However, before too long I got a phone call from Starr in London to say that Michael Manley had called, asking him to give his permission for Yvonne to come back to Jamaica for a year during which he wanted her to head up the Jamaica Festival Commission, part of the portfolio of the Office of the Prime Minister. Starr suggested that *if* he seriously wanted to be in with a chance he should telephone again, ask to speak to Yvonne and then ask her.

Starr was absolutely right. I know my daughter and if she had ever learned of MM's approach to Starr for permission, there would have been absolutely no chance of her even speaking to him, much less agreeing to leave London.

For once Michael Manley took the proper advice. In no time at all Yvonne was back in Jamaica for an eventful year as director of the Jamaica Festival Commission, a large quasi-governmental organisation employing hundreds of people throughout the Island. Its prime objective was the weaving of local cultural values into the everyday lives of the population as a whole. With young Julian in tow, Yvonne rejoined the Jamaican workforce under contract to the Government.

The Festival Offices were within walking distance of Queensway where we lived and she set to work with commendable energy. Each of the twelve parishes in the country had to have an office and staff to organise the competitions. There were competitions for everything under the sun. For instance, local foods cooked in local ways became a category for recognition: Culinary Arts. I remember the excitement when Mrs Enid Donaldson first made an apple pie with cho cho (christophine to some). Some of the people from those days in 1976 like Bari Johnson, Joyce Campbell and Tony Laing are still making stalwart contributions to the culture. Jean Binta Breeze, who was employed by Yvonne to work in a Festival Office in western Jamaica, is now a major international poet and novelist.

Many interesting people passed through Jamaica during that time. Yvonne, who is at her very best meeting people, had a really exciting time. She used to regale me with snippets. 'Did you know Andrew Young's wife is Puerto Rican? They really liked the ceramics at Devon House.' Or 'Winnie Mandela's speech caused uproar in the Sheraton – you should have seen the manager's face,' and so on.

The work was hard, especially the travelling and the constant public appearances. She set herself the target of visiting every parish at least once every two months. They then gave her a driver. The Office of the Prime Minister must have heard how lethal she is on the road and may have wanted to protect their investment. Whatever the reason, I was extremely glad of this. Driving in Jamaica is another thing only for the brave, the foolhardy or the suicidal. They accuse *me* of driving in the middle of the road. I find it safer there. Especially with my hand on the horn.

The director of the Jamaica Festival Commission was expected to make speeches. Lots of them. One day early on in the job, out of the blue, two young movers and shakers in the world of public relations and marketing, Carmen Tipling and Burl Francis, offered to help Yvonne with the public relations aspect of things, the speeches especially. They spent Sundays and some evenings writing and editing every major speech for her, tailoring the content to suit the audience. I cannot imagine what her life would have been like if it hadn't been for these two sainted women taking her on as a project. You see, she could deliver the speech and get the message home, but as someone who can't even write a

111

decent letter, she would have been up a gum tree without this act of spectacular generosity.

Suddenly (most things happened suddenly) she was off to Cuba to accompany Arnold 'Scree' Bertram, Junior Minister and rising star in the Manley firmament, his wife and Corinna Meeks, CEO of what was then called the Agency for Public Information. What to wear? Castro's Cuba was at the height of its militaristic might, but this delegation, coming from the sun/sand/sea/sex capital of the West Indies, would not cut the mustard in sensible clothes. I mean, they didn't sell battledress in Kingston. Sensibly, they kept to what was comfortable for them individually: Corinna in her designer gear, Yvonne in her ethnic compilations, Scree in jeans and Mrs Bertram in a head tie. This motley crew was charged with paying cultural respects to Fidel's Government, and he had sent a plane to collect them.

One must remember that during this period, very few aircraft could fly over Cuban airspace. Expecting a kind of Air Force One number or at least Air Jamaica One, there were a few undiplomatic comments as they boarded the rusty old transport plane with benches, no seats. The 'in-flight meal' was a rough-hewn sandwich of bully beef. Not Scree's usual fare. 'Well, ah mean a patty would have been all right but me no eat bully beef.'

The noise of the engines discouraged further conversation, which was just as well. However, things started looking up once they were on Cuban tarmac. First they were relieved of their passports (all red – Yvonne wanted to keep hers once the visit was over, but the powers-that-be knew better), which they were promised would be returned on the return flight. Raúl Castro, brother of the main man, was there to greet them, amongst an embarrassment of really good coffee which alternated with the best frozen daiquiris ever made.

One half of a glass of wine sets my daughter's spirit

free to roam, so she couldn't remember much more of the arrival except that she kept asking for her passport. However, they were eventually dispatched to the 'casa protocolo', Scree and Mrs B, Corinna and Yvonne each in a separate car with an interpreter, a driver and a guide. Big time. As the cars swept up the long and impressive drive of the house, they all had to do some swift personal re-evaluation of the Cuban Revolution. The magnificent house, now a 'casa protocolo' for important guests of the Revolution, must once have been home to some very rich people who probably left in a hurry. All the furnishings were top-of-the-range Macy's, the double staircase up to the first floor was wide and gently rising, the bedrooms were to die for and as for the sheets . . . Well, we don't usually sleep on linen at home, so they were cause for comment from Madam. As was what she saw when she attempted to open a window which wouldn't. It was sealed. Tight. As her eyes got accustomed to the dark she swore she saw men in camouflage dress concealed in the trees that surrounded the house.

Next morning, the silver place-settings competed with the sun. There were six courses. Nine at lunch and twelve at dinner. Socialist Yvonne was appalled but I had to tell her to grow up. There is always one rule for the rulers and another for the ruled.

For the few days of the visit there was a busy round of visits to people of importance. Corinna's designer style went down the best. Most of the ladies they met were wearing the latest Christian Dior shades – no army fatigues for them. For the men, yes, as they knew they looked appealing. Especially Fidel. My daughter still keeps a photograph of him in his prime given to her on that occasion, pinned up on the notice board in her kitchen at home. Heady days. The visitors were shown the boat 'Granma' which brought the Revolutionaries from Mexico to Havana; it is on prominent and permanent display in the centre of Havana. In Santiago de Cuba they met Juan Almeida the only Negro Comandante, head of the armed forces and hero of the Revolution. They also did the tourist stint at the Cococabaña nightclub.

During this trip, Yvonne got a lesson in flag art for crowds (you know, the orchestrated wave at football matches which is quite popular now) from a Chinese expert and she used it to good effect in her Grand Gala at the National Stadium which was the climax of the year's celebrations. Having assisted Wycliffe Bennett in the Carifesta Gala, the Festival Celebrations were not funded to compete but they acquitted themselves rather well. It was the forerunner of the Festival Grand Gala Annual Independence celebrations which, I believe, still happen every year but which at my advanced and vulnerable age, I no longer frequent.

The diplomatic mission ended and the passports returned, the little group flew back to Jamaica. Among the lasting impressions Yvonne still sometimes mentions is the fact that, although the shops were pretty empty of food, clothes and furniture, the roads were so well kept, well lit and pristine, the bus stops and the buses so regular, the people so committed. There was no grumbling. 'Perhaps not on the diplomatic beat,' I ventured, only to be harangued by another fact – that every afternoon at three her driver was relieved by another. He had to go to his university classes. This was expected of all those whose education was not up to scratch. He was studying for a science degree.

Yvonne's year as Festival Director was drawing to its close. I had got accustomed to having her and Julian staying with me at Queensway and was facing the fact that they would have to return home to England soon, but not as soon as they did, nor in the manner they did.

It wasn't till she was safely back in London that I got

the full story. A couple of days after the Gala she was in the office sorting out the handover to whoever was to take on the rôle for the next year when the door burst open and a familiar face around town greeted her with 'Ah come for mi town-crying money.'

Now this was a gentleman who was used to being obeyed: you didn't mess with him.

Let's just say he had had a lot of target practice.

'Town-crying? I don't know about this. Tony Laing arranged that side of things, so if you did any town-crying you had better talk to him.'

'But ah wha do dis woman sah? Look, lady, just pay me mi money an' mek me go bout mi business.' Mrs Scott, her senior secretary, could be seen gesturing wildly in the background with the two first fingers of her right hand pointing to the ceiling, out of sight of the gentleman. Yvonne twigged.

'I don't pay bills here,' she said. 'Let me just go up to the office and arrange this for you. Might take a little while, so make yourself comfortable.'

Leaving her car keys on the desk in plain view she left the room, and ran like hell as soon as she was out of sight. You see, she couldn't bring herself to pay this man for work he hadn't done, just because his friends were powerful. So she risked her life. What can I tell you? The clever bit was to leave the car keys. Nobody who is anybody walks anywhere in Jamaica. As I say, neither did Yvonne. She ran the short distance to Queensway, grabbed Julian, the passports, tickets and a few other things and was on her way to the airport in minutes. I think Neville drove her there, but I can't remember. She was given refuge in the British VIP lounge when they realised how terrified she was. To cut a long story short, that's how her year as Director of Festival ended. She did get an effusive letter of thanks from Michael Manley. Ironic.

115

So I lost them, Julian and Yvonne. Back to Blighty they went. My house here in Queensway went dead. I moan when she is here but in truth I quite like it, as no two days are the same. That reminds me, she is due, isn't she, so I'd better tell Mervys, my sainted house-keeper, to start on what I think they call in England a spring-clean in preparation for her ritual rearrangement of my furniture. At least we won't be embarrassed by any stray cobwebs and the like when Madam arrives.

Done that.

Where was I? We lost touch for a while as domesticity took over. Starr had managed to secure another, margin-ally larger, flat in Kipling House but the location was not really ideal for a young child, especially one who had never known the restriction of living in a flat five storeys up, where there were no puppies to play with and where 'play outside' meant dressing up in layers of warm cloth-ing, manoeuvring a pushchair into the nineteenth-century lift, then fighting through the crowd of city folk to get to the nearest green patch in Embankment Gar-dens or, failing that, the half-mile walk past Trafalgar Square onto the Mall and to the green opposite Clarence House.

With heavy hearts they decided to move away from Kipling House.

Here's Yvonne's letter from the summer of 1979:

Sounds impressive to say that St James's Park is our local but the lift in Kipling House is the original which means it is out of order more often than not. Six flights of stairs with a push chair, perhaps not. I think we have to move. Starr can't contemplate this at all. His socialist values prevent him from house ownership but honestly, Mummy, that's all right for him but I can't imagine life without a place which one owns. I guess I get that from Daddy. Anyway, Starr succumbed enough to agree to a search just so long as we didn't end up in suburbia.

So, as committed Central Londoners we put a compass on a map using Marble Arch as the centre and prescribed a two-and-a-half-mile radius. This was as far out as would be considered central. Mayfair, St John's Wood, Primrose Hill, Maida Vale were all out. Too expensive. Kilburn just creeps in under the wire. We're going to look there. Wish us luck.

More time,

Yvonne.

PS: I can hear you say, 'Surely there are only Irish bedsits in Kilburn?'

Next letter.

The hunt did not take long. One afternoon we came upon a smartly dressed older woman scrubbing the steps of a large end-of-terrace Victorian house. Most other doorsteps in the neighbourhood certainly didn't show any signs of having been scrubbed clean in decades. It turned out she was French and had lived with her father in this house for many, many years but now she is alone and scared.

She had rented out rooms but had been traumatised by vicious tenants. She is absolutely desperate to sell but doesn't know how to go about it. Even after so many years in England her accent was very pronounced and she preferred speaking in French with Starr who has promised to help her find somewhere easier for her to live in. That's a whole heap of work, you know, but we have become a bit like Mrs Hale's family. She says when she has somewhere to go to we can buy her house. My God, it's bigger than we were thinking of, a largish semi-detached corner house in

Kilburn. It <u>is</u> in bedsitter land. But there is a lovely feel to the neighbourhood.

Householders – us? If everything goes well we will be. Starr is not really impressed.
Love,
Yvonne

Everything did go well and I even broke my vow never to return to England and paid them a visit one Christmas. Five bedrooms, two living rooms but no dishwasher, no washing machine! I had to put that right before I left.

'You'll never get an au pair to live here.' This from Elizabeth, mother of Starr. She was so wrong, unusual for her. Kilburn certainly wasn't out in the stockbroker sticks like Buckinghamshire, say, or Surrey, which meant seriously curtailed social life for the young European girls. The last trains to Chalfont St Giles leave from Marylebone Station before midnight, but there are buses all through the night to Kilburn. There was never any difficulty in finding an au pair, as you can imagine. Starr and Yvonne have never moved, although there is talk of it. They are spread all over that house like an infestation. My daughter says she loves Kilburn. No accounting for some people's taste.

Hilda Isaacs

Mr and Mrs Sam Isaacs

Sam Isaacs

Alice Clarke and Yvonne

Charles Nathaniel Clarke

Kathleen Vanessa Clarke on her wedding day, 1937

Kathleen in her forties

Yvonne, Valerie and Neville: siblings

Yvonne at five years old

Yvonne's first day as a drama
student at Rose Bruford, 1956

Linstead Market Yvonne's first production at St. Hilda's
Diocesan High School

Parents Kathleen and Claude at Yvonne's sweet sixteenth birthday party

Yvonne's graduation photograph from Rose Bruford, 1959

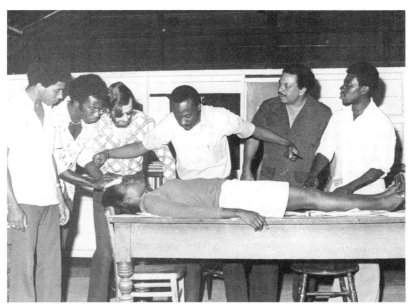

School's Out by Trevor Rhone. Premier production at the Barn Theatre

Rehearsals for Dennis Scott's *Echo in the Bone* for Talawa, 1986

Rudolph Walker and Mona Hammond in *Two can Play* at the Tricycle, 1984

Rehearsals for *King Lear*, Cochrane Theatre, 1994

Greta Mendez, Yvonne and Ellen Cairns: creative collaborators 1985, onwards

Curtain call, *The Importance of Being Earnest* at the Newcastle Opera House, England, 1988

Yvonne, HRH Prince Andrew and Malcolm Frederick, Royal Gala of Edgar White's *Moondance Night* at the Arts Theatre London, 1987

Julian, Yvonne and Starr, Buckingham Palace, 1993

Yvonne as Nurse Ruth in the long running BBC TV series *Doctors*

Yvonne and Willard
White, 1996

Kathleen Vanessa Clarke aged 90 with Bertha Clarke 2003

Chapter 14

She Likkle but She Tallawah

During this period of the late 1970s Yvonne was doing odd bits and bobs in television, including the series of something called *Maybury* for the BBC, set in a psychiatric hospital. She played an almost silent nurse to Patrick Stewart's doctor. He's now a *Star Trek* millionaire and look at her! All she's got is the *aire*. She did some directing but nothing too spectacular. It was all fringe stuff with no money and in the end too depressing.

Typical experience was directing a musical version of Barry Reckord's play *Skyvers* called *Streetwise* which was received very well by the critics; indeed, Denise Black (formerly Nixon) won the Best Supporting Actress Award from *Plays and Players* the same year Dame Judi Dench won Best Actress. She, Denise Nixon, was forced to keep the name she had acquired for the purposes of working with a black company!

But money was in short supply and in addition to directing the play Yvonne had to drive the van with set, props and six actors. After striking the set on the last night in Bristol, loading the van and driving all the actors home, she arrived back in Kilburn in the early hours to find no parking space. By leaving the keys in the van, and the van in the middle of the road, she anticipated that by morning either thieves or the police would have removed it. No such luck. At about ten o'clock there was

Ken Chubb, founder and Artistic Director of the Tricycle Theatre knocking at the door.

'I have parked the van,' he said, 'and yes, you can't go on using up your energy so foolishly. There is a job going at the Arts Council of Great Britain for a Drama Officer. I'll get you the details and you must apply.'

Big joke. She thought no more about it but Ken was good to his word, produced the forms and buzzed around until eventually she gave in, applied, did the interview and got offered the job. Ken was delighted. The point of working at the Arts Council would be to learn what she could about the funding system from the inside.

'I can't accept this job,' she objected. 'I can't go to an office every day. No way. I can't.'

'I dare you.'

'Nobody dares *me*.'

Ken won. She began work at the Arts Council of Great Britain on 1 October 1982 and, having sworn to stay no longer than two years, left on 31 September 1984. These two years later she did know a bit more about how the funding system worked. Jean Bullwinkle taught her everything worth learning, and was delightfully witty, as was her boss, Director of Drama, ultra-refined John Faulkner while others were larger-than-life characters like Ruth MacKenzie and Peter Mair. One or two were excellent at the art of losing friends without influencing people.

The story she dines out on from those years was when she went down to Guildford's Yvonne Arnaud Theatre to attend her first board meeting as Drama Officer. She enquired of a member of staff where the board meeting was being held.

'Up on the second floor, but you need the canteen entrance. You have come for the kitchen job, haven't you?'

'Well, no, as a matter of fact. I would have hoped the theatre could offer its new Arts Council Officer a cup of coffee without her having to make it. Could you please tell me where the board meeting is taking place?'

When a few months later the Arts Council decided to cut its grant in aid to the theatre, some small minds thought that her initial greeting by the theatre staff was the cause. Very insulting to think that my daughter for one thing would have stooped so low, and for seconds that the Arts Council would have thought this incident significant enough for such drastic action. The productions at Guildford had been for too long simply pre-run West End fare and not of spectacular vintage. So off with their heads.

On leaving the Arts Council, freelancing suited Yvonne and some good work was achieved, including the first production in England for many decades of Lorraine Hansbury's *A Raisin in the Sun* with Carmen Monroe as Mama for the Black Theatre Co-operative, two productions of Trevor's *Two Can Play*, with Rudolph Walker playing Jim on both occasions – once with Mona, once with Carmen – *Blood Sweat and Fears* by Maria Oshodi, *Moon Dance Night* by Edgar Nkosi White in downtown London at the Arts Theatre in 1987, which was attended by Prince Edward. She even found time for acting in the National Theatre's production of *The Crucible* when it transferred to the Comedy Theatre in London's West End.

Life was good. Then Mrs Thatcher decided to neutralise the Greater London Council. The reverberations can still be felt in many areas of the capital's life but Black Theatre has never recovered from the shock. The GLC had been instrumental in encouraging black and other ethnic minority artists to be courageous, and the flowering of talents was spectacular. When it was certain that the writing was not only on the wall but had been read and translated, a number of final grants were made for work in the minority sector.

In response to a phone call from Lord (Michael) Burkett ('Isn't there anything you want desperately to do?'), Yvonne wrote up a six-page application for funds to produce CLR James's *The Black Jacobins*.

Why *The Black Jacobins*? CLR James, one of Trinidad's most eloquent and elegant of thinkers, was getting old. He was in his eighties and this play, which he had adapted from his seminal novel of the same name, had been produced only once before in England, some fifty years earlier. In 1935 there were few black actors in England, so Paul Robeson came to London to take the role of Toussaint L'Ouverture. Most of the others in the twenty-five-strong cast were obliged to black up. It therefore seemed a fitting tribute to Nello (as CLR was affectionately known, his middle name being Lionel) to produce his play fifty years on without having to resort to white actors blacking up.

The application was accepted in her name. She has to thank Parminder Vir, who was a GLA Arts Officer, for supporting the idea. Yvonne didn't have a producing company; enjoying life as a freelancer was enough for her. Starr pointed out that she had better form a company quickly, as if this harebrained scheme went pear-shaped he had no intention of selling the house.

Phone calls to Carmen and Mona resulted in them agreeing to be founder members, but they weren't much help with a name. 'Something round,' Carmen wanted. Mona, 'Something Jamaican.' There is a wonderful book called *Jamaica Talk* by F. G. Cassidy which is a treasure-trove of Jamaican words and sayings, so starting from the back of the book *zuzuwapp* appealed but she thought it would sound too African maybe, then after a while *tallawah* became a possibility. Three Caribbean women all past the first flush of youth, all formidable in their way, surely represented the Jamaican saying 'She likkle but she tallawah.'(She may be small but she's not to be messed with)? Why not use the phonetic spelling, which looked more sexy and had more graphic possibilities, Talawa? So Talawa it was and is.

The production of *The Black Jacobins* called upon the talents of the late great Norman Beaton who, with Mona Hammond, led the cast. Many actors who are now well-known, some even household names – Gary McDonald, Brain Bovell, Trevor Laird among them – were also part of the twenty-three-strong cast. It was Jenny Jules's first professional production and Carmen Monroe's first exposure to directing. She assisted Yvonne.

Tommy Pinnock, the inspired choreographer who had begun life under the wing of Rex Nettleford, came over from the United States to work his magic. Almost too well. Voodoo cannot be ignored in Haiti and the scene in which Dessalines, played by Trevor Laird, summoned up the spirits to aid their fight against the French was always a highlight for the audience. Tommy warned everyone never, repeat *never*, to close their eyes during this movement sequence. One gentleman actor, who always knew better, did exactly that during a performance: the sequence took on a life of its own with him wielding his machete not in the rehearsed manner but with an abandon which caused the rest of the cast, especially Brain Bovell, to leap then duck for cover. I believe in some circles this is referred to as 'catching the spirit'. Luckily no one was hurt, but the tension lingered on. Live Theatre. We'd be dead without it.

The production sold out for the three weeks of its run at the Riverside Studios. Many dignitaries saw it, including the Haitian Ambassador to the Court of St James's, a M. Duval who unfortunately had to leave at the interval as the second Haitian revolution had just begun in Port au Prince.

Yvonne's original budget for the production did not anticipate any income, an oversight she wouldn't be able to get away with nowadays. However, as the production did very well at the box office, the new company Talawa had money in the bank! The gals soon decided to produce a second play, Dennis Scott's *An Echo in the Bone*, a compelling, thought provoking-piece, the echo being that of slavery and the bones those of the inheritors. This also did well – it was probably a matter of supply and demand – so yet another play was produced: Derek Walcott's *O Babylon!*. Difficult play, difficult playwright. I think this was Yvonne's way of testing the play's magic after the bad experience at Carifesta a decade before. Derek Walcott and Galt MacDermott turned up for the latter part of the rehearsals. Yvonne was in her element. She said at the time that she would put up with anything just to be around truly creative people. Half an hour with Derek and Galt was worth a month of Sundays with many she could name. The atmosphere was electric as the cast could feel the special vibrations. The actors took the criticism well and produced a quite wonderful show. Some people still talk about the Four Horsemen of the Apocalypse, choreographed by Jackie Guy, and the amazing voice of Malcolm Connell, as well as Ellen Cairns's evocative set.

Mind you, all the peace and love was very nearly ruined by the delivery of Galt's score. The Musical Director insisted on pre-recording the music and having the musicians mime . . . Miming a congo drum! Derek's comments are unprintable. And as for Galt's! However, all things considered some compromise must have been worked out, as the company was offered an annual subsidy on the strength of this production. This meant Talawa could plan work in the knowledge that the money would be there to produce it.

'So, Yvonne, what will your first production as a revenue-funded client of the Arts Council be?'

'*The Importance of Being Earnest* by Oscar Wilde.'

Pity there wasn't a camera on hand to record the dropping jaw of the Drama Director. 'The *what*?'

'Oh yes, we will now do the plays which established black actors want to have the opportunity of exploring. Mona Hammond wants to play the relatively small part of Miss Prism, the governess. But of course, she must play Lady Bracknell. This raffia ceiling which keeps black actors' horizons so low must be challenged. Why else would one of the finest actors in England feel she must play the supporting role?'

There were some very worried funding officials who agreed to what they saw as this crazy scheme, but it was too late to take back the money. Yvonne had been wily enough not to admit to the political reasons for producing *The Importance*. Oscar Wilde had been forced by toffee-nosed upper-class English to abandon his Irishness in his desire to be accepted as one of them. He worked hard at eradicating all signs of his origins: 'My Irish accent was one of the many things I forgot at Oxford.' This rang loud bells in the head of someone who had been failed verse speaking by Rose Bruford because she would not speak verse in Standard English. Yvonne saw *The Importance* as Wilde's way of getting back at the barely hidden vulgarities of English snobbery in his masterpiece. What better playwright to inspire black actors, themselves treated as stereotypes, to break with tradition?

When the brave Artistic Director Andrew MacKinnon offered Talawa a co-production with his Newcastle theatre company housed in the lovely Opera House, some jaws recovered from the dropped position. These were testing times but Yvonne never had time to listen to what was being bitched about – which is just as well, as some of the guardians of the purity of English theatre were talking in apocalyptic terms. Most critics were unkind but the audiences couldn't get enough.

In fact, I am now in possession of the book in which Oscar Wilde's grandson Merlin Holland wrote the following: *Yvonne, you've done more for the Importance than anyone in 20 years!* I was supposed to be impressed by this. Actually I was. Being a pioneer is lonely work, inadvisable for the faint-hearted. Some think vision is the only component part of success. To me, a modicum of blindness and deafness helps, too.

Chapter 15

Kathleen's Ghosts

Now that she is older and, if not wiser, certainly less erratic, Yvonne and I have better conversations. In fact, we have developed over the years a protocol of interviews. This began with the advent of the video camera. She brought out a video copy of one of the plays she had directed for me to have a look at. Then she started fooling around by pretending to interview me on tape. I was fascinated to see how, just by pointing that small machine in someone's face, it could immediately record not only the face but the voice as well.

We did a mock television interview with me as the candidate. Once you start with these things it's actually quite difficult to stop. A sort of innate vanity spurs one on. I found myself spilling the beans but then so did she. Dressed up as experiment, a bit of fun with new technology, these recordings are a comfort, a reality check, a grounding force in my diminishing years as friends die, photographs fade and no one will talk to you without shouting, or, worse still, speaking very slowly as if to a stupid five-year-old.

At the very soul of my lonely survival is the ability to be able to enjoy these past moments of simple truth flickering before my eyes. I sometimes wish I had some tapes of other people. Of Claude and his brothers, of Marjorie my sister and Bonny my brother, especially now they are all dead. Perhaps I could more easily lay their ghosts to rest. Unsettling unfinished business, especially Bonny, Claude's brother Alvin and Gramma, all three murdered. My recurring nightmares. I should have spoken about them to the camera but then it seemed too difficult, too sad.

I'll talk now for the first time about having so many murders for everlasting brain company. And I will start with Gramma, as I promised earlier. My mother's mother, Gramma Caroline.

When age forced her to seek refuge under the roof of her lucky wealthy daughter Hilda, now Mrs Sam Isaacs, who had done so well in the world, Gramma Caroline made herself almost invisible, realising that anything that reminded Hilda of her origins in the cane piece would not be welcome. I remember having to sneak down to her little room to listen to old storytime. She managed to stay out of sight of her daughter Hilda and did many of the daily chores as soon as milady swept down the drive in her motorcar.

Gramma Caroline was a tiny wiry woman who moved with the speed of the wary wise, with East Indian sharp features emphasised by the way she scraped back her hair in a bun. Her natural curiosity helped maintain her, in her below stairs existence. No drawer was safe, no letter unsteamed, no parcel unpoked, no conversation unheard. Papa, her son-in-law, provided her with never-ending challenges in this regard. One day the chauffeur made a midday trip up to Orange Grove with a number of important-looking parcels to be stored in the garage. With them safely stowed, he drove back down the hill to the office in Kingston.

Of course Gramma was watching, and no sooner had the car disappeared from the driveway than she was rooting around in the garage. Unfortunately, she was not the only one observing the delivery. Unemployment in Jamaica is the rule rather than the exception and some of our beloved out-of-work layabouts had been watching from afar. They also wanted to see what was new in the garage and came upon Gramma, in her element checking out the parcels. Both searching parties must have been scared. When Gramma was threatened with violence she reacted bravely but unwisely and was killed in the struggle. An outhouse or privy (outside pit toilet) was nearby and in panic they dropped her in it. This is how the police said it must have happened when they eventually were alerted to the murder.

The afternoon rolled by and no one had missed her. Mother arrived home from babysitting Yvonne, followed by Papa, who liked the old lady and, missing her, started the hunt. I was summoned and it was I who found her, dead, in the pit toilet. The memory has stayed with me to this day.

I loved Gramma. She and I used to gang up together against Mother. We used to play childish tricks on her, Gramma and me. But then they killed her. It was a hell of a way to go. This was my first murder.

The second was Claude's youngest brother, Alvin, who had been, if you remember, the family's war hero. Handsome and debonair, he managed to woo and win the prettiest, sweetest girl in Jamaica – Dorothy Alberga. Unfortunately, she became victim to a strange disease of the heart for which there was no cure. Her early death led to his second marriage and his politicisation. He always did speak a trifle too loudly, and laugh a trifle too long, but he never meant anyone any harm and was always the life and soul of the party. Especially the party on the veranda of a legal bigwig in the Jamaica Labour Party, who was annoying people with his rhetoric.

The gunshot, intended we think for the bigwig, missed its real target and there was Alvin. Dead. Another hell of a way to go, but nothing like the case of my brother Bonny.

As I have already mentioned, Bonny was not the most pleasant of men in his dealings with others, especially those whom he considered beneath him socially. The approach to his house by the sea was blessed with a very wide straight stretch of road. He could always be relied upon to exceed the speed limit by as much as possible before turning in to the gate. That way he killed a lot of goats which, as everyone in Jamaica knows, have the right of way. And a small child too, once, the story goes. Small bones, goat or human, are no match for speeding Cadillacs.

One afternoon three men came into the Sam Isaacs & Son office in downtown Kingston.

'Which one of you is Bonny Isaacs?'

I am he.' I heard three shots ring out and arrived to just catch a glimpse of the men leaving and Bonny bleeding on the floor. At that moment one of the gunmen returned to the scene to search Bonny's body for the gun everybody knew he carried as a matter of course. I challenged the gunman. He took a pot shot at me. Kenneth, one of my adopted sons, apparently threw himself in front of me and the bullet lodged in the doorframe above my head. I don't remember any of this.

Some say that the gunmen were American hit men who had been employed to take Bonny out for reneging on a drug deal. He was, they said, bringing in cocaine in the coffins. Impossible, I think, as he never had anything to do with the overseas shipping and anyway he wasn't bright enough to think up, much less bring off, such a scam. *I* think they killed him because of the goats. And the boy. We'll never know. Yet another hell of a way to go.

Yes, too many murders in my life. Not one of them solved so there is no closure. The Lord sure moves in mysterious ways. I was saved but have not been the same since. The images won't go away and they mix themselves up now. Gramma in the pit-toilet, Alvin on the veranda, Bonny on the floor and the bullet over my head. I put up a good show and people don't talk to me about it. It's been a bit traumatic putting all these deaths together. It's far more discreet to pretend they never happened. But they did, as a sort of personal prelude to the everyday senseless violence which we in Jamaica now take almost for granted. Who out there wants me to be a nice old lady, then?

But back to this visit from Yvonne. Time goes fast when you're having fun. I am really getting into this writing business. Her room has been thoroughly cleaned from top to bottom. I hope she brings some more tapes of what she's been getting up to in England lately.

In the past her Talawa stories have kept me amused. It seems that taking on the burden of running a company was something she was loath to do. It meant that she had no time to dream. There were Arts Council forms to be filled in, petty rivalries to be ignored and bitchy backbiting from the less imaginative to be endured; this was a great price to pay for her peace of mind. But she continued in the face of strenuous opposition. I once asked her why she did it, 'to be suffering so much in England when she could live the life of Riley back here in Jamaica and do what she wanted to at her own theatre, the Barn'. Seems the greater the challenge, the more she feels she must meet it. Or the further away the challenge, maybe?

For seventeen years she continued to run the Talawa Theatre Company. I believe the situation has changed now: I can't wait to hear from her when she arrives if this is indeed the case . . .

Let's get back to the earlier Talawa years. The success of *The Importance of Being Earnest* was impressive. It was even sent by the British Council to Ireland as part of the Britain in Europe Festival. The country of Ireland is divided into two parts: Northern Ireland which is

British and Eire, the Republic of Ireland, which is not. The play was scheduled to be performed in the old Opera House in Cork – a lovely city in the Republic with a river running through it.

The elaborate set got in quite smoothly and the buzz in the town was almost tangible. The British Ambassador was due to attend the first performance and he did. Everything went smoothly until Lady Bracknell's line 'Perhaps it was the result of a revolutionary outrage', upon which the entire audience of Republicans turned and applauded in the direction of the Ambassador. Those unfamiliar with the politics of Northern Ireland and the Republic might miss this point. The good citizens of Cork enjoyed themselves mightily and the cast and crew were all given 'the freedom of the City' . . . free Guinness for the duration of their stay. Luckily this was only a week.

Talawa now had to plan work well in advance. Gone was the laidback casual programming: one had to have a concept, a plan, a strategy. It was no longer any use saying simply 'This is a good play,' one had to look at who else might think so. Would it meet with the approval of the army of assessors on whose secret advice the funders relied so heavily? One also had to persuade white Artistic Directors to agree to have the productions in their theatres. More than once Yvonne was told by these privileged people that such and such a play was not the right thing for the black community. They knew, of course!

So to Africa she went. 'Why Africa, Yvonne? You don't know anything about that continent.'

'Good time as any to find out if my teachers at St Hilda's were right when they told us there was nothing in Africa to bother learning about. Oh yes, Mummy, don't pretend you didn't know that's what went on. Remember we learned all about the Yorkshire Dales and the sweetly flowing River Afton, but Africa was considered a waste of time for nice West Indian girls from proper families to worry their pretty little heads about. So it's as good a time as ever, don't you think?'

Couldn't argue with that. I must admit she had a point, although I worried about her safety all the time she was in Nigeria. Would she be kidnapped? Would she be able to eat the food? There was a lot of heavy stuff going on in Nigeria at that time in 1989, as the military ruler Babangida's antics were meriting some international headlines. Every morning at eight o'clock I was tuning in to the BBC World Service to find out if there was any news from Nigeria. Just like Harry in Greece!

Aren't we funny people? I was so worried about Yvonne being in hostile, violent Nigeria when on my doorstep here in Kingston, Jamaica, we are past masters of the art of the gun crime. She was probably safer in Lagos than in Kingston. Apparently Wole Soyinka once told Yvonne that he was so happy, felt so at home in Jamaica directing his play *Area Boy*, because downtown Kingston was the closest city in feel to downtown Lagos. Ponder on that for a while.

The trip to Nigeria proved a turning point in my daughter's approach to theatre. As she had actually found an African play which fascinated her, there was some method in the madness. *The Gods Are Not to Blame* was hidden away in the children's section of Waterstone's in Charing Cross Road. It first caught her attention because the entire ghastly yellow cover was taken up with a photograph of the playwright's black face. A mischievous black face. Ola Rotimi. As she glanced through the pages it became crystal clear that this was a very serious play, not one which should have been nestling undisturbed in the children's section. It was, in fact, the Yoruba interpretation of the Oedipus myth. Ritualistic and oozing with proverbs, it demonstrated that the Yoruba approach to tragedy was quite different from the tradition she had learned at Rose Bruford. The individual's fate is in *his* hands. He chooses at birth to kill his father and marry his mother, making the tragedy *his f*ault, not that of the gods. The gods are not to blame. Whereas in the Greek approach, the individual has no power over his destiny.

I suppose after so many years of European indoctrination, she had to go to Africa to sort this one out for herself.

Chapter 16

Africa

Yvonne's anecdotes about her visit to Nigeria in 1989 have been, I am told, well documented. All I have is this journal.

The Nigeria Airways plane from Heathrow was comfortable enough and when Kole Omotoso spied me sitting in Economy from his First-Class seat it became even more comfortable. By the way, Kole Omotoso is a Nigerian scholar who is married to a Barbadian. He also wrote the best reference book on Caribbean Theatre, *The Theatrical into Theatre*.

Anyway what was good was that Kole had a car picking him up from the airport, and as he was heading for the University of Ile Ife, which is where I was going, he offered to take me along. I had been thinking I would take a bus. Everybody laughed like mad. Bus! Just like they would have done in Jamaica. I keep making the same mistake, thinking that the wonderful long-distance bus and coach service in England will be replicated everywhere I go. Never learn.

Kole had to make a brief stop on the way to visit his boys' boarding school, which was run by a Colonel of immense proportions who entertained us lavishly with those typically Nigerian gigantic bottles of Star beer, being most grateful for the pair of golfing shoes all frilly brogue-ish and bright white with which Kole presented

him. Very large size. Then on to Abeokuta where he
hoped to catch a glimpse of Wole Soyinka his mentor
and friend, but that didn't work out. Eventually we
arrived in Ile Ife. A garden of tranquillity and softly
spoken buildings, purring trees, landscaped houses.
Where Ola Rotimi was waiting to receive me in his
professorial residence.

I have to tell you what happened on my first morning
walking on campus with this group of very distinguished Nigerians (and me!). To my dismay, beautiful young men kept falling to the ground in front of us.
At first I thought that some strange affliction was rife on
the campus as I rushed forward to help them up. Good
thing Professor Elufowuju (I think it was him) explained
to me that this was how the young men showed respect
to their elders and betters. Prostration. I have to say I
could get used to this.

Then we went into a music lecture where the tiniest
frailest elderly man you could ever imagine was in
charge. A distinguished Master Drummer. As I came
into the room this amazing sound of some fifteen or
twenty drums beat out some very serious music which
got to me right in the solar plexus. When they had flourished to a finish everybody looked at me. Well, I just
knew I had to say something. I felt it had been for me. So
I said, 'Thank you. Thank you. Thank you. It is good to
be here.'

Ola whispered to me, 'Very good. How did you know
they were beating you a welcome? That it was *your* name
they were playing musical variations with?'

Never to be forgotten.

But the food. I couldn't get my head round this food.
The fufu, which is yam pounded till it is quite fluffy and
a bit like very good mashed potato, that's all right, but
the green slimy ochro sauce I find a big turn-off, especially when it covers the bush meat. Now this bush meat

'something' is something else. I am trying to find out what animal it actually is and Ola is always pointing it out to me as we drive along the highway. It looks like a small animal which is killed, flattened out and dried in the sun and is for sale by the side of the road. 'Agouti,' said somebody – but that sounded too much like rodent for me to listen up too long. Bush meat is a great delicacy but this poor soul can't eat it. Just cannot. The smell is something I just don't want to get accustomed to. The only way out was to become a vegetarian, which in Nigeria is next to being in need of care and protection. This cramps my style quite a lot but I have to pass on the bush meat luxury. I suppose curry goat must seem equally horrible to some people.

Ola is very kind and has driven about the place taking me to see the sights. Before setting off on one of the big journeys he explained in his wonderful way, saying, 'Apologies, my dear Yvonne, but we must first visit the Professor.'

I thought: Not another Professor! As the car left the splendid gates of the University and we began to negotiate the less-well-kept roads, we came to a very flat clearing of hard-packed earth with only a large scrub tree for shade.

Under it were two men in immaculate white overalls.

Slowly we bumped over the dry ground before coming to a halt. The senior overall gave the ritual greeting to Ola: 'Kabyesi O.' Ola then said, 'Yvonne, I would like to present the Professor of Peugeot. The best mechanic in these parts. Before I risk the roads, the Professor must see that all is well with my most important asset, my Peugeot.' Pronounced Piggot. It's a bit like at home in Jamaica: when someone is a good politician we call him Gladstone or Churchill.

We went to Oyo where the crossroads of the world meet, to the market in Ibadan to buy the cowrie shells, cloths, beads and fetishes we need for the props in the play. Talk about scared. We went into a dark little hut kind of place with a crocus bag over the entrance to buy the dried monkey heads. You heard me. Touching these things took some determination but I am resolved not to fail any more tests. Bush meat yes, but no others. My pride is at stake. So I took the monkey heads into my hands, felt slightly sick, especially when I met a monkey eye, but managed to keep a straight face. After that it was plain sailing. Mistress of my environment? Not very likely.

Ola decided that I should see not only Central Nigeria but that we should go to Port Harcourt where he held the Chair of Literature. As an Ibo he came from the south and was anxious for me to experience the difference between the Yoruba and his Ibo people. The roads to the south are not good. They are bad. The potholes are so enormous they make ours in Jamaica look like teacups. Also there is no street lighting. As we came closer to the oil area I saw what looked like gigantic torches blazing in the night. All around, the leaves of the trees were scorched, leaving only spectral black shapes to give substance to the eye.

So just hear this idiot, your daughter: 'So Ola, are we approaching the tourist quarter?'

Never have I felt so stupid and useless as he replied: 'No, my dear, this is the south where they burn off the gas which the oil produces. The oil is piped straight to the north. The south gets the burned forest, oh yes and the potholes. I don't think we will be able to get out of this one so we will have to wait until some people come by.'

'Come by? This is a very lonely place.'

'Yes, but it has eyes. They are watching us as we speak. They will make us wait a bit longer and then one by one they will appear in order to lift the car over this native swimming pool. Best if you wind up your window and sink down in the seat. On no account speak. Here comes number one.'

Mummy, believe me it happened exactly as he had said. After about forty-five minutes we were on our way again, twelve men having lifted the Peugeot station wagon over the abyss in the road. A human Bailey Bridge. Ola was considerably poorer. Immediately my mind went into overtime about the return journey which Ola promised would be taken in the day. Whew.

I had been asking after Carol Dawes – Neville Dawes's wife who you might remember was formerly Carol Morrison, the woman I did *Suddenly Last Summer* with. I think she is the best black director in the world. She studied under Peter Brook – but we don't hold that against her! Lucky woman. I had heard she was in Nigeria somewhere but found people cautious when her name came up. 'Oh yes, your countrywoman' was all they would say. And change the subject. I was getting really curious, so I tried again with Ola. It was a long journey and conversation lurched from pillar to post. 'So, Ola, you do know Carol, don't you? It would be very nice to see her.'

'No be small my sister, you have been rooting around in that yam hill for long enough. In fact, we are travelling in her direction. You see, she is covering my lectures for me while I am at Ile Ife. Truth now, she is one of the main reasons for my visit to Port Harcourt. I am keen to see if the story will change here and not be the same as at all the other universities in Nigeria where she has taught.'

'What's all that about? Come on, tell me.'

'All lizards lie prostrate: how can a man tell which lizard suffers from bellyache?'

'Eh?'

'Carol is an extremely talented person. Many universities here have gladly opened their doors to her. Unfortunately, as night follows day, she turns unhappy and off she goes again, from the north all the way down to the south of the country. The feeling among the academic fraternity suggests she is simply unable to cope with us Nigerians. That's easy to understand, is it not, my sista? Sista Carol is now in Port Harcourt, on one edge of this vast land of Nigeria. One more move and it's into the sea. So, my little sista, no more questions. We shall see what we shall see.'

And so we did. There was to be a student performance directed by Femi Osofisan of Wole Soyinka's *The Strong Breed* the night we arrived. Very well done as the director pursued the drama relentlessly. There was Carol seemingly not a day older. She recognised me and we greeted each other rapturously. The first Jamaican in three weeks and not just any old Jamaican – the legendary Carol Dawes. Happy hour lasted about forty-five minutes. Was it something I said? Probably. But all of a sudden in a moment she clammed up, walked away.

I can hear you saying it *was* my fault, Mrs Clarke. However Ola, with his famous dry proverbial wit, chuckled, 'The moon moves slowly but by daybreak it crosses the sky. We'll all get over it. Not every shoe fits every foot.'

He's full of these sayings, which ring a distant bell. I now realise many are in his play! Quoting himself, what a thing!

And with that the journal arrives at its end.

Some say the Talawa production of *The Gods Are Not to Blame* is the best thing they have done. I haven't seen any of the productions except *The Lion*, which the British Council toured to Jamaica. That was so good I stirred myself and gave them a cast party. I remember liking Madge Sinclair and Dennis Charles rather a lot. She was so elegant and he made me laugh.

But people assure me *The Gods* was worth seeing, I have never been able to read an African play without falling asleep, so that is not for me to judge. It did the company a world of good playing first in Liverpool and then at the Riverside Studios in London. Yvonne imported our splendid Leonie Forbes to play the Queen to Jeffrey Kissoon's King Odewale (Oedipus). Leonie always waxes poetic about the experience.

The playwright was particularly pleased with Leonie's portrayal. After the first performance he spoke to the assembled company, who were anxious to earn his approval. For many this was the first African play they had acted in, and to have the playwright there in living colour was very exhilarating. He said something along these lines:

'Ladies and gentlemen, I have now been part of an audience which has experienced this production of my play. I want to thank you all for the time and care and trouble everyone has taken with my inadequate work. I have, as you can imagine, been present at many, perhaps *too* many, performances of this play.' (By now the assembled company is busily staring at the floor.) 'I can't tell the number of times I have heard this play, but tonight for the first time I saw it, I felt it and I heard it. I stood to applaud you and want to thank you from the bottom of my heart. No be small, my sisters and brothers. *Oluri! Kabeysi O!*'

I guess he liked it. The company certainly enjoyed doing it. Many now familiar faces played their part in the success, especially Ian Roberts (now Kwame Kwei Armah, actor, playwright and raconteur), who portrayed an old seer and was particularly compelling. Yvonne always mentions Peter Badejo and Ellen Cairns, without whose inspired help in this production, she would probably have drowned, she says.

Some years after the production the BBC commissioned a radio version which Yvonne directed with some of the original cast, who were joined by Sir Trevor McDonald as the narrator in one of his few acting roles. Very detailed and punctilious in his approach, which paid off nicely; and the late Sir Robert Stephens, who was keen to play his first African role, that of a 100-year-old Yoruba priest. His presence in the studio raised the odds, as a more professional attitude would have been hard to find. 'He's so humble, Mummy,' the dear girl kept saying.

The Government of Ghana had for some years produced and promoted a Pan-African International Festival of the Arts (Panafest) in which performance existed side by side with colloquia. Ghanaians apparently look just like Jamaicans – much more so than Nigerians. They are more contained in their behaviour, with a sense of humour which is light and witty.

Yvonne was invited to give a paper at the Second Panafest Colloquium, on the connection between Ghana and Jamaica. She used as her metaphor the trickster figure of Anansi, a West African, Ghanaian mythological character who crossed the Middle Passage with the slaves bound for the West Indies. Anansi has over the past few centuries become endemic to the psyche of the Jamaican.

Anansi is a spider survivor who uses his brains to good effect. For example, he enters a room with five people at table enjoying a meal. He is not expected and there is no food for him. He protests that it doesn't matter but agrees to share with one diner, and another and another until he has had two and a half helpings and everyone else has had a half. If someone accuses you of having an Anansi mentality, think carefully before you take it as a compliment. However, in these days a little bit of Anansi mentality might mean the difference between life and death.

The paper was well received as the links between the two cultures, which may have seemed tenuous at the beginning, became less so as the dialogue between the participants revealed more and stronger ties. The hospitality of my daughter's Ghanaian hosts knew no bounds. She was given the services of a driver and interpreter who would take her wherever she wished. So, being no laggard, she managed to see the Golden Ashanti region from where the Kings of Ghana originate, was presented with a fabulous 'Queen Mother' Kente cloth in silk, bought another in one of the unbelievably complicated markets, and visited the Gold Coast but got cold feet at the thought of Elmina Castle where so many slaves had begun their one-way journey to the Americas and the West Indies. Not sure if I would have wanted to see this place, either. Man's inhumanity to man is too much on show in this my beloved Jamaica for me to want to gawp at slave pens where our ancestors were kept in readiness for their forced migration.

The Kwame Nkrumah monument in Accra came in for great praise. 'Very imposing, rendered gentle and appealing by the abundance of water.'

Africa seemed to have got into Yvonne's psyche as she chose an impenetrable play, *The Road* by Wole Soyinka, with which to open the Cochrane Theatre on a windy corner in London WC2. The story goes that Derek Walcott had come over to London to check out her production of *Antony and Cleopatra*, (of which more in the next chapter) and during the after-show festivities, he persuaded Yvonne to do this play, referring to it as 'one of the best plays in the English language'. Said Professor Walcott: 'I tried to understand it, I tried to direct it and failed. Now it's your turn.'

Apparently most people found it hard going, but there is a school of thought among experts and scholars of the Nigerian canon which regards my dear daughter's production as one of the definitive ones. 'The perfect misreading' is how it was referred to in a conference on the works of Soyinka in Toronto, Canada, in 2001. At first Yvonne's nose was a bit out of joint until she realised that this was a compliment. She smiled serenely thereafter, basking in the glow from Biodun Jeyifo's approval. She has never attempted another African play since then. Wisely, I feel. Biyi Bandele's *Resurrections*, commissioned by Talawa, won a prize in one of the LWT competitions for playwriting and she did direct it. But it seemed somewhat derivative, sort of sub-Soyinka, and was in the end a quite dreadful production.

Win some, lose some, that's what I say.

Chapter 17

Pomp and Circumstance

—◦◎◦—

Talking of winning, is it always possible to win with Shakespeare? One tries, but win or lose the energy and application the old man demands are never wasted. I can't think why Yvonne chose *Antony and Cleopatra* as her first stab at Shakespeare as a director in England. Her explanation is that she had tried to get into the Tutankhamen exhibition and failed, so her consolation lay in reading something about Egypt. She did go to Egypt on a fleeting visit with Mona once, and the famous postcards from her were sizzling with excitement. They had got into the museum in Cairo which housed the exhibition with no fuss at all and saw all of it, not only the parts which had travelled to England, in comfort with a proper Egyptian guide. Apparently the casual acceptance of the people of so many years of culture, so many years of history, left a lasting impression. *This is our city, our history. Take it or leave it. This is us.*

She described the City of the Dead, which played casual host to hundreds of homeless citizens who took up residence in the elaborate tombs and sepulchres of the once-fashionable graveyards. This interested me immediately, being in the undertaking business, and I hastened to double security up at our Shooter's Hill Crematorium and Burial Park. The idea might catch on in Jamaica! Apparently, however, we draw the line at taking up residence in graveyards. Too much duppy and

145

not everyone is a duppy conqueror. Which is just as well.

But back to *Antony and Cleopatra*. Since the latter was Queen of the Nile she must be an Egyptian and therefore North African. Shakespeare says she was dusky. I mean, he didn't call her fair or an English rose so why not get Donna Croll, a versatile actress of Jamaican origin, to get her teeth into the Queen of the Nile and see if together they could extract some of the juice from the play. Jeffrey Kissoon, who had been appearing as the Prince of Morocco, the 'mislike me not for my complexion' golden casket-fancier, in the Dustin Hoffman *Merchant of Venice* in London's West End, was happy to exchange his flowing white robes and Elizabethan vocal quiver for the even sexier Roman dress of Antony.

This production had its moments. In fact, HRH Princess Anne graced it with her presence for a gala performance in aid of the University of the West Indies. There was a distinct danger of more drama off stage than on. I do like her small talk to my daughter as they sat in the auditorium waiting for the curtain to go up.

'This is a play about a man leaving his wife, is it not? Jolly good for me to see such a thing at the moment. Sermons in stones, what?' Very wry, as she was at the time, according to the media, having a bit of local difficulty with Captain Mark Phillips. This remark endeared her to Yvonne, who will not have a word said against her. Ever. In the interval, all the elaborate plans were thrown into disarray as the lift taking them up to the first floor for refreshments malfunctioned; the doors closed too quickly and became well and truly stuck. There was no movement up or down for quite a few minutes.

There was Missis Queen's only daughter stuck in a lift with Trinidad and Tobago High Commissioner Ulric Cross and Yvonne Brewster. Ulric can pass muster

anywhere as he is one of nature's most sublime sophisticates and managed to keep the conversation going as if
nothing out of the ordinary had happened. All Yvonne
remembers is the fact that HRH's children rather liked
baked beans for tea. The lady-in-waiting was heard
banging in vain on the lift doors for quite some minutes
before off it took suddenly, jerking them up to the next
floor. Rapid footsteps on the stairs and many very red
faces. After the show the cast was introduced to the fine
royal lady and she was so cool and gracious in her pretty
yellow dress.

While we are on the royal wavelength let me tell you
about an Edgar White play, *Moon Dance Night*, which
Madam directed for the Black Theatre Season at the
Arts Theatre in London. During rehearsal I would get
the odd phone call, even one letter which made me thank
my lucky stars I was dealing with the dead and not with
living luvvies.

Here's what I remember of a long phone call about
two and a half weeks into rehearsals: 'Mummy, I can't
go on. Edgar White turns up most days dressed in
sombre clothes, a Fedora hiding eyes already hidden
behind dark lenses. He rarely speaks. However, sometimes he starts to play his flute. Plaintive wailing flute
from the back of the rehearsal room, always behind me,
always unsettling. I have twigged he does this when he
thinks it's going all wrong. It's a difficult play, a good
play but challenging. Politically outspoken about the
influence of colonisation, immersed in ritual. The challenge is to make sure the balance is kept as it's all too
easy to go all out with the ritual, which the English
critics will love as its so ethnic, but if we succumb to
this we do the play an injustice by undermining the
substance.

'Edgar White writes a mean play even if he will play
the flute instead of talking to you. He also seems to be

unduly fascinated by Jean Breeze. This affects her concentration but not as much as it may have done others'. Then this actor is invariably late. "I don't set out to be late, it just seems to work out that way." The cast refer to him as 'Late Bloom'. If I kick up too much of a fuss which everybody is wanting, defying me to, the atmosphere will become even more charged. If I don't, then I'm done for.

'Isabelle (Lucas) is in danger of losing her confidence as loud remarks about her Canadian accent are sometimes thrown around the place like confetti. She is actually very good in the play, better than some who would undermine her.

'Look, I am going on like this just to unburden. You see, I have to go on with this thing. Nil desperandum.'

'OK, darling, call again, any time,' I reply, 'but not collect, remember.'

I thought, Give me the dead any time. Anyway, the play in spite of everything was ready on time – just as well as lots of tickets had been sold especially for the Royal Gala Night with another of Missis Queen's children. This time it was Prince Edward. He too was charming, seemed appreciative of the good-looking girls, which was OK. They, the royal party, sat up in the balcony at the Arts Theatre in London's West End with Julian waving at Yvonne like mad from the stalls. Beside him was the lovely French au pair who was also gaping upwards.

'Who is that?' asked the royal personage.

'My son Julian.'

'And who is with him?'

'Isabelle.'

'I hope they are joining us in the interval.'

They did and au pair Isabelle enjoyed a few moments of right royal appreciation. Her family back home in France was ever so impressed.

Let's have all the royal bits and bobs together, shall we?

Prince Charles was to visit the Riverside Studios to see a play and in the interval he was expected to have a look at the current exhibition. Yvonne was on the Board of Riverside Studios at the time and it fell to her to walk HRH around the show. It was really avant-garde work — you know, the kind of stuff that has a small coloured dot luxuriating in an otherwise large blank canvas. Yvonne says that was why the Board gave her this job.

'Ummmh.'

'Aaaaahhh.'

'Yaaaaaah.'

'So what do you think of this one?' Pointing to another shape lost in space.

'Actually, Your Royal Highness, I don't understand this kind of art and so I wouldn't know if it's good or bad. I'm a total philistine.'

To which HRH replied, 'Whew, I am so pleased to hear that.'

The rest of the tour around the exhibition went swimmingly.

And finally the OBE. We back here in Jamaica were over the moon when we heard that Yvonne, Starr and Julian would be going to Buckingham Palace to collect Yvonne's OBE from the Queen. She, Yvonne that is, has lived in England so long that she has adopted some of the slightly embarrassed way of dealing with success or recognition. As far as we were concerned, there she was being recognised for her services to the Arts. Not to Black Theatre in Britain but simply the Arts. She thrashed around as to where this had come from, why would 'they' give her such a thing, what had she done etc until some senior patriarch told her to stop faffing around and accept the thing.

The arguments put forward the points that in those

days, ten years ago, you couldn't suggest yourself for an OBE, nor was it up to your community to put you forward, so this was a surprise honour for someone not born in the country. Also, think of the role modelling for younger people of Caribbean origin. In other words, either put up or shut up. She put up and we were, as I said, over the moon. I have a photograph of her holding up her insignia in front of the Palace and smiling sheepishly – you know, the picture which is the stereotype of those occasions. Stereotype or not I like it.

Pretty pink dress she wore. And no hat. Apparently the only women in the room on that occasion without hats were Her Majesty, Kate Adie the BBC reporter, and Yvonne. Her argument was that it was indoors so why a hat? Honestly, though, it was because she is short and wide and hats make her look like a mushroom.

'So what do you remember about that day then, Yvonne?' Deirdre Forbes the *Voice* newspaper reporter asked.

'I remember the dapper Lord Lieutenant's pep talk to the assembled company of people who were to receive recognition. "A few pointers: Her Majesty should not be referred to as Maaaaaam with too long an a, but preferably as something more closely related to Mum with a very short a. You must listen for your surname before you begin walking on the red carpet towards Her Majesty. For instance it will be: 'Smith, Adam Michael, to receive the Office of the most noble Order of the British Empire.' Walk when you hear your surname. Repeat surname. Stop in front of Her Majesty and walk four steps towards her. You will only speak when spoken to, your decoration will be pinned on you by Her Majesty, and when the exchange is at an end Her Majesty will give your hand a little push which indicates your dismissal. Immediately walk four steps, backwards, turning sharply to your right after this has been achieved."

'Now, this sounded quite easy for someone who has been embroiled in the business of stage moves, but when push came to shove it was terrifying. The "exchange" went on longer than I had expected. HM actually spoke to me as if she knew me. "Your citation is for services to the arts. What arts?"

'"Black Theatre, Your Majesty. Sorry, Maaam, I mean Mum."

'"And what is that?"

'"Theatre produced with the interests of Black people in mind."

'"Exclusively for Black people?"

'"Everyone is welcome, Mum. Two of your children have seen my work, Princess Anne and Prince Edward."

'"How very interesting. And what were these plays . . ." and so on.

'HM had seemed so interested in what I had to say. It's an art really to make the person you are talking to believe they are really fascinating. One somehow forgets that there are three hundred other hands to shake and a similar number of breasts to pin.

'At one moment, I looked up and saw these two Yeomen of the Guard with pikestaffs standing on either side of the Queen. Those were not friendly eyes, much more eloquent with centuries of authority than anyone in the Metropolitan Police. It struck me there in the middle of this important personal moment that they were there to protect the Queen and were not tourist attractions. No wonder HM was so relaxed with guys like that on call, standing guard.

'When the push came I felt quite elated and managed to walk backwards but it was made much more difficult by the thickness of the carpet.

'Forwards is one thing but backwards is quite another as your heels catch in the pile. I made it, just, but a lot of others didn't do so well.'

And they say ritual is dead.

'So how does it feel to be an OBE? What's it like to get a gong?'

'Don't know yet.'

'Oh go on.'

'O bloody 'ell or maybe just a touch of obeah. Get it? Ethnic? Obe-ah? Never mind.'

'Is the Queen really tiny?'

'Yeah, and very pretty.'

To me, proud mother, one of the real highlights of this episode is that she made the front page of the *Voice* newspaper in living colour! No accounting for what turns one on. Seriously, I am very proud of Yvonne for having survived in a world in which it is easier, nay safer, to be invisible, inaudible. Can't accuse her of either of these graces. I keep the photograph of my daughter and Missis Queen on my dressing-table to show off, of course. I do sometimes wonder if Her Majesty will ever consider changing the name of these honours, though, as Officer of the British Empire is a little wanting. Didn't the sun set on the pink map a long time ago? However, I suppose part of the British charm is its eccentricity.

Things royal are jumping into my mind in the form now of Talawa's *King Lear*. It may not be putting too fine a point on it to say that this production sorted out the liberals from the conservatives. All in lower case. Drama and crisis are never far away when people are creating work which is not predictable and which seeks to find its own systems, its own signals and significances, in the face of barely disguised racist pre-judgement – prejudice, if you like.

Norman Beaton had often phoned Yvonne in the middle of the night to discuss among other things not his desire but his *need* to play King Lear. Not only were there late-night tipsy phone calls, sometimes he would turn up at the house. One Saturday morning around ten o'clock a large white chauffeur-driven Bentley pulled up outside the Brewster residence in Buckley Road, causing a minor sensation. Out fell Norman dressed in white linen, which must have been quite stunning when he put it on the night before, holding aloft a half-empty bottle of white wine.

Starr and Yvonne debated whether or not to open the door, but as a small crowd was gathering, discretion overcame valour. Three hours later the chauffeur, who turned out to be a long-suffering friend, persuaded Norman to leave. In the intervening hours he had raided the house of its small stock of wine and had, amazingly enough, read most of Andrew Salkey's *Anancy's Score*. Aloud. Beautifully. He was auditioning, he said. He wanted to play King Lear. He felt as the most senior, most easily recognised and most talented black actor working in Britain at the time, that one of the large well-subsidised companies might offer him this opportunity. They did not. Nor were they likely to. His reputation for courting headlines probably put them off. Truth is, maintains Yvonne, that 'When he was working, Norman Beaton was the most punctilious and professional of actors. You just had to beware of his out-of-hours behaviour.'

His recurring theme was that Talawa, as the only Black British theatre company with the resources to mount his King Lear, had a responsibility to do this. Yvonne didn't like the sound of duty and responsibility but she did fancy Norman in the role. They had worked together with great success in *The Black Jacobins* when he re-created the role of Toussaint L'Ouverture. Great actor. Difficult, obsessive, embittered human being with a malignant wit, but his talent, his timing, his intelligence, his scrawny enfeebled body, plus his life experience of family and its ties made him a perfect King Lear.

153

The pair of them plotted and planned the production over many months, usually over an Italian meal in Sicilian Avenue near the Cochrane Theatre.

Norman's King Lear was going to draw heavily from black traditions. He saw him as the founder and chief executive of a large successful Friendly Society or Credit Union. This made sense, as Caribbean people are hooked on Credit Unions and 'partners'. All was looking good. An impressive set of actors had agreed to appear in the production, including Cathy Tyson (Regan), Lolita Chakrabarti (Goneril), Diane Parish (Cordelia), David Harewood (Edmund), David Fielder (Gloucester), Karl Collins, David Webber (Kent), Dhirendra (Edgar) and Talawa stalwart Mona Hammond as the Fool. Then Norman fell ill. The posters were printed, the theatre booked and Norman was in hospital. The doctor said, 'This is a serious admission.'

What to do? Yvonne talks about her sleepless nights, but the buck stopped with her and she had to make the decision. She had three options. Cancel. Recast older. Recast younger. Cancellation was like giving in. This is not her style. Recast older? In the light of the relationship which had built up between Yvonne and Norman she had great difficulty in discussing the role with the few, the very few, older black actors willing and able to take over the role. There was a lot of angst around. To this day, well over a decade later, one senior actor will never forgive her for not offering him the part. It remains a chorus with him.

So it was recast younger. Donald Wolfit had played the part in his forties so it was not unheard of. Yvonne decided to go with Ben Thomas, whom she trusted and with whom she had worked regularly. Most of the acting company decided to stay with the production, even though it would now be something quite different. Markedly post-contemporary street culture, all decked out in black leather and opportunism. A complete rethink, but as the cast was up for it, the production brought alive *King Lear* to a young, vibrant black audience and gave David Harewood, for example, the opportunity of playing a challenging Shakespearean role. Of course, since then he has had no shortage of offers but one has to start somewhere.

I often wonder what would have happened to Yvonne if the critics had been kinder to her work. They often reserved a special kind of spleen for her which might be summed up in the words 'Who does she think she is?' One bright spark commented on the bad role model for all the impressionable black male youngsters in Brixton by having such a successful (read sexy) portrayal of Edmund by the handsome David Harewood. They might think that fratricide was now OK and take to killing their brothers in Brixton.

I heard the tape of her riposte to this when Jenni Murray asked about it on *Woman's Hour*: 'Don't you find it strange that the critic didn't laud the good example given to the impressionable young black women in Brixton by seeing Cordelia portrayed by the charming Diane Parrish as a blameless, loving daughter?'

Another pink-shirted critical gentleman wondered in print why a red blooded member of the audience would be interested in what the Nigerians ate. This was his only contribution to the appreciation of Wole Soyinka's play *The Road*. A basket to carry water. I must not go on about the critics, as Yvonne never does. Don't think she reads them much.

Thus Norman Beaton never got to play King Lear. Our loss. He crept into one performance but was too ill with a coughing fit so saw only a very little of it. When Yvonne accompanied him outside she noticed he was crying.

155

It was during the Second Panafest festival in Ghana that Norman Beaton's death was announced one day during the lunch-break. The noise was deafening but when the details of his demise came over the Tannoy silence fell: 'Norman Beaton, who always expressed the hope that he would die in his native land, Guyana, managed to achieve that wish. His plane landed. He came down the steps. Fell into waiting arms and died on the tarmac. He died as he lived. On the edge. A moment of silence for a great actor.'

According to his son, however, he died on the plane on his way home but Yvonne prefers to believe the myth. I too think it's nicer, don't you? Sort of 'I will live and die an actor man', with apologies to Evan Jones.

Chapter 18

What Time is it Now?

Oh my great goodness – planes! The day has come when my elder daughter is due. The London planes are usually late, especially in the winter, but who knows? House is ready, flowers in place, fruit, coconut water, bammies in the fridge, me ready in the best dress I can find, Valerie to drive. I hope Trevor is going to meet her, as I would like to see him. He only comes round when she is here but that's life. I have to make some notes about some things I need to talk to her about. You see, time is running. Writing these jottings has taken my mind off the impending visit until now.

Normally I would not have the spare hours in the day to be idly pretending to be Jane Austen, but it's becoming increasingly difficult to get down to the office. If a day passes without my going to work it does so at a snail's pace. Yes, I realise I am very nearly ninety years old – but so what? I am fit. I do my yoga every day, eat my steamed vegetables, drink my coffee with too much condensed milk. I am as steady on my pins as anyone, yet the feeling is that I should stay at home. What am I to do here? I, who have never bothered myself in the kitchen and delegated the smooth running of the house to a series of capable housekeepers. Exactly what am I supposed to find that fascinating to keep me at home?

My orchids used to interest me when I was busy

winning prizes with them, but they have all given up the ghost and I really don't care to start on all that greenhouse business again, even if I could. My days of winning prizes are over. Both my daughters suggest I use the greenhouse . . . I should get some little pots and plant some little exotic herbs, thyme, basil, sage and so on, and then sell them to John R. Wong supermarket. How boring. Little pots of little herbs instead of large carnivorous dangerous orchids? No.

I must tell the truth. I am having a bit of trouble with the time of day and this may be why they want to ban me from the office. I am not always sure whether the sun is coming up or going down. Six o'clock is the most difficult hour. It's hard getting it clear whether the darkness has just gone or if it has just arrived. Everyone in the house humours me. 'Now, Mrs Clarke, it's another twelve hours before the chauffeur comes for you. Time to go to bed now.'

Something in me doesn't trust them. Silly. I know if this confusion was not so real and present I wouldn't be such an embarrassment. However, on no account am I giving up going to the office, as they need me to add a bit of style to the place. None of them know what they are up to, and if I am not there the funerals will simply not be presented properly. The wrong bodies will be in the coffins, people cremated who should have been buried, the hearses won't start, the money won't be collected. They need me but they don't know it.

I will simply have to continue doing what is necessary. For example, the dress code has got really loose – imagine jeans and T-shirts! This is the beginning of the end. So to work I must go every morning, seven days a week. In case they are trying to be clever and leave me at home twiddling my thumbs I have obtained the cellular phone number of the driver, and if he is not here by six in the morning, I call him incessantly until he comes to fetch me. Or if that doesn't work, I start walking down the road by myself and that sets the cat among the pigeons – someone has to be found to ferry me back and forth.

The day I stop going to the office is the day I die. Believe. Enough of me; I've said too much already. Better get back to the safer subject of the imminent arrival of my house guest. Some producer from the Jamaica Information Service just rang to speak to her. I told them that they would be able to catch to her tomorrow. Apparently they are planning to film a full-length programme featuring Yvonne in their series *Masters of the Arts*. Jamaica gets in on the act a little bit late – although, as they say, better late than never. Internationally there have been a number of such television programmes, documentaries, articles, seminars and so on, but seeing as how Jamaica has never seen fit to award my daughter even an order of the OF . . . What is the OF? I hear you ask. Old Fool, of course. This figures.

I bet they get a good programme out of her, but does anybody here care? Except maybe Trevor. She has been working all the hours available to adapt his autobiography into a version for the stage, which if they don't quarrel too much will be presented at the Barn this year end. I have seen the script, which is really one man's struggle against the odds to become and remain an artist. From Bellas Gate in deepest Clarendon to Britain and back.

This is deeply important in the developing world, where cable television presents such a never-ending parade of American culture that to continue believing in the strength and importance of native talent is more difficult than one might imagine. Work like Trevor's autobiography, *Bellas Gate Boy*, is an important yardstick for this generation, as well as a reminder of the possible for others.

Before I get into deep water – and I can't swim – excuse me for now, y'hear? I am going to meet a flight.

Chapter 19

Sweat is Salty

Norman Washington Manley International Airport lies at the tip of that long strip of land the Palisadoes, which helps form one of the great natural harbours of the world, beautiful Kingston Harbour. The sound of the surf and the sight of half-sunken hulks of ships make the journey rather romantic. I like to imagine those gorgeous pirates of the Caribbean whose shenanigans in the eighteenth century made Port Royal justly deserve its name as the wickedest city on earth. Can almost hear the doubloons clinking in the treasure chests, shiver mi timbers.

However, to all intents and purposes, I appear to sit quietly in the back of something called a people-carrier which my grandson Gordon owns, and hope the plane is on time. It is. One of the first London passengers to emerge is Yvonne, looking in need of a tan but otherwise all right.

Here beginneth my ordeal: celebrate is the word on her lips, tolerate is the word in my head.

In the people-carrier it's all small talk and excited chatter as she strips off almost every article of clothing while commenting on everything in sight. The sudden tropical heat does something to the traveller from the north. However sophisticated he or she may wish to appear, the Kingston heat exposes us all. Brings us back to basics. Sweat is salty.

When I was scribbling down my bits and bobs of memory, I gradually realised there are huge chunks of darkness I wish to enlighten, to tickle the bottom of. I must try and get this information from Yvonne without, of course, letting on or seeming too interested. If I let down my guard it will put me at a disadvantage and I don't like being at a disadvantage. Ever. I have worked out how to do this, and go over the plan in my mind as we jolt along our way home.

I am disturbed from my reverie when Yvonne deposits a large bag of my favourite nut and honey-coated popcorn in my now ample lap. I am very fond of honey and nut popcorn and this brings a smile to my face. I'll tolerate that quite happily. The next comment wipes the smile off said face: 'So, Mrs Clarke, what you want for the party, eh? I've brought some of your favourites out with me – asparagus tips, lovely olives, and maraschino cherries for a start, but we can plan it all together, can't we, Miss Val?'

Silence. No reply from Valerie and I am all of a sudden admiring the sunset. She lets it go, but I know it will not go away. I must get myself together, act my age and simply tell her that a birthday party is the thing I want least in life. I will wait until she settles. In a couple of days I know I'll wonder what all the fuss was about.

If I must, in the end, put up with this party foolishness, the upside will be, now that she is here, I can get on with my newfound interest: my research project into what makes Madam tick. Methodology: I will simply take the relevant theatre programmes, articles and videotapes she has sent to me from time to time over the past forty-something years, scatter them casually around the house and use them to lead the conversation into the areas of darkness I mentioned earlier. This will kill two birds with one stone. I will get the information and she

162

will be talking about herself. Making us both happy. And she might, you never know, forget about the party. Yes, I know that is wishful thinking but it helps.

The journey from the airport is over, the nut and honey popcorn quietly scoffed, and we all pile into the house. I am relieved when everything appears to meet with first-glance approval. I have a bet going with Mervys about how long it will be before the furniture starts to move. But we are safe for now, it appears.

As I leave for work at six o'clock the next morning, my daughter is still asleep and I leave the programme for *Othello* lying about on a coffee-table in the flop room. She is sure to come upon it and I will casually bring the production into conversation when I come home. This programme is most informative, with a strange yet compelling introduction by the Barbadian novelist Austin Clarke (not related to us in any way), whom she met in Toronto, where he lives.

On hearing Talawa was producing *Othello* he gave Yvonne permission to use an edited version of his paper *Orenthal and Othello*, which looked at the parallels between OJ Simpson and Othello in 'an examination of two black lives, two black heroes, two persons used as symbols and both victims of a racial epidermal schema'. Heavenly coincidence should be accepted, never be questioned. Yvonne had been using that very comparison in her preparation for the play, while also including black General Powell in the Gulf War, which was on everyone's lips.

She was equally impressed, I must tell, you with Clarke's famous recipe for the best martini in the west: 'They say, the experts that is, that a true martini must be made from Bombay gin, with Noilly Prat vermouth, with olives that do not have those little red things in them; and that it must be pure and dangerously strong;

163

and that you must spend *eight* minutes to drink it in; and that it should leave you with a kick.' She's tried it out on me. Very good.

The image on the cover of the *Othello* programme is fascinating but a little risqué, I think. It has this black man almost kissing a white lily. I suppose it's clever and the young man *is* very good-looking. I expect it's intended to attract audiences to this sexy play . . .

Othello has always fascinated me. As a girl growing up I would hear my father reciting purple passages from Shakespeare in his strong and heavily accented voice while shaving. Each stroke was accompanied by yet another famous line: 'Vaulting ambition, which o'er-leaps itself' (razor action) 'and falls on the other' (razor action). 'Screw your courage to the sticking-place' (razor action) 'and we'll not fail – no, baby, we'll not fail' (razor action). And so on.

Papa was particularly fond of Bottom in *A Midsummer Night's Dream* and joyously bellowed forth: 'Masters, you ought to consider with yourselves: to bring in' (razor stroke) 'God shield us!' (razor stroke) 'a lion among ladies, is a most dreadful thing. A most dreadful thing, *n'est ce pas?* (razor stroke). So he played with the texts in his early morning capers with the razor. The only one which did not get the razor stroke treatment was *Othello* or *O-to-hell-go*, as he called his favourite General. You could hear the catch in his voice when he recited

> *Speak of me as I am; nothing extenuate,*
> *Nor set down aught in malice: then, must you speak*
> *Of one that lov'd not wisely but too well . . .*

And here Sam's voice would trail off. I think he was considering his own marriage. He may have been contemplating his life as a stranger in an even stranger land.

164

He often said Shylock played by a black man would make the ultimate sense. I am interested in finding out how his granddaughter approached *Othello*. I know as a girl she always delighted in his 'Shaving Shakespeare' as she called it. She used to ask him to recite it for her.

'Come on, Ba. If I start, will you continue? "Soft you; a word or two . . . ?"'

Funnily enough, the other day I came across Papa's ancient well-worn copy of the *Complete Works* given to him by his Shakespeare collaborator then, a young Jewish solicitor practising in downtown Kingston. The inscription reads: *To Dear Sam, with best wishes from a true and loyal Friend, Leroy Murad.*

Old Man Sam and his disciple used to meet in the lunch-hour in the Funeral Home's Chapel of Rest, where they would read aloud a bit of the Bard, their only audience the uncritical dead awaiting burial. Ha! That's one way of getting a good review. Very funny, Kathleen. Sometimes I make myself laugh, but I must remember – snuff isn't allowed to sneeze.

Congratulate me. On day two of the visit I've done it. I simply asked her. 'Tell me about your *Othello*,' I said. Leaving the programme lying around had done the trick. It had brought it all back to her.

The answer took very little time and was interesting, I must admit.

'Mummy, as you know I do not like adaptations or so-called versions of the classics. I have always resisted setting the Scottish play in tribal Africa as what that suggests is a little too problematic for me, if you get my meaning. Anyway, too many others have tried this.

'But you asked about *Othello*. I suppose I wanted to attempt *Othello* partially because I couldn't get the sound of Ba's' (my father and her grandfather) 'voice out of my head and more specifically because of the Gulf War and the OJ Simpson trial. Colin Powell, the lone black General in that theatre of war, and almost simultaneously the court case of OJ Simpson alleging the murder of his Desdemona. It seemed to me that this complicity of global circumstances demanded an exploration through Shakespeare's *Othello*. Was it written in the stars?

'Also, Mummy, I wanted to test Ba's theory about Cassio played by a black man providing a more believable cause for Othello's jealousy. He felt this would make the Moor less irrational, less childlike, than he is often portrayed. This made sense even those long years ago.'

'So did you adapt the text to suit this idea?' I asked, although I knew the answer already.

'Absolutely not. We never changed one word. I don't approve of changing playwrights' words to suit other purposes. We, the interpreters, must find a way of making them work. If this is beyond us, then we should leave those plays alone. Or go and write our own.'

'So you are not one of these directors who think they can do better than the playwright?'

'As you well know, Mother dear, I can't even write a decent letter much less a play, which incidentally is a very difficult thing to do, to write a really good play.'

'Did your *Othello* work?' I was genuinely interested.

'The audiences were good, with a lot of younger black people joining our faithful core audience. Ben Thomas was brave and beautiful in the part. The thing looked good, sounded good and elicited long and heated after-show debates and discussions in the bar, which I always feel quite happy about. For me, leaving the theatre without a question in one's mind means it has been a waste of time. Hearing members of an audience say the awful four words – "It was all right" – is my idea of hell. I'd much prefer to hear them say, "What a load of rubbish"

166

than condemn with "It was all right." Of course it's much nicer if they say "How brilliant!"

'A good number of mainly older white theatre people turned up. Some found it to their liking but many dwem – dreary white English male – critics amongst them objected strongly to aspects of the production.'

'Oh, like what?' I wanted to know. How dare they criticise my girl?

'How long have you got?'

'The rest of my life,' I said tartly. 'Everyone keeps saying I am retired now, don't they? Anyway hurry up.'

'You asked for it.' Yvonne shrugged. 'First off, Desdemona. I cast a lovely English rose of an actress in her full-blown thirties, not a teenager. The text says that Desdemona has turned down all the suitors her father thought suitable. It also suggests that she left the bosom of her small family and went off to join Othello. She got drawn in by the stories he told. You can see this happening today in any High Street in London.' My daughter was warming to her theme now – I could tell. 'The exotic, the different, the exciting, prevail in spite of every obstacle. She fancied him big time. This does not suggest some little adolescent flower, this suggests a *woman*.

'One white man wrote me twelve pages – I think it was twelve pages – of prejudice on this aspect alone. In a nutshell, for him *Othello* was about an ugly old black ram defiling a flower of Anglo-Saxon virginal youth. It was Shakespeare's way of warning people against entering relationships with inferiors.'

'Inferiors!' I spilled my cup of over-sweetened coffee.

Yvonne explained: 'You see, you are tackling centuries of prejudice against the black male so you have to expect this and worse.'

'What other faults did they find?' was my next question, once she had mopped up the mess.

'They didn't like a black Cassio. Said it shifts the natural balance of the plot. If there are too many black people hanging around Othello, he is not as marginalised as he should be. And anyway who would believe that the authorities would appoint *two* black men as Governor of Cyprus in such immediate succession? You see, one black swallow must make this summer. Black must be strange. Rare and slightly risqué. Too commonplace and it threatens to become an accepted part of society.'

'Theatre is that powerful, I suppose. OK, so you are turning *Othello* into a love story not a tragedy?'

'Yes. A tragic love story. Black and white.'

So that was that. Sounded like hot stuff to me.

Ladies and gentlemen, didn't I do well and wasn't this a good beginning? I've never tried anything like this before. I am quite puffed up with pride – which comes before a fall, I know, but don't be so boring. I think it augurs well for the visit. Can I get her to wax equally lyrical on the other topics which interest me? Fingers crossed.

But then I spy my living room, which has been transformed from a mildly comfortable nicely sterile room into a tropical jungle of greenery and loosened curtains flapping in the wind.

Patience, oh Lord.

Chapter 20

Southern Comfort

If there is one part of the world which has always fascinated me, it is Louisiana and in particular New Orleans. I
love the idea of brass band funerals with plumed horses
and jazz everywhere. I wonder if Yvonne saw one of
these when she was there? This is my next target. I know
she's worked in that neck of the woods.

Yvonne says she has never made any money, but
doing what she wanted to do for all her life is riches
indeed. I agree. And I envy her just a little bit. I wanted
to be a nurse, but ended up a keeper of the books. I
wanted to help and to heal the living, but ended up
burying the dead. The only way to come to terms with
this was to try to help and to heal people in their distress
at death, to see it sometimes as 'the necessary evil' which
must come when it will come and at other times as the
welcome gift. To help them see beyond the grave. Many
have been kind enough over the years to attribute this
quality of mercy to me. I hope in some small measure
this is true – or else what has it all been about?

It is early evening and the sunset is brilliant. So quick
is the sunset in our tropical paradise that sometimes you
blink and the cacophony of colours is gone, leaving navy
night behind. We time the sunset with an eight-minute
Austin Clarke martini. This evening's sky is particularly
encouraging, with violent oranges and pinks loudly
clashing. Forget subtle sunsets, give me the hairy

169

tropical magic. I decide to broach the subject of Louisiana as Yvonne is not going out tonight and the magnificent sunset has made her all dewy-eyed.

I think I am getting quite good at choosing the right moment, before there is time to mention the party. I am rewarded with this conversation. We were on the topic of to Love Bird or not to Love Bird. 'Loving the Bird' is flying with Air Jamaica. A national pastime.

'So how did you get to Louisiana from London?' I asked. 'Love Birds don't fly there, do they?'

'You're right. I needed to get to Baton Rouge. I was to direct a new play by Femi Euba for the University of Louisiana. The airlines often don't fly their big planes direct to Baton Rouge in spite of the fact that it is the main city of the state.'

'Why ever not?' Seemed plain silly to me.

'Often in the States the capital cities of the state come a poor second to a more vibrant city. Sacramento is the capital of California, but San Francisco and LA have the buzz. In Louisiana, Baton Rouge is the capital city but New Orleans gets the votes, doesn't it? Therefore it's much easier to get an international flight to New Orleans on a proper-sized plane – you know, with nice solid-looking engines and more than one air steward. I'm a bit of a coward in regard to the tiny planes that frequent the American domestic schedule. Much safer, I know, but then New Orleans didn't look too far away on the map and I thought it would be chickenfeed to hop on a bus to Baton Rouge. I never learn, do I, Mother?'

No you don't – but I am feeling too charitable to agree. So I politely say nothing.

'Femi was kind enough to drive all the way from Baton Rouge to fetch me: When I mentioned taking the bus, he said, "Bus? What's the matter with you, woman? There are no buses from New Orleans to Baton Rouge."'

I interrupt. 'Just a minute. You were in New Orleans. Did you get to see the place?'

'It was dark and I was tired and very anxious to get to Baton Rouge. I must tell you that at first I thought with all the French influence, folk would pronounce this town's name with a French accent. But my best Parisian was met with "Huh? Bahun hooge? Huh?" I soon learned to say Batt'n woooge with the best of them. Anyway, kind Femi drove me to the faculty residence where I was to stay. Nice room, computer socket, great bathroom, good view. I'm in business. I have a good night's rest.

'In the morning I take in what I had missed the night before. I am billeted in nothing short of the set for *Gone with the Wind*. Huge staircase and all. Nice. As I prepare to descend this imposing piece of wrought iron I spy two black sisters, one on either side of the staircase at ground level, who are obviously most upset, to judge from the akimbo position of their generous arms and the dangerous look on their faces.

'"Now lookie here, sista, you done use the wrong stair. We suppose to use the back. Huh!"

'Didn't take me long to twig. They just couldn't imagine from the looks of me that I was a bona fide guest. Probably thought I was a jumped-up new cook, cleaner or lady of the night. Praise be, my wits did not desert me. Replying in the best, the very best, upper-class British accent I could muster, I said, "I'm so *aw*fully sorry but I don't understand a word you've said. My name is Yvonne Brewster from London, England, and I am here to direct a play for the University. Where *is* the dining room, please?"

'They got the message and almost lifted me into the dining room. I could hear them telling other members of the kitchen staff that I was on the Faculty, yes indeed, as they took turns to peep surreptitiously through the

171

serving-door hatch. From that moment on I was to get the most perfect dining-room attention for the rest of my two month stay.'

Madam settled herself more comfortably on the couch and took a swig of our special martini, smacking her lips in approval. It's the Austin Clarke Happy Hour – again!

'As the weeks went by I spent quite a while telling them about life in England. They were genuinely surprised to learn that there were black people in England. They had to make out they were pointing out the quality of the muffins, the pastries, the juices and the coffee. They were, you understand, not encouraged to converse with the guests except on matters of the menu. And to replenish the free crackers. Don't look at me like that, Mummy. On the tables of all the restaurants in Baton Rouge you get a generous supply of small packets of free crackers. You know, like saltines. Ironic. Quite a few crackers roam the streets free.'

'Say that again.' Am I going deaf or daft – or both?

'Crackers? That's the name the black folk give to white folk who would rather they, the black folk, did not exist. Maybe when we say someone has gone crackers, crazy, we are localising the Deep South phrase – who knows? For example: the play I was working on was not that political but it pulled no punches on the topic of the influence the white preacher men of the South have on the hearts and minds, souls, wallets and even the bodies of the black women in their congregations. It wasn't the most comfortable of subjects in Louisiana.

'I was met one night leaving a popular restaurant by a phalanx of white-shirted Bible-bearing fundamentalists who made it quite clear that they did not approve of the play. Not too safe a feeling.'

'Fire crackers, eh?' I said thoughtfully

'Just so. Anyway, my dining-room ladies were fascinated by the idea of such a play with a racially mixed cast dealing with religion and above all written by "that African man" being put on in the big theatre on campus. Curiosity got the better part of natural suspicion and the front row of the theatre was filled with these ladies dressed to kill in all their finery for the first night of *The Eye of Gabriel*. Not one of them had ventured into that theatre before. Not to sit in, anyway. Not that they couldn't have, I guess, but perhaps they hadn't previously seen the point of doing so.

'Baton Rouge is in the South and many customs die hard. I agitated until I got Femi to drive me over to visit the other university in the city, called Southern. Southern caters exclusively for African-American students. I found them very talented, enthusiastic and full of humour which I recognised and appreciated greatly. I, however, couldn't get over how different the whole feel and look of Southern (pre-fabricated and low on the ground) was from that of the manicured lawns of Louisiana State (columned and domed Washington replica).

'Southern University was literally across the tracks. I had read and heard the term "across the tracks" in relation to housing ghettos in Southern American cities, but when the car bumped over the tracks it took on a whole new meaning. However, politics not being my bag – well, not on this assignment – I concentrated on getting *The Eye of Gabriel* rehearsed and ready for performance.'

'Yes, yes, yes.' My daughter can be so interesting when she gets into her stride – especially after some gin! 'But did you ever get to New Orleans?'

'What's up with you, Mrs Clarke? What's all this New Orleans thing?'

So I told her about my fascination with the brass band plumed hearse and jazz funeral thing. Could it work in Jamaica?

173

She laughed long and loud. 'You really think I accepted a job in Louisiana, in February, to go seeking out brass bands, plumed hearses and jazz band funerals? Mrs Clarke, I'll have you know February is Mardi Gras in New Orleans. I sure enough went to New Orleans every opportunity I got. Its spirit took me over completely. The jazz floating out from shuttered parlours, the market where African masks and trinkets competed with clothes with attitude, mountains of silver jewellery, rare and newly minted music, and I must not, *cannot*, forget the food.'

My daughter smacked her lips. 'The dish étouffe I just couldn't get enough of. The main ingredient is fish but the sauce and the pancakes that accompany it are simply delicious and irresistible. And gumbo is almost too nice. The restaurants are temples dedicated to food. No rush is allowed. The palm-fringed rooms always, it seems, have interesting art covering the walls. There is a kind of mix-up of sensations and cultures and sounds and images that defy being put in the box of any one description. It's a case of chill out, eat out and find out.' Yvonne grinned, then added: 'And pretend you're in a Southern Comfort ad.'

'You were telling me about Mardi Gras,' I prompted her.

'The day of the Mardi Gras is the Fat Tuesday before Ash Wednesday. It is the day of the procession of floats and outrageous behaviour. Getting out all the avarice, lust and gluttony in one "fat" day in preparation for the constraints of Lent.

'We set out early in the morning,' my daughter began dreamily, 'so as to get a parking place within the city limits. As we approached New Orleans, even the eerie mangrove swamps of the bayou so particular to this part of Louisiana seemed to contribute with an electric vibe.

'Many of the streets, already closed to vehicles, were

174

lined with spectators from all over the world. To warm up the gigantic crowd came the coconut men walking behind enormous Cadillacs filled with these objects which they offered to the most beautiful, the oldest, the youngest, the baddest in the crowd of thousands who begged the best. I got one. I'm not sure why I qualified but you know I don't do things in half-measures so I am sure I deserved it – as the loudest, maybe. It was interesting to see one of these trophies close up. It's what we call a dry coconut, smoothly husked to within a whisker of its life, painted black, polished and elaborately decorated to represent African masks and deities.

'Next came horses with riders costumed in the full monty. Cowboys, sheriffs, officers in the Confederate Army – you name it. There was plenty of top gear lassoing, bucking bronco-ing and marching to the bugles. I found these intimidating, knowing what mounted police can do to a crowd.' She shuddered.

'What about those float things?' I asked.

'Oh yes! Monsters of papier-mâché and extruded foam designed to the last sequin, piled high with costumed revellers themed to the eyeballs, some drawn by heavyweight vehicles and tractors, others by horse. These paraded around the streets for some four to five hours, continuing the ritual of throwing beads to the crowd. At first there was easy banter among the crowd but when the real bead throwing began, then it became deadly serious.'

'Bead throwing?' What on earth is she talking about? Better have another sip of my cocktail.

'Well, you see, some floats represented the French ruling class in the eighteenth century – a time when they were top dog. These floats were peopled by whites and the blaring music was European classical eighteenth-century. I was told that, in earlier times, during Mardi Gras it was customary for the French nobility to throw coins down to the peasants from their chariots.

'The sport for the chaps upon the floats was seeing the underlings on the ground fight one another to get at the money, thereby maintaining control and supremacy. Nowadays beads have replaced money. The larger the bead, the more valuable and desirable as a trophy. And believe me, the onlookers do fight to get them. Human nature red in tooth and claw, responding to the idea that there *is* such a thing as a free bead.'

Yvonne grinned, and went on to tell me: 'There I was in the middle of the scrum trying to catch only the large beads. If they fall to the ground, no one wants them. No small little foolishness for me! You then wear your day's spoil around your neck. It felt like a rope around a cow's neck! When you think about it in the cool light of day, the analogies and images all this brings to mind are rather frightening: was that really me? But hey, it was Mardi Gras . . .

'Other floats had mainly African themes, usually heroic, historical and revolutionary. I found it quite interesting that not one of the floats flaunted an African-American theme or identified in any way with that history. Except in the case of the music, which was not Mother African but deep New Orleans jazz. Ooooh, the energy! And the naughty tongue-in-cheek designs triumphed, especially in comparison to the died-in-the-wool traditional floats inhabited by the white folk.'

'You mean to tell me in this day and age there is such an obvious colour line?' I tut-tutted.

'Yes, mam. The rules of engagement in Louisiana are: peaceful parallel co-existence until some lynching takes place, then it's heads down for a bit. When I was in Louisiana there was a case in the neighbouring Texan courts of a black man being tied to the rear of a truck and dragged to his death. Some crackers stood accused and were on trial. There it was on the front page of the *New York Times*. A genuine one-day wonder for the papers and the television news – they were both full of it. Terrible, shiver down the spine stuff. Not to be ignored. Everyone was talking about it.' Yvonne turned to me.

'It made me think of the problem we have in Jamaica. We know how few people go around with automatic weapons, we know not everyone is high on or selling crack cocaine or whatever on every street corner, but to judge from the media representation one could be forgiven for thinking that this was the rule rather than the exception. So it is with the South. Every incident of lynching should, and appeared to, concentrate the collective mind. The same should apply to Jamaica. We are our own worst enemies if it does not. But will we? Can we?'

'You always say you are not political, so why are you entering this fowl yard, Miss Cockroach?'

'I'm not. This is just a common or garden commonsense comment.'

Fools rush in, I thought but said, 'Right. So, you didn't hear any jazz?'

'Of course. When catching beads from the floats lost some of its appeal we made our way to the French Quarter through streets thick with discarded beads of green, purple, yellow and some white. On the wonderful wrought-iron ornate balconies stood hundreds of men with really gorgeous strings of the better class of beads. Some were gyrating; others were blowing kisses and so on to the women gathered below in the narrow streets. The men encouraged the women to expose their breasts (some came bra-less, prepared for this annual ritual) and those who found favour would get thrown the best beads. Stuff went on you can only imagine. But Mardi Gras is Freedom Hall time in New

177

Orleans, as traditionally the police turn a blind eye to everything.' She winked. 'Someone should make a ballet.

'Anyway, my latent feminist principles hurried me away from this almost Roman spectacle and towards the sound of a piano. What looked like an impromptu (I think) session had just started up in one of the kind of bars you see in the Southern Comfort ads. This was not Ronnie Scott's. It was deeper than that – in the bone. You felt that these guys didn't know how to do anything but play jazz and with one another. The anticipation was incredible. You, Mummy, as a musician would have appreciated it. I sat there for hours. The sadness. The seductiveness. The sexiness.' She looked nostalgic.

'I'm not a musician, I just play the piano,' I objected. 'So, no jazz funerals on any of your other trips to New Orleans?

'Sorry. There was some saxophone, some trumpet but no plumed horse-drawn hearses. Will you please give this a rest? And I had me some great food,' Yvonne told me, brightening. 'Gumbo.'

'Gumbo!' I repeated, 'Terrible name. Doesn't sound like something I would like.'

'Yes, you would, Mummy. It doesn't look appealing but the taste makes up for that. It's the staple dish of the Creoles.'

'You haven't mentioned them before.'

'Surprising, as I like them. They remind me of our middle-class Jamaicans who feel so under threat from contemporary, cruder Jamaica. The Louisiana Creole bridges the gap between the two extremes of Southern existence but I didn't feel or see any Creole presence in the Mardi Gras. They were more like slightly amused beautiful onlookers.

'Femi's wife Addy, who is the most elegant, beautiful Creole lady, preferred to join in these revels from the

178

safe distance of her elegant front garden in the old quarter of Baton Rouge with a dozen or so hand-picked guests who would make the odd sophisticated attempt at catching some beads. But the emphasis was on the gumbo, the crab cakes, the frozen daiquiris, the conversation, the gentle fun. You could easily have been in Martinique without the croissants and *Le Monde*.

'However, I did get taken out to visit the property of a well-known Creole family, about two hours' drive from Baton Rouge. Isolated, imposing, set in what looked like hundreds of acres of very flat uncultivated-looking prairie-like land, three Creole matriarchs lived in an ancestral home in an area which bears their name, a large version of a shotgun boardhouse crowded with memorabilia and photographs of generations of people who looked just like you. Shade and colouring are of the utmost importance and these three ladies were light coffee, with what would be called fine features and straightish hair. They were tall, dressed in floaty pastel-coloured material, perfectly coiffed and bursting with old-time stories. It was pretty interesting, listening to them politely contradicting each other in soft musical voices from under the most flattering glamorous over-the-top droopy hats trimmed with tea roses. These confections were put on whenever the possibility of venturing outside might occur. This didn't happen often. Ladies' Day in Creole Louisiana County.

'They took to me as they thought I could be adopted as a Creole. This was definitely intended as a compliment. Unfortunately, no way could I deal with the constant elegance, especially the flimsy white diaphanous dresses – not to mention the hats. These, I swear, are meant to keep the demon sun from the light-brown faces. I could of course be wrong.

'I knew instinctively we would be given gumbo for lunch. Thought I could smell the cooking before it had even started. You say you wouldn't like it but I sure did. I'd often heard it spoken of and once or twice I had tried it in the University cafeteria but I wasn't at first that keen. The real thing had to be better than this stuff.

'So, in *carpe diem* spirit I asked if I might be allowed to watch the process in these ladies' house. This had to be the real McCoy. They slowly looked me up and they even more slowly looked me down. Then:

'"OK, honey, this here is what you do. You want to make gumbo, you gotta have patience. We just about to start the roux. Say, you wanna watch? No, honey, you can *do*. Here's the flour – the best flour you can lay hands on; here's the corn oil – the best quality you can afford. You've heard of the French base for white sauces – roux? Well, it's the same thing but done different. Takes forty-five minutes of you stirring that there roux until it gets to the good brown colour we need. Not too dark and certainly not too light. A little like us, if you please. Keep stirring or it'll burn black and you'll have to start all over again. That would never do." And out of the kitchen they swept.

'My big mouth! Let me in for forty-five minutes of constant stirring of the flour and oil. But the roux was pronounced fit for gumbo with lots of heys and hollers. The other ingredients had been bought fresh at the market that morning. Great big crabs, langoustine, lobsters, shrimp and white fish, and most important lots of ochros, all of which had been cut up and prepared. In they all went, including a small amount of chicken and a special sausage rather like chorizo (for the taste), and in no time the gumbo was ready. It's like a very thick fish stew, served on a bed of fluffy rice. Very very more-ish. I'll do some for you if you like, Mummy.'

'No, thanks, child, we would have to take out a mortgage to get all those ingredients here. I believe you that it tastes good, though thousands of others wouldn't.

Ochros! And no brass bands and no mention of the Mississippi. Remember learning to spell this in school. M I crooked letter, crooked letter I, crooked letter crooked letter I, hunch back hunch back I.'

'Oh yes, I remember crooked letter I! There was the time I went on a Mississippi paddle-steamer which had been converted into a gambling casino, *à la* Las Vegas but made special by the fact that this casino was floating on the Mississippi river. After the first shock of the ten-foot-high plastic crayfish and lobsters hanging from the ceiling as decoration I believe, and the noise of the machines as the coins rattled down the chutes to greedy hands, I was able to take in the scene quite dispassionately.

'I looked at the river: not really anything to write home about, I thought. It's certainly wide, so wide in fact I couldn't see the other bank, which was impressive, but it's very brown and languorous, not seeming in a hurry to go anywhere. It struck me that that's why they call it Old Man River. Actually, I felt just a tiny bit disappointed really. Yet somehow the name Mississippi still conjures up mystery and excitement for me, even though I now know it's sluggish and ugly. No accounting for sentiment.'

Yvonne looked me in the eyes. 'I tried my hand at the slot machines, Mummy, but they won. They always do. I was very content just watching the roulette players, seeing the expressions on their faces of greed, need and speed. Gambling is not my thing and cynical me was checking out the methods the management used as successful ploys to help keep open unsuspecting wallets and relieve the punters of their cash, like the too easily accessible potent frozen daiquiris on sale cheaply for a dollar and the fever-pitch furious music.

'I kept looking at this slow-moving brown river, willing it to be more exciting but it's too deep for that kind of superficiality. The bayou is more spectacular. All those skeletal trees in the swamp with no leaves but cobwebs to catch the sun, roots hidden in water. They say crocodiles lurk in the waters of the bayou. They well might but not too many people are seen looking for them. The unreal scenery doesn't seem to have a purpose except to make this part of the world even more mysterious.' And after a moment: 'Look, where is dinner? Let's eat.'

And that's about all I could get out of her. I still wonder about those brass band and plumed-hearse funerals though . . . Oh, when the Saints go marching in . . . Do you think I might persuade her to take me to New Orleans for my birthday? I'd soon find what I was looking for there. I guess nobody is going to get the hint and there is no way I would ask. Pity, but there it is.

I have met many Americans in the course of my business. They will insist on renting cars to drive in Jamaica, which apes mother country England and drives on the left. Accustomed to driving on the right, too often tourists end up being shipped back home in urns.

Southerners, though, have always fascinated me because their attitude to so many things there seems to fit into the Jamaican mindset of my youth. I can't say if that much has changed in the second millennium as I have been out of things, but I do know that Jamaica was as stratified a society as Louisiana's when I was a girl, and I don't think much has changed. Just as, in Louisiana, under the surface the plantation seems to be humming, the legacy of slave society here is still an almost open wound, and it takes very little to expose the lingering explosive malignancy.

In my youth there would have been very little possibility or interest in having a Jamaican national motto, not to mention one which suggested *Out of Many, One People*. What's Mine is Mine, What's Yours is Mine might have met with more approval as a national motto from the expatriate landowners and ruling backra class. It was the 1940s before anyone took any notice of the people's need for representation or even stopped to consider who these people were. Sure, there were bloody rebellions in the nineteenth century, but the only people to die were the poor and the politically misguided. Some of the leaders of those uprisings and movements for rights and recognition are National Heroes today.

However, has this representation come at too great a cultural price? A mild-mannered, delicate, artistic, polite people have morphed into such irritability, anger, distrust and violence. And in so few decades. Perhaps it won't take longer to recover that earlier equilibrium than it did to lose it. Although I think it will take longer than we've got.

I am an old woman who knows nothing. However Trevor, who does know what he's talking about, said to me the other day, 'Mrs Clarke, if you sow corn you get ears. If you sow guns you get tears.'

Chapter 21

Sunny California

—•◦◦◦•—

The United States of America. I had a green card once but as the years wandered by I gave it up. Seems I'm only travelling towards my grave. Now, you may find this lacking in ambition and imagination. Perhaps. But since shopping in Miami is all that is really on offer and I can't afford to go further these days, quite frankly I've been there, done that and don't care to do it again, so I will close the book on travel except if someone gets the hint about Louisiana.

In the meantime, however, my armchair voyager appetite has been whetted for more of Yvonne's wanderings. I believe she had a whale of a time in California once. I was keen to see what I could extract. Must be more interesting than shopping in Miami.

Before I could do this I had to endure a planning meeting for the party. I thought this nonsense had gone on long enough. I fondly remember other parties she has thrown but the truth is at ninety it's different. How many people realise this? You don't want to be the centre of attention: you want to look on. All the wasted energy being poured into this wretched party! I just wanted to be allowed the freedom to pursue my new career as investigative journalist.

As it happens I didn't have long to wait for the California story to emerge, as during her visit Yvonne had been in contact with the University of California who were tying up possible dates for her to visit to direct Tennessee Williams's *A Streetcar Named Desire*. She was very excited about the prospect and therefore happy to talk about her first visit to UCDavis.

Davis is one of the many colleges of the University of California. Some of its sister institutions like UCBerkeley and UCLA are probably more famous but Davis tutors over thirty thousand students and has its own distinctive style. Although it is primarily known as an Agricultural Science institution it also has a very active proactive Arts programme. The United Kingdom television company Granada has sponsored for many years two or three English professional directors annually to work with the UCDavis graduate theatre students.

Some years ago, out of the blue Yvonne had been asked to go out there. On that occasion she directed Derek Walcott's *Ti Jean and His Brothers*. At that juncture the student body in theatre did not boast any members of colour. This she welcomed as a challenge and had probably featured in her choice of play. She wanted to do something Caribbean, and Walcott's play was his take on the famous European cautionary tale of *Three Billy Goats Gruff* – sometimes known as *The Three Little Pigs*. It is perhaps his most accessible play and lends itself well to international interpretation.

However, you will remember that one of Madam's rules which must not be broken is never to change words in order to fit an interpretation. This provided one of the more culturally interesting challenges and a testing of the practice much admired in England of 'blind casting'. This was an extreme example – an all-white cast doing an all-black play. A case of total blindness? No half-measures here.

In the play there are, as one might imagine, three brothers (instead of the three goats of the original), Gros Jean (Big John), Mi Jean (Middle John) and Ti Jean

(Little John, called Tie Gene in the States). Gros John was to be played by a charming student, Tel from Texas, very tall, very blond, very right for the part – except that there was this line: 'Because I come from that mountain forest don't mean I can't come like you, or because I black.' With the best intention in the world of co-operating with the concept of blind casting, this was difficult for Tel. Yvonne, as his director, and the other members of the cast used this as the focal point. With support Tel eventually managed this speech with conviction, now really enjoying the part, and they all knew the process had worked.

In the end, the actor's humanity, his understanding (or as the Rastafarians say 'overstanding') allowed him to be totally convincing.

Success made Yvonne rash and she later did some text work on Lorraine Hansberry's *Raisin in the Sun* with this group of Caucasian students. She thought this was the only way they might be encouraged to contemplate this African-American masterpiece. The students were marvellous. For many it was an opportunity to approach a major text which would probably have evaded them in the normal scheme of things. A few of these students keep in touch with my daughter to this day.

But how did California impress? She arrived on 2 January and was collected by Bobbie Bolden, who was to become a great friend and ally. It was cold and rainy. Apparently they have a weather system peculiar to the West Coast called El Niño which heralds rainstorms, high winds and treacherous snowdrifts. El Niño doesn't turn up every winter but he showed up in grand style this year. Yvonne had imagined California to be the 'State of Perpetual Sunshine', so her packing had not included thick winter woollies.

Yvonne was shivering from the word go and had to quickly buy a comforting weather-proof down-filled coat at the insistence of Betty Canton, an old friend from Jamaica who now lives in California. This unbecoming garment never left her back – not the sort of thing she would have been seen dead in normally, but needs must when the devil says.

Lucky she had this coat when Bobbie and her husband Barry invited her to see Yosemite National Park – thousands of acres of unadulterated but controlled wilderness containing bears, foxes, sun-capped mountains, a Native American reservation and great waterfalls. The awesome size of everything helped to keep the traveller humble: the master plan is so obviously at work. Coming from a small island I think the impression America made on impressionable YB could well have been confidence-shaking. Difficult to come to terms with the idea that one National Park is bigger, much bigger, than your entire country. That one relatively small university campus of thirty thousand or so students can have more than one larger better-equipped theatre than any existing in the Caribbean gave pause for thought.

A similar feeling never arose in England. I wonder why? There is grandeur there. Maybe it's in the ancient careful detail and therefore less intimidating.

One outcome of the UCDavis visit, apart from a great experience with the students, was that the University invited Derek Walcott to visit soon after. And now Yvonne herself has been asked back so it can't have been that bad. Skip Gates also turned up to give one of his electric if short lectures and he was gracious enough to be nice about the show and, even nicer, take her out to dinner *à trois* with Fahizah Alim, journalist on the *Sacramento Bee*, making up the party. This little rendezvous helped her profile in Davis quite considerably. Celebrity is what celebrity does.

She had met Professor Gates in London when he interviewed her for the *New Yorker* article on the movers and shakers in Black Britain, and again at the impressive exhibition of art of the Harlem Renaissance in London where he was giving another of his lectures.

It occurs to me, as I heave myself to my feet, now that this session has ground to a natural halt, that this Professor from Harvard is really a one-man industry. Jamaica could use his foresight and talent for getting impossible things done.

Oooh! My old bones are creaking. You know, this a small world if you can live comfortably in it. Small things stick in the mind. Yvonne remembers perhaps too little of the detail of the Professor's lectures, the interview or the dinner, but she does remember that he kept a London taxi cab with the meter running for a whole day and her amazement at 'Skip's cool acceptance of this as an everyday occurrence'. Fringe theatre people in England are paid far too little, obviously.

I must say Papa would probably turn in his grave at the thought of this. Secretly I am also appalled. I guess you could call this a moment of truth – both undertaker's daughters agreeing on something. Are we really such economic peasants? Maybe.

My goodness, look how late it is and all we've had for hours is liquid refreshment. Time for rice and peas, jerk chicken for the others but a nice big vegetable salad for me. Mmmm.

I hear Mervys rattling the cutlery. Her way of drawing attention to the fact that she is missing her favourite television programme. Gotta go.

Chapter 22

Every Little Breeze

The Jamaica Information Service filmed their interview with Yvonne today. Madam was looking forward to being grilled by Fae Ellington, whom she has known since she took her first steps on the path to media glory in Jamaica. She says Fae is a shining example of hard work and stick-to-itiveness. (Is this a word? Probably not.) Another plus was that they were going to film the little interview in Hazel and Wycliffe Bennett's delightful indoor garden.

I don't often hear such praise from my daughter but on her return she was full of how extensively Fae had done her research, how excellent the camera crew were and how smoothly the whole exercise had gone. I have now seen the programme and she was quite right. It's a very professional affair, notwithstanding the raw material . . .

I asked what else had she expected? Wasn't she accustomed to this level of professionalism? Touchy subject this turned out to be. I gleaned from her brusque answer that yes, she had been subjected to an abundance of interviews all over the globe, in all media, but that too many times, particularly in England, they had started with: 'So tell me about yourself.' I got the feeling that the major culprits were the exploding number of people trying to write up, very quickly, theses on Black Theatre. Many hadn't bothered to do the necessary research, expecting to turn up, turn on their tape recorder and have the work done for them.

This kind of interview rightly brought out the devil in Yvonne and she had to fight the urge to tell them any old rubbish, any old fantasy. If they couldn't be bothered even to check the website before expecting her to spend what was usually promised to be half an hour but which could take anything up to two or three hours, then they shouldn't complain. True, the professional reporters especially from *The Voice* newspaper, the BBC, *The Guardian*, *The Gleaner* and so on came in for praise. I thought slyly, Well, you can't accuse *me* of not doing my research, young lady – and I'm not even trained.

As expected, my house has been thrown into turmoil but I am bearing up well. The sofas have been sent for re-covering, the ceiling in the flop room is being painted white, a cactus garden is springing up, a new painting has arrived and is gracing the kitchen, if you please. Ah, but then there are also dogs in my life again, compliments of my son-in-law Lloyd, Valerie's ex. Seven heavenly puppies and I am allowed to choose two. In honour of Rottweiler dad Caesar, I decide on a pair of beautiful little ladies: one will be Cleo and the other Patra.

Most of Madam's alterations to my house, if I tell the truth, are a marked improvement and are in preparation for the threatened birthday celebration. I wish I had thought of them first. But of course I will reserve praise. It's my way. I am a reserved woman who was taught by my father to say only what I meant and then only *some* of what I meant. That is now my protection from those who would bully me just because they think I am past my sell-by date. I've got news for them. I may be ninety years old to them but I am ninety years *young* to me.

My daily yoga keeps me positive. I am determined I'll remain so as my mother, having successfully negotiated a major operation, died by simply giving up. For weeks she lay on her back and looked at the ceiling until she was no more. But my father, although he was bedridden for years with crippling arthritis, still kept abreast abed of world news and local gossip, the latest book, who was flavour of the political moment. I have decided I, too, will be restless until the grave beckons. No easy submission, no drifting into the calm tomorrow, but, like our national poet Claude McKay, fighting back. Very annoying for those who would curtail my imaginative life.

My scrapbook helps my quest. I have been secretly keeping a scrapbook of whatever clippings and photographs I could get hold of. Together with letters, tapes and videotapes they make me realise that, far from helping to reveal the jigsaw of life, especially around the dark areas of the soul, they obscure. For instance, in Yvonne's case her real relationship with Talawa and with England as a whole needs probing. I need to know what was the survival guide. I can't get this from clippings and printed CVs, I need to get it from her. And I will. I haven't done so badly so far.

The phone rings and Carroll, daughter of our war hero Alvin, answers. It is Louise Bennett calling from Canada. She asks for Yvonne. Everyone in the house is excited. Ms Lou has always been a hero in my house but she has never called here before. Ears grow invisible elephant wings to aid the not-so-subtle eavesdropping going on. It's fascinating how art has the power to change lives, countries even, and it is Yvonne's theory that Louise Bennett-Coverley's impact on the Jamaican psyche has been greater than that of any other single artist.

During the phone call the torrential rains, which were making the place look so good that even Hope Gardens was green, were mentioned. 'The only thing is, you see, Miss Lou, everybody's roof is leaking.' On cue Miss

Lou recites 'Dry Weather House', that old-time Jamaican ditty:

> *'Dem nuh worth a cent*
> *Man ah shouldn't pay*
> *So much fi mi rent*
> *When the rainy weather was raisin Cain*
> *The dry weather house dem*
> *Couldn't stand the strain*
> *All o' the house began to leak*
> *And the whole foundation get very weak . . .'*

And after a few more jokes – including her reaction when threatened with vertigo: 'Mi just tell him 'Verti, go way' – and much love it was 'Ah mi chile. Bye bye.'

Yvonne looked so happy and relaxed after the phone call that it was child's play to encourage her to wax lyrical.

'Every time I hear her voice it's a special moment,' she told me. 'From a long time ago. I have a lot to be grateful to her for. I remember when I came back to live in Jamaica in 1974 and the Fowlers asked me to direct the National Pantomime. Before that I had had only one outing with the Panto. I had been taken on as assistant to the director Rex Nettleford for the production of *Morgan's Dream of Old Port Royal*. I learned a lot from him, but before the run of the show had ended I had played most of the leading female parts at one time or another.

'The first of these was Jezebel. I wasn't cast to play her but the role sort of stuck during rehearsals. I'll never forget my gorgeous costume as the naughty girl who made the pirates pay for her services. With her song "The ships are in, girls, get down on your knees, girls", she unionised her fellow practitioners. Next Norma Woon, juvenile lead, was out of things for a few performances so I did her part.'

'I recall her,' I said. 'Butter wouldn't melt in her mouth – ha!'

This made my daughter give a peal of laughter. 'The third and really big moment came' she went on, 'when Miss Lou was due to leave the show to represent Jamaica at an international festival of the arts overseas. Everybody presumed that the show would close down for the duration of Miss Lou's absence. After all, whoever heard of a Jamaican pantomime without Miss Lou? They hadn't banked on the Fowlers. The show was doing good business, it had been written by Henry Fowler and there was that Jill-of-all-parts, Yvonne. So Miss Lou's costume was taken in to fit me and there I was ready to rock and roll. In those days I had no fear and learning lines came very easily then.'

Thing was, Miss Lou didn't after all go to the festival so my daughter's efforts would have been in vain. This wasn't a problem for her, I remember, but Louise, sophisticated, thoughtful and kind lady, stayed at home in Gordon Town the night Yvonne was due to perform. And she did.

'Lois Kelly-Barrow and Ranny Williams (Maas Ran) were fantastic, and with their help and that of the whole cast this first performance went off well.' Yvonne stopped for a moment and we both listened to the rain. I think she was lost in the past. I'm much happier to be in the present, thank you very much.

'With hindsight, I realise what a moment that was in Jamaican theatre. It's a good thing I didn't have time to think about the audience reaction to me turning up on stage when they had expected Louise Bennett. Give it to them, they didn't boo or slow handclap which I expected. In fact, by the end they had sort of accepted me. The applause was not for talent but for guts. Mine.'

Thus was an understudy culture in Jamaican theatre born, my daughter informed me. These days, Jamaicans are well accustomed to turning up at a performance not knowing which actors are going to be seen. Back then it was unheard of. It was not that long after this episode that Pauline Stone started alternating with Miss Lou, Oliver Samuels with Maas Ran and Leonie Forbes with Lois Kelly-Barrow.

Let's move on to 1974, when she was directing the Pantomime at a time when Barbara Gloudon was at the beginning of her meteoric rise as the undisputed Queen of the Jamaican Pantomime. The script Yvonne was asked to work with had been drafted by her and was called simply *The Witch*; it was loosely based on the classic Jamaican slavery story of Annie Palmer, the White Witch of Rose Hall plantation in St James.

The Fowlers were, they admitted to Yvonne, 'trying a thing' with this one, putting a team together which was new or nearly new to the Pantomime experience. Laura Facey, notorious now for those controversial Emancipation Park nude sculptures but always talented and visionary, was to design costumes and set. Doing away with the ubiquitous bandanna-tied heads, she introduced subtle, interesting costumes in quirky fabrics. She went mad and designed a metal minimalist set which did not boast a single cardboard cut-out flat or, oh horror of horrors, any cut-out houses.

I remember this going down like a lead balloon with the traditionalists but it was too late to turn back. The text was presented as a draft, meaning there was work to be done on it which Barbara happily did, working out on the back veranda of Starr and Yvonne's Kingsway townhouse. Material was cut and cleaned, resulting in a script which would not run for four hours of unnecessary repetition.

Rex Nettleford was to choreograph. Now that was scary. Rex quite simply inspired a sort of brain stun. The man was so elegant, so witty, so decisive – so *just so*

– it meant screwing one's courage to the sticking-place in order to make sure that what Barbara had written and what Laura and Yvonne created on stage would survive intact. They needn't have worried, Rex was so helpful and collaborative that even Barbara Gloudon shut up and got positive.

'Peter Ashbourne would be Mr Music,' my daughter recalled. 'That was cool from the beginning as Ashes is a consummate and imaginative musician. Oh yes, and this was slipped in quite casually by the Fowlers: "as Louise has retired, this production will usher in a new era."'

I can just imagine Greta Fowler delivering that knockout punch while waving to a 'houseboy' in the dim shadows of the leafy veranda, the signal for a new round of Rum Collins. I never did manage to stand up to Greta. When Yvonne told me years before that Greta had told her she had 'great promise of bosoms' I was too easily restrained from rushing over to her house with a broomstick, by the thought of my shame and anger at the lofty, inevitable put-down. I think they call this sophistication.

Yvonne, who had been caught up in her story, now opened her eyes and made a face at me which really did nothing for her looks. 'As far as I was concerned, everything else was copacetic, but not the absence of Louise Bennett! I knew that this was the only time I was ever going to direct a Jamaican Pantomime. I had already sussed that one would probably be more than enough for them and for me. I was devastated that there would be no Miss Lou. To cut a long story short, she was persuaded to come back for one last show. *The Witch*. Thank you, Miss Lou. Again.'

Yvonne did a little pantomime curtsy of gratitude. Sometimes it seems to me as if that girl is never off stage.

I got up to close the window behind me: there was a draught on my neck bringing with it a faint sprinkling of rain. We moved into the sitting room and Yvonne brought me some ginger tea. 'What else do you recall?' I asked.

'The fact that Barbara must have been pleased with *The Witch* as she has programmed it again. This makes me think that we ought to respect past achievement more enthusiastically. You know, without the past there is no present, and certainly no future . . .'

Oh my goodness, here she goes again. 'No future? What exactly do you mean?' I ask, hoping the explanation won't be too lengthy. She ignores this and rushes on.

'Let's deal with past recognition. A few years ago when Norman Beaton died I suddenly realised that there was no in-depth interview with him for the actors and others who come after to hear how he saw life, to share whatever secrets he wanted to share, however outrageous. People needed to know that Norman was a professional, that he was a distinguished scholar, whose studies on the racial genesis of Beethoven and Pushkin were well argued if contentious, and that he was generous to a fault. Not that this would wipe out his sometimes anti-social behaviour but it would allow a more rounded picture of the man to emerge.

'I determined to strike while the iron was hot and find the money to video the reminiscences of at least some of the other Black Theatre elder statesmen and -women in Britain who were growing into the third age and whom we might lose to the Grim Reaper without recording their stories. It was as vulgar a thought as that,' my daughter confessed.

'I wouldn't expect anything less from you.'

'Look, you asked me to tell you about these things! So either rest up the wit or . . .'

'Lost your sense of humour with your tan in England, have you? Oops. *Do* carry on.'

'Heading it was Louise Bennett.' There was a sulky silence.

'Who else was on the list?' I prompted her, pretending not to notice the sulk.

'As you can imagine, it was very difficult with such limited resources at Talawa deciding who to interview. We had to be selective. There was a fair portion of high dudgeon floating about in the ether but there we are.' My daughter sighed. 'I find it most frustrating that when you actually see an opening, manoeuvre some action into it and miraculously manage to complete a project, there are always the Jeremiahs who would have done it differently, who are upset. What's a girl to do? Stop doing? I think not. Perhaps I *could* listen a bit more. That's what Michael Abbensetts keeps telling me . . .'

'Could I please have an answer to my question?'

'I'm ignoring that. However, with one thing and another, including a lot of really positive help, especially from Jill Evans at London's Theatre Museum in Covent Garden, there now exist fifteen half-hour videoed interviews with people, all of whom have contributed immensely to the fabric of Black Theatre practice in England over the past half a century.

'The roll call is quite impressive, with playwrights Barry Reckord, who had three plays on in London at one time in the 1950s, and Michael Abbensetts, whose first play *Sweet Talk* – a modern Black British classic – was first directed for the Royal Court in 1972 by the now famous Stephen Frears. We also filmed actors including Rudolph Walker, whose "steady as she goes" approach has seen him become a British household TV name, Thomas Baptiste, Corrienne Skinner-Carter, Alaknanda Samarth, Ram John Holder, Earl Cameron – one of the first black faces on the London West End stage – and, of course, Mona Hammond. Trinidadian Pearl Connor, the first black theatrical agent is there, plus cultural activists Naseem Khan and Cy Grant, joined by theatre founders Frank Cousins and me. Fifteen!'

'I'm quite impressed. Don't look at me like that, I really am!'

Yvonne rolled her eyes and, very slowly, poured more tea.

'There were others who were on the list but for one reason or another we did not manage to film them,' she said regretfully. 'For instance we had to do without South African Alton Kumalo, who together with Trinidadian Oscar James founded Temba Theatre Company in 1972. Temba was the first Black British Theatre company to get an annual subsidy from the Arts Council and its history is an important one. You see, Mother, when the subsidy to the company was cut as a twenty-first-birthday present Alton ceased to have anything to do with Black Arts in England and still won't. I was asked to try and persuade him to attend the closing-down party for the company and his response was: "You are asking me to attend my funeral."

'Yet another important interviewee is missing: Mustapha Matura, whose contribution to the development of Black Theatre in Britain in the 1970s and 1980s was phenomenal, but you can't win 'em all and those we did manage to film are a pretty interesting bunch, don't you think? It is the Talawa project I feel a warm glow about. The people told their stories and these stories are now helping another generation to stand tall. Until the lion tells its own story the hunter will always win. Nigerian proverb.' She grinned. At me, I think.

'Let me write that down,' I said. It took a while. Old age is so troublesome! 'Never heard of any of these people except Mona and Louise, of course, and I don't expect many Jamaicans have,' I commented as I wrote,

'It's strange to think of so much work going on in England and here we knew nothing of it. Sounds like we should have. Anyway, how come Louise was top of this list? I didn't know she ever worked in England?'

'Oh yes, she did a lot of work in Britain. In fact, she enrolled as a student in London at the famous Royal Academy of Dramatic Art in 1948. She was the first black person ever to do so. Her obvious talent very quickly came to the attention of the men from the BBC and she was pulled away from her studies to do the real thing only weeks into the course. She says she was only at RADA for a short time, long enough to learn "to teach drama games to children", which was probably her "backative" for *Ring Ding*. She continued to do more and more work for the BBC at both Broadcasting House and Bush House. Very soon she had her own radio programme and was one of the first people to broadcast live from the spanking new television studio in Alexandra Palace, where the first ever television transmission in the world was made.

'There was other work in Britain touring in theatre productions to the provinces, mostly playing maids, she told me. "Remember, there are maids and there are maids, mi chile." You can see there wasn't much time left over for drama school studies. She had made her mark so quickly and so professionally.

'I was asked who my hero was by Hannah Pool, a *Guardian* newspaper reporter in England, not so long ago. Fancy, it had never before crossed my mind to have a hero! But somehow Louise Bennett's name popped out of my mouth. I thought about it for a while. Maybe my hero was Miss Johnson but in the end I stuck with Miss Lou.'

'To tell the truth, and let me whisper this,' I confided, 'I am convinced that Bob Marley is actually a cultural child of Miss Lou, although I can't say I am too fond of the untidy Rasta hairstyle. She made it OK to speak the dialect proudly. He made it OK to sing it proudly.'

'Amen,' my daughter echoed. 'When I was Jamaica Festival Director and my duties took me to nooks and crannies of this land, I don't think one visit anywhere was complete without at least one person reciting a Louise Bennett poem, or singing a Bob Marley song. Make no mistake about it, these are comforts a long way from home.

'Maybe we here in Jamaica should think like this. I mean, after all we erased the recordings of *Ring Ding* . . . Sorry, I shouldn't have brought that up! Miss Lou lives in Canada now, doesn't she?'

'Yes, enthroned in a veritable cocoon of Jamaican Heritage, paintings, awards galore, memorabilia and the sweet smell of Jamaican cooking. The Canadians love her very much and have heaped praise and support on her. Nice.'

'You mentioned a Miss Johnson,' I suddenly recalled. 'Who she?'

'Don't you remember her? She was Deputy Headmistress at St Hilda's and one of the few black members of staff. I will always remember Miss Iris Johnson,' Yvonne said with a smile.

'I never met her. Remember, I didn't do school trips, your father did.'

'Always too busy, I know. She was our tall elegant teacher of English, trained in England and training us. One of the few Jamaican teachers on the staff, she held her head very high as she out-Britished the British. Most of the other teachers were from England and were thought to speak with the preferred accent. At the time, how were we to know that Miss Tweed, the Headmistress, spoke with a thick accent which in Britain would mark her out as a native of the northern county of

200

Every Little Breeze

Yorkshire and working-class to boot? But this was what was on offer and we didn't know the difference. Us talking, thinking we were sounding like the King of England when we were aping Yorkshire lasses.' A rich chuckle preceded a discreet yawn. It was getting late, and we were both ready for bed, but she kept on going.

'Miss Johnson knew the difference. In fact, she sounded really up-market, but she had to keep stumm to keep her job. She would prowl the quadrangle in order to chastise "gels" who were failing to conduct themselves in a manner befitting daughters of quality. Some of her declarations to me I remember still.

'"Yvonne, please be so good as to refrain from laughing in that manner. If you persist you may be mistaken for a dray person." Yvonne giggled like the naughty schoolchild she really is. The years rolled back

'"What's a dray person, Miss Johnson?"

'"Try not to test my patience, gel. A dray um, *man*, if you must, is a peasant who sits side-saddle on a donkey which pulls a wooden cart on wheels. He advertises the services he offers by offending the ear in a most raucous voice."

'"Thank you, miss."'

And:

'"If you continue to ignore the finer points of English grammar, you won't make the grade, even as a hussiff." This was spelled *housewife* but pronounced in the Elizabethan manner, *hussiff* – can you credit it? In all my long years in England I never once heard anyone pronounce *housewife* as *hussiff* except in Shakespeare.

'Fay Lowe, good friend and irrepressible spirit, would always race around the quadrangle in defiance of all the strict rules.'

'"Ladies never run. Ladies never hurry. Ladies never sweat – they perspire. Ladies dress in white demure dresses and thick woollen blazers all the year round in spite of raging tropical temperatures. Ladies speak in quiet voices," and so on.

'Miss Johnson, who seemed to have taken a set on Fay, would regularly stop her in her tracks with this rebuke: "Fay Lowe, Fay Lowe, Lowe in name, Lowe in name, low in nature, in nature low. Say after me . . . Lowe in name . . . " Not that Fay ever succumbed to this attack on her confidence.

'Most of us were made hardier by the very presence and attitude of Miss Johnson. Although it may not have seemed so at the time to Johnny, as she was called behind her back, many of her "gels" secretly admired her for getting to where she had and realised that she couldn't go the whole hog. We instinctively knew that being so black she couldn't sound common as well, even if she wanted to! It would have been more than her job was worth. Succumbing to being a bit of what they call in England a coconut (black on the outside, white on the inside) was the easier, wiser route for those times.' Here I was treated to one of Yvonne's less attractive snorts.

'Here they say roast breadfruit,' I put in. 'Aren't people unkind?'

'Goes with the territory, Mrs Clarke. The twinkle in Miss Johnson's eye almost always gave the game away. Thanks to her, St Hilda's Diocesan High School of the 1950s did not produce many rubber-stamper "gels". There were tennis champions, ambassadors, leading United Nation members of staff, PhDs galore, entrepreneurs, Rhodes scholars, pioneers and artists . . . but not many blind followers of fashion. Johnny definitely had something to do with this. It's a kind of "in spite of" mentality that she engendered.'

'So you are the exception that proves the rule?'

'Touché, sweet Mama! Seriously, though, it's good to have icons like Miss Johnson, Claude McKay and Miss Lou, to keep one going.'

'Now just look at this, eh? You are telling me this. I, who was responsible for drumming into your thick skull the significance of Claude McKay's celebrated sonnet, used – without its authorship being credited, I might add – by British Prime Minister Winston Churchill to revitalise flagging British spirits during the Second World War.' That made her sit up and take notice!

'Yes, Mummy, I can still quote you: "If we must die", the sonnet reads, as Churchill repeated, "Let it not be like hogs hunted and penned in an inglorious spot". He famously encouraged his kinsmen to "meet the common foe" with dignity and even when "pressed to the wall, dying" . . . to fight back. It's the sort of thing you've got to know if you are going to survive in England. How's that?'

I suppose I should be quietly grateful that something stuck.

Chapter 23

August Gentlemen

The next morning the sky was its normal baby blue I so love. It is always like this after the rain. I could sit and look at it for ever. *The Gleaner* has arrived and I have been joined on the patio for early morning coffee by Madam. I expected last night's session to have worn her out, but here she is, Venus rising from the foam!

She spies an item in the paper, reporting on the introduction of some ultra-sophisticated security system for use at our airports. 'Airports used to be fun but nowadays getting through security is very heart-stopping. With every electronic beep my heart races. It doesn't matter if you are innocent as a baby, you feel nervous. In California the other day, we had to take off our shoes as well as all the other prodding and poking . . . I got quite confused and flustered, as I wasn't expecting to have to walk barefoot on the filthy carpet. Came out of that with very little dignity.'

'Of course, you know my days of travelling are over,' I remarked, looking up from the paper. 'If one of those women with bleeping rods came near me to look for bombs on my person, that's the last thing she would ever do. I'd best keep at home, then, yes? But I do like to know what going on and you are always on a plane. Tell me a story before the man comes to take me to the office.'

'What about?'

'Anything.' I shrugged

'Mummy, you can be really irritating when you act the innocent. Although, you know, talking about Miss Johnson at school last night reminded me that I saw Betty Andrade from school in Toronto the other day. Remember her?'

'The other day.' Huh! Jet-set Woman 'What were you doing there, if I dare to ask?'

'I think I have a conference relationship with Toronto and I always try to see Betty – now Morris – and her husband John whenever I'm there. Canada always seems in control yet there are so many conferences questioning everything, and in that way the place is very alive and invigorating. I was invited to give the opening address at the first AfriCarib Theater Festival in Toronto in1997. It was here that I heard this for the first time: "Afro-Caribbean? Oh no, darling, Afro is a hairstyle. We are Afri-Caribbean."

Neat thinking. Then I was introduced to the Canadian use of "visible minority" instead of the phrase "ethnic minority". It has been widely adopted now.

'Jean Binta Breeze was performing during the conference and I asked her to point out Kwame Dawes to me. He was billed to appear.

'"So, Jean," I asked, "how do I recognise Kwame Dawes?"

'"Just look for a cuddly black teddy bear."

'Some fun was to be had seeking out cuddly black teddy bears but Jean was dead right. I spotted him soon enough. I went up to this young gentleman who fitted the description.

'"Kwame Dawes?" I asked.

'He looked nonplussed.

'"Binta Breeze said to look for a cuddly black teddy bear."

'Bingo! That was the beginning of a collaboration

which peaked with my commissioning and directing the first production of his musical *One Love* in Britain's oldest theatre, the Bristol Old Vic.'

'Some said it couldn't be done, didn't they?' My memory is a little dim for more recent happenings. Never for the days long gone. They glow.

'There's always them that say it can't be done. Takes all types. Some say, some do. It was done. And done well. It was a great hit with the audiences who filled the important theatres where it played. In Bristol and in London at the Lyric Hammersmith, another beauty of a theatre.

'*One Love* opened up the idea of live theatre to a much wider black audience. Sometimes the height of the audience's headgear gave a little trouble to the people sitting behind the brothers and sisters, but most times all was Peace and Love.

'It was great working with Peter Straker, who I had first seen baring all in the fabulous musical *Hair* in the sixties, Jackie Guy, and most of all the lovely diva Ruby Turner. What a performer! Hey, we had fun and so did the audience. Can you ask more? Before you say it: yes, I know you can!'

'So you first met Kwame in Canada?'

'Yes, and lots of great people. I came down to breakfast one morning and seated in a far corner of the room was a distinguished, elegantly cravated tall grey-haired man. Jan Carew. A name to conjure with. He spied me and from then onwards for the duration of the conference we had breakfast every morning. I would get down to the dining room as soon as it was opened, as I knew he was an early riser and I didn't want to run the risk of missing out on my early morning education. For just listening to Jan Carew is an education. His breadth of knowledge and experience, his sophistication and his wicked sense of humour, illuminated the rest of the day.

'He was always full of memorable quips. Once when we were joined by an over-enthusiastic and boring visionary theorist, Jan, I thought, was in danger of nodding off. My mistake, as he eventually stage-whispered to me, "Vision without action is mere hallucination." The man ceased.

'Having breakfast with Jan for those few mornings brought me introductions to some of Toronto's most famous black cultural icons, the most enduring of them being Austin Clarke.'

I interrupted, 'He of the magnificent martini?'

'The very same. It's too early for that, Mrs Clarke. Listen up and hear what happened when I met him. To my dismay I had never heard of him or his work. I don't know how it had escaped me before, and when Jan introduced us he presumed that I was familiar with everything he had done. I learned a long time ago that honesty is the best policy and admitted my ignorance.

'What a refined cussing I got. Jan said, "I was under the mistaken impression that you had received an education, Yvonne."

'Austin was cool. He cooked some exquisite food and gave a stunning dinner-party in my honour – to introduce me to him, he told the guests. I have since bought everything I could find of his and am now a great fan of his work. His prose is so intimate one almost reads in a whisper in the head to keep it so. Trivia is the stuff of his memory, it seems, until the layers expose themselves and what was trivia is now elemental. And he writes like he wants you to read it. I am grateful to have met him and, more important, to have met his work.

'Oh yes, remember I mentioned that he had written the introduction to my production of *Othello*? Well, that came about as a direct result of this meeting.'

Canada, Yvonne informed me, is now also home to the extraordinary Honor Ford Smith, whose vision and tenacity saw Sistren Theatre Company achieve Olympian heights of working women's theatre. Madam always tries to see her at least once on every visit to Toronto, where she is doing her doctorate, but still manages to be the yolk in most Canadian/Jamaican theatrical eggs.

'You seem to have a good time in Toronto,' I said mildly, hoping for more revelations. For once I was not eager to go to the office. It was fascinating sitting here listening to Yvonne throwing light on the parts of her life hidden from me until now.

'Yes, none better than when I was invited by the University of Toronto to give a keynote speech at the conference dedicated solely to the works of Nobel Laureate Wole Soyinka. I was quite surprised to be asked to participate, as the Nigerian, Canadian, American and English scholars who devote themselves to the study of the great man's works were all expected to give learned papers at one time or another during the conference. Very academic, very theoretical, very analytical. Not my scene at all.

'I had directed *The Road* (if you remember I followed Derek Walcott's suggestion), had found it very challenging and had, sacrilege of sacrilege, actually *edited* the play! It seemed to me to be too repetitive for an English audience unfamiliar with the heroics of African tragedy, and too long.

'Kole Omotoso, who had introduced me to Wole in the first place . . . Did I ever tell you what he said as an introduction?

'No.' Couldn't wait for this.

'Must tell you. "Wole, may I present Yvonne Brewster, Artistic Director and Founder of Talawa Theatre Company, who is here to research Ola's play *The Gods Are Not to Blame*. Yvonne, this is Wole Soyinka, who I must warn you has an anthology of wives."

'Mummy I don't know if I was I was behaving in a particularly rapacious way or whether he saw something in Wole's eyes that I missed. I expect it was simply elevated Yoruba hyperbole in action. What I do know is it was a wonderful way of describing one of the most attractive and spell-binding playwrights it has been my distinct pleasure to have worked with.'

'I like that. See if I can remember it: "An anthology of wives", eh? Was he very sexy-looking?'

'Behave yourself, Mrs Clarke! Yes. Very sixties, with a great halo of greying hair. Where were we? Kole. He was himself finely attuned to the cultural niceties and subtleties of Yoruba drama and had kindly assisted me and the cast with the academic preparation of the production. On the matter of editing he had remained noncommittal – but quietly supportive, I felt.

'The playwright turned up to see his butchered play on the first night at the newly refurbished Cochrane Theatre. I was in a state of frazzled nerves.' My daughter shivered.

'Firstly, here we were opening the first ever home for Black Theatre in London, nerves enough on that score. Secondly, handling the generally hostile white press, who were cynical about the need for self-determination in British Black Theatre which this black-led, black-run company Talawa promised to deliver. These people felt we should assimilate, acculturate – any kind of ate – which really meant in practice continuing to put on a good show for the few white artistic directors with buildings that they might be persuaded to let us use if they liked the play and judged it was right for us. The epitome of colonial containment.

'And thirdly, having in the audience Wole Soyinka with his famous inscrutable face. It was too much for one poor director, who should only be thinking of her lovely cast and technical crew and wishing them luck. I sat beside Wole for the entire performance. Every time a cut I had made in the text came up I stopped breathing. He remained inscrutable.'

Do you know, for a moment there, I almost felt sorry for Madam?

'The interval passed with polite meaningless chatter. I could see Angela McSherry, my close colleague and administrator of Talawa, checking out the scene from afar, gesturing madly and mouthing, "Does he like it?"

'At the end of the performance he took me aside and said simply, "Yes. Good. Actually better than my production in Chicago. Yes. Were there a few lines missing?" And he giggled momentarily. *Whew!*

'I certainly never expected to be asked to speak at such a prestigious affair as the Toronto conference. Of course, knowing how much I like Toronto, I accepted the invitation to talk about the Talawa Theatre Company production of Wole Soyinka's *The Road*.

'My offering concentrated on the difficult search for the characters, the people in the play, the drama in the play. I said that the dense scholarship which surrounded the play was at first discouraging as it concentrated so much on the ritual. Some say that to direct a Soyinka you must have a PhD in Yoruba culture! As a mere theatrical interpreter of text I had to have the courage to ignore some of the more abstract theoretical and philosophical aspects of the Yoruba gods. Too much of this threatened to kill the play dead—'

I had to interrupt, 'Watch your English! How can you kill a play dead, if you please?'

A withering look and a couple of pouts later, she continued. I had very nearly blown it. 'You run the risk of *killing the play dead* for a non-Nigerian audience. One should, I tried to suggest, be actively encouraged to open up the classical works of Soyinka to the influence of differing artistic and cultural norms.'

August Gentlemen

I must be careful here, so I put on my wise look and ventured, 'Do you know, I reckon there's a lesson to be learned from Shakespeare. His plays are constantly being re-interpreted by "an anthology" of cultures – each culture creating its own individual Shakespearean scholarship, aren't they?' All I got was 'Of course!' So much for my bright moment.

Yvonne continued, 'At the back of the hall loomed the famous mass of electric-grey hair. Soyinka. Much excitement among the delegates. He promptly summoned Femi Euba and myself to join himself and his wife for lunch. As I walked toward him I thought: Oh Lord, why don't I just keep my mouth closed? But I needn't have worried: lunch went off swimmingly. What's more, talk about profile being enhanced. From that moment I was looked at with different eyes.'

I thought, There she goes falling on her feet again, but heard myself saying how proud I was of her. She smiled. One of these days we will be able to cut out the ritual between us. Life may be simpler but less interesting. I will continue to keep my own counsel.

'Later on in the conference,' she continued, 'there was a session scheduled to concentrate on three well-documented productions of *The Road*. I was not at all worried, not for a moment anticipating what was to come. Turned out it was three well-documented *non-Nigerian* productions of *The Road* that were scheduled to be dissected. The productions were one directed by Derek Walcott with the Trinidad Workshop Theatre in Port of Spain, another directed by Professor Gowda in a translation of the play into Kanada – one of India's main literary languages – in Mysore, India, and the 1992 Talawa Theatre Company production in London directed by – oh my God – Yvonne Brewster!

'Enjoyment ceased forthwith. My old friend and fellow latter-day Rose Bruford College survivor Femi Euba

211

had to restrain me as I was bent on leaving the scene. But I needn't have worried. Indeed, I should have been feeling very happy.'

'Really? Why?' I wondered out loud.

'They say that theatre in Jamaica suffers currently from the lack of properly informed criticism. I overheard a conversation just recently during the interval of a play at the University theatre up at Mona which went something like this: You must admit that Jamaican theatrical criticism is essentially narrative and somewhat superficial in nature, does not challenge, nor does it lead, thus allowing the standard to fall below the level which it is capable of. Time was when this was not so, but Archie Lindo and Harry Milner are no longer around to tell the sometimes unpalatable, indigestible truth. Just so. Selah!'

'Yvonne, will you get on with it? Do, I beg you.'

'OK. Constructive criticism is one of the most precious gifts any creative artist can receive and this is what the erudite Nigerian scholar and gentleman Biodun Jefiyo had lavished on my efforts. I sat spellbound and extremely flattered to think that such a person could have taken such care, paid such attention to the motivations, the choices, the cultural "misreadings" which he found so profound. The misreading bit, I was made to understand, was in fact a compliment, as the directorial choices I had made were thought to have been the result of my cultural background, you know, my "broughtupcy".

'The design of the mask we used had overtones of Johnkunu and Carnival, not the Egugun. It would apparently have been quite different in a Nigerian interpretation. There were other detailed observations which were equally amazing to me. Remember, this was a production which the gentleman had seen over a decade before.

212

'Even more detailed academic attention then focused on the treatment of the lead role of Professor, especially at his death. Do you remember Ola Rotimi's Professor of Piggot? Well, I had tried to use my memory and emotion then, to help the London actor place and centre his performance.

'But there were subliminal influences at work too, it appears from my Jamaican experiences, especially in the murder of Uncle Bonny – sorry, Mummy, I didn't want to remind you of this – of the gunmen who, after they had shot him, came back to rummage around for the firearm he may have had on his body. That callousness in the bone was there somewhere in my production. In the end, as soon as the Professor is dead his closest allies spare no time in stripping him of everything saleable. Those who, moments before, would not have dared speak to him in tones above a whisper, quietly scavenged his body, still warm. So political, don't you think?'

I said nothing, but nodded sagely.

'Apparently this was a major triumphal misreading which would not have occurred to a Nigerian director because Caribbean and Nigerian rituals of the dead are so very different. So the London production was perfectly proper but different, and I was admired for taking the play into another place. Still a misreading!'

'Why not take some praise for a change?' Oh dear, had I really said that? I pretended to fan away some mosquitoes to hide my confusion.

'Stop that, Mummy. I am *your* daughter. The chip hasn't flown far from the block, so why do you think I would be able to accept praise, eh? To continue, you live and learn how much your roots guide if you give them a chance. I learned then that my instinct not to do tourist theatre – you know, dressing up in foreign clothes of the country of origin of the play and kidding yourself that you are being true to the spirit of the thing – was

213

probably the right decision for me to have taken so many years ago. The thought of Shakespeare in doublet and hose doesn't work for me. That so often negates the contemporary cut and thrust of old Sheik el-Subair as Wole Soyinka calls him.'

I hadn't heard that one before. Very amusing. 'Looks like you have learned to listen in your old age,' I said. Uh oh! My car is at the gate and there is Coke the driver politely bowing, hoping to get my attention. I drag myself away – I must never shirk my duty. 'I promise I'll be back home in no time,' I said, and left my daughter with her precious memories, more of which I hope to plunder later today.

Chapter 24

A Road Well Travelled

Everything seemed to be just fine and dandy at Sam Isaacs & Son when I arrived. Somehow I get the feeling that they would be quite happy if I stayed away altogether. That'll be the day. I didn't linger today, however, and was soon on my way home to Queensway. I wanted to make sure I caught Yvonne before she went out gallivanting.

When I arrived the house was still and cool. The shutters had been closed against the glare of the afternoon, and even the dogs were reluctant to greet me. I followed the sound of Miles Davis to find Mrs Brewster getting ready to go out to tea with some 'old girls' from school. Tea! St Hilda's throws a long shadow.

Looks like I shall have to kill some time and waylay her when she gets back. I wondered around, poking about in the kitchen, trying out the newly upholstered sofa, which I must tell you is now covered in natural linen. I ask you! This is not New York. Anyway, what really has my senses reeling is the bit of sculpture which Yvonne has stolen from Valerie's house. This is very expensive, I was told by Mervys, who, seeing the perturbed look on my face, had joined me. 'Miss Kathleen, *you* think people should pay so much money for this little piece of screw-up barbed wire?'

'Mervys, this is beyond you and me, my dear. Did Miss Von say when she would be coming back?

'No, she just say "Later."'

And much later it was before the tea party ended and a whole gang of her friends turned up. I organised some Austin Clarkes. I really wanted to pick up from where we had left off, but you know I have to be subtle about these things and pounce at the right moment. This arrived not long after all the ladies of quality had departed. We had had a quick salad and were both putting our feet up outside in the walled patio I love so much.

'Bedtime is fast approaching, dear Miss Von. Can I have a little story before I go to bed?' I cajoled, hoping not to sound too foolish.

'You are incorrigible, Mrs Clarke,' Yvonne responded to my attempt at charm, 'but I give you full marks for trying. OK. Where do you want me to start?'

That was all the encouragement I needed. 'You mentioned Lloyd Richards once in one of your letters. Did you mean Lloyd Reckord?'

'No, of course not. I meant Lloyd *Richards*. The Arts Council of Great Britain decided that I needed some exposure to a really accomplished and experienced black theatre director. Somehow, Drama Director Ian Brown at the time, who knew Lloyd Richards, managed to arrange to bring him across from New York to London where I was rehearsing *The Gods Are Not to Blame* in a draughty church hall in Pimlico.

'Another case of the jitters for me. Lloyd Richards coming into *my* rehearsal room. This is the man who discovered Lorraine Hansberry and directed the first production ever of *A Raisin in the Sun* with Sidney Poitier and such delights. He who directed the Yale productions of nearly every August Wilson play, most of which transferred to Broadway.

'Look, Mummy, I had read books about him, studied his production philosophies, and now he was turning up

216

at a rehearsal room of mine. It was scary. If you continue to laugh at me I'm going to bed.'

'I'm really sorry, Miss Von, but I just can't imagine you scared!' I said quickly, blocking the doorway.

A few tense moments later: 'I have a photograph of me pretending to be assured as he gave me his notes . . . I was anything but. However, these encounters help to ground you. He was attentive, quiet as a mouse sitting at the back of the hall, so much so the cast almost forgot he was there, forgot to continue auditioning! Broadway is a good address. He and I had lunch together in a most basic pub nearby and he started by saying, "How do you get actors to experiment so unselfconsciously, like they were doing just now with those three bits of cloth? I need some help here."

'Could have hugged him. I think I may have. Having put me at my ease, he could then give the help he had been drafted in for. "You must persist in making the play belong to *you*," he told me. "You must make it the company's property, which it must selflessly guard against those who would generalise, not particularise. OK, so it's set in AD 400 or whatever: we live at the end of the first millennium and that's where it's travelled and survived. Find out why. And hey, Yvonne, you still have to tell me how you get a dozen actors who have never worked together before to do those things with that cloth."

'How could I not be influenced by that, Mummy? All of a sudden I understood how he managed to be so very low-profile and yet be so seminal to twentieth-century African-American theatre. I mean to say, Lorraine Hansberry and August Wilson! That's not bad going for one human being.'

'So now I know who Lloyd Richards is. Who is this August Wilson you keep on about?'

'He's a playwright. Some years ago he started writing

a play for each decade of the twentieth century from the point of view you might say of the African-American. They became instant classics, although some are better than others.'

I nodded wisely to show that I was following.

'*Fences* seems to get the winning vote when theatre people gather, but the impressive thing about Wilson is that he continues to work on his plays until they are as near-perfect as he can get them. For instance, in August 1997 when I was at the Black Theater Festival in Winston Salem, North Carolina, to get my award, I saw *Jitney*.

'Excuse me, not so fast. What award?'

The first I'd ever heard about any such thing. My daughter likes to keep me in the dark.

'I'll get to that later, but let me tell you about *Jitney*, one of his proposed decathlon of plays. It had been produced by Crossroads Theater Company in New Brunswick, New Jersey, had travelled to the Festival and was billed as one of the highlights. That made sense, as August Wilson was scheduled to deliver a version of his famous response to American critic Robert Brustein's ideas on non-traditional casting: *The Ground on Which I Stand*.

'As I say, Mummy, Wilson had already made his suitably rigorous response at an academic conference earlier in the year, but now here he was in August in Winston Salem at the largest gathering of Black Theatre people possible – so why not do an encore of *The Ground on Which I Stand?* This audience was ripe and up for it.'

Yvonne's eyes were sparkling as she re-lived the scene.

'The National Black Theater Festival is one hell of a platform for practitioners working in Black Theatre. Hundreds of thousands of fans of Black Theatre turn up in the small town of Winston Salem to feast on a choice of over thirty plays which are on offer over the six

218

days of the Festival – festivities really. The fanatic could possibly see about half of what's on offer.

'The whole town is, for the first week in August on alternate years, completely taken over by the event. It's quite something to see in this part of the world – which you must remember is part of the tobacco-growing Carolinas, if you get my drift. It takes the genius of someone like the eccentric founder, Larry Leon Hamlin, to pull off something as mind-boggling as this. "No" does not feature in his vocabulary and gainsayers are probably frightened off by his shimmering golden mode of dress.' Yvonne gave one of her rich chuckles.

'As well as the many plays, there are also innumerable workshops, street parties, an enormous craft market, celebrity press conferences, signings and sightings: "There's Debbie Allen from *Fame*, there's John Amos, is that Ruby Dee? Miss Shange can I have your autograph, please?" Amiri Baraka glimpsed in deep conversation with Cecily Tyson and Ed Bullins, and so on. It's a good buzz.

'A prestigious International Colloquium is held as part of the Festival. This year the keynote speaker for the kick-off lecture on the first full day was to be August Wilson.

'By some quirk of fate I was asked to chair the event. Know the saying, Fools rush in . . . ? The gargantuan dining room in the largest hotel in town – the Adam's Mark – was cleared to make room for over two thousand souls, all crammed in to witness this epoch-making moment. The platform was heavy with dignitaries, who all had to be introduced, and in turn introduce others. Finally I had to get up and introduce August Wilson.

'I had a bunch of biographical notes to read out as his introduction, but with the lengthy preceding features of this affair the vast crowd was by now getting a bit restless. I thought if I read out this whole history there would be a riot. After all, there was not one soul in that room who did not know who August Wilson was. That's why they were there. That's why they had come early and queued to be sure of a seat. Luckily for me, one of those rare moments when the right words just pop into head, into mouth and out of mouth happened. I kind of saw it flash before me. I simply got up and said, "Ladies and gentlemen, it is my extreme pleasure to introduce your key-note speaker for this afternoon without further delay. It is an august moment: in this month of August, I give you the august August Wilson."

'He obviously was expecting a long introduction and when it was over in a flash he gave me a big smile. This is something he doesn't do in public too often and I treasure the memory. He was even kind enough to comment favourably on my introduction.'

'I know how you like these moments of drama, but what was so special about the speech this time around?' I ventured.

'We were experiencing it in living colour, not from the pages of a newspaper, even if the speech was more or less similar to the now famous *Ground on Which I Stand* original, which had argued the case for an end to integration as a easy solution to lack of real and specific opportunities for the development of African-American Theater. No more colour-blind casting, no more non-traditional casting, just the real McCoy would do. No more, no less. Quite uncompromising.

'The audience reception was wild. Almost ticker-tape. The question and answer session afterwards which I had to do my best to chair was pretty predictable, as most speakers took the opportunity to "agree with everything that has been said".

'There was one hairy moment, however, when a very brilliant scholar called Nefertiti Burton asked a question which lots of people would have liked to have been

220

forthright enough to pose: "Why are there never any persons of mixed race in your plays when you so patently are of mixed-race origin?" (Which of course he is. I think we would call him "very high brown" in Jamaica.) "Why do you never address the concerns of this very large section of your natural audience?"

'He didn't appreciate that question one little bit and his reply was unsatisfactory, as he abruptly maintained that he wasn't in the business of autobiographical treatises. The question needed a proper answer which it did not get. I could feel his hypertension beside me. I was a little disappointed, but we moved right along to happier, more conventional questions and observations.

'Of course, after that sensational lecture tickets for Wilson's *Jitney* were hot. Now, too often people do not tell the truth in theatre. They will gush in dressing-rooms, "Oh darling, what can I say?" Or "Words simply fail me!" Or "Your performance was really something else." Or "You really stunned me," and so on. The same people will gush out minutes later, "Oh God! How awful. I need a drink."

'It was quite extreme in this instance; the truth is the version of *Jitney* on offer in Winston Salem clearly needed a lot of work. There were also a few heretical mutterings debunking the idea of black actors only playing black roles. *We gotta eat, man.* At least in this, another "cockroach in the fowl yard" situation, I managed to keep stumm.'

There was a long silence during which I, too, decided that to keep 'stumm' might be my best policy at this moment.

'About five or so years later *Jitney* was presented by the National Theatre on the South Bank of the Thames with its original African-American cast. I went to see it as a matter of course. It had been transfigured into the

most wonderful evening of theatre I had experienced for
many a moon.

'As it was sold out and I needed to keep on seeing it, I
queued, I begged, I pleaded, and got to see it again and
again. My point is that the play was not allowed to rest
on the laurels of the playwright's distinguished name
but had been moulded and edited, worked on until it
reached perfection. We can learn a lot from this, you
know, Katie. Fame needs living up to. It requires work or
it will be as a passing train. One big noise and it's gone.'

'What about this fellow's other work? You said some
of the plays were better than others – but this *Jitney*
seems to have got under your skin.'

'I like the August Wilson plays and have seen most
of them in production, have discussed the work with
Lou Bellamy, who is his mate from the Penumbra
Theater in Minneapolis, among others, but let's say I
like to read them, I like to see them, but have never
felt the urge to direct any of them. Don't know why.
Probably scared of the look I remember in August
Wilson's eye when he wasn't well pleased . . . Seriously, though, I lack a deep enough understanding of
what makes the African-American tick, and without
that attempting August Wilson is just a teeny bit
suicidal.'

'That's never stopped you before! So now I have an
idea who the man August Wilson is and how much in
awe you are of him. So what about the award?'

'There is a great dinner given in an enormous barn of
a place to mark the beginning of every Festival. People
flock from all over the United States and further afield
for this event. There is a ceremonial entry parade of the
celebrities which entails stilt walkers and African
drummers. The drums and the celebrities carry the
magic for the week of the Festival.

'These celebrities are the stars of small screen, large

screen, and the proscenium. They proceed up the aisle to an avalanche of flash bulbs and outstretched arms until they arrive at their destination, the raised platforms at the other end of the room. This procession can take up to fifteen minutes. Many of the celebrities will be given awards in recognition of the work they have done, and there are thank you speeches for the entertainment of the crowds of diners sitting below.

'Into this amazing arena I found myself sleepwalking,' mused Yvonne. 'I am still asking why. But I would not have missed it for the world. Larry Leon's office had sent me a very imposing letter to say that the Festival organisers had decided to bestow upon me the distinction of a Living Legend Award for my services to Theatre. At first I thought it was a joke. Then I took a look at the list of people to whom this honour had been paid in the past and it read like a Who's Who of African-American household entertainment names. Sidney Poitier, Denzil Washington, Cecily Tyson, Harry Belafonte and Maya Angelou, for starters. I thought: Wow! Why me? You must remember I have worked in England for most of my life and this was a very African-American affair.

'Irony is king in London so the quips were predictable, as in, "Darling, I thought one could only be a legend if one was dead." And "*Is* there something you haven't told us?"

'I determined to find my way to North Carolina and there I was, part of the celebrity parade, among the glitterati, mounting the raised platform and finally presented with my Living Legend Award for my lifetime's work in theatre, of which I am inordinately proud. Those who scoff are probably never going to be offered one. A quite mind-boggling experience, especially meeting and beginning to understand how the African-American approaches to life and art differ from those of the Black British, the African and the Caribbean. Selah!'

I find myself chuckling in sympathy and say: 'Right, when the "Selah" comes out I know that you need a drink. I certainly do. Where's the cognac you have surely brought for me?' She always brings some fine Rémy Martin, along with my Dr Scholl Weekenders. I do like a drop of cognac, you know, but suspect they are hiding it away from me. If I sound like an alcoholic, don't worry: the heat works wonders. And I do appreciate the finer things in life. It is quite extraordinary that when you get old enough to know your own mind that's when everyone else knows what good for you. You've got to be cunning to survive, and this takes up too much of the little time you have left. Speaking of time, 23 January approaches and I haven't heard a peep out of anyone about this ninetieth birthday party. You see, that's another way of controlling you. Withdrawal of information. I keep reminding myself: Kathleen, *nil desperandum*.

Chapter 25

The Tail of Talawa

＝•☉•＝

Yvonne always disappears into the 'country' for a few days every time she comes home. Everywhere outside Kingston is referred to as the 'country' in Jamaica, even though some really stylish entertainment goes on there, especially in Savanna-la-Mar. She loves visiting her good friends Merle and Freddie, who insist on at least one visit to the seven miles of prefect beach at Negril. She always come back in a very good mood from Sav.

Thus too many days go by before we have another little chat. I look forward to them, not so much for the information but as a way of really getting to know Madam. I now realise that parents think they know their offspring but nothing could be further from the truth. It's only now, when it's too late, that I have found the time to find out. I am sure a lot of parents make this mistake. Or perhaps they don't. I'm not a particularly motherly model.

I saw her watching the six o'clock evening news on BBC World Television in the flop room. As soon as the news bulletin ended I switched off the set, ready for another long awaited session. Old age! I realised I didn't have my tape recorder with me. So, in for a penny in for a pound: I shall attempt to write this next bit from memory, which as you know is getting a bit unreliable these days, but here goes.

She keeps saying she has retired from Talawa. My

reaction was: 'You say you have retired from Talawa. Explain, if you will be so kind, how you can retire from something which is so much a part of your life. You know I will never retire.'

Wrong move.

'No, you will keep going down to the office, as you call it, until they wheel you out in a chair to sun you. Dead woman walking. Different strokes for different folks, Mummy.'

Ridiculous woman. The gist was: she knew when enough was enough but it had taken her much too long to throw over the traces at Talawa. Even now, she says she hopes she has finally managed to do so. Finally. Took her nearly five years. Now, when anyone enquires after her they are told she doesn't work there any more. Get it. She's left. She hasn't retired. She was bored. Now she must learn to click the Delete button.

Freedom. That's how she sees it.

Freedom! That sounds so African-American. What have we here? I needed to get this bit accurately down so I took a chance and asked her to get the tape recorder for me.

'Tape recorder? What tape recorder? Mummy, you haven't ?'

'Yes, I have. There's a good girl.'

Won that one.

'Let's get back to freedom,' I persist with tape recorder spinning. 'You've always been free, so what's this foolishness about freedom?'

'Let me tell you why: I have never had too much ambition. When I wrote up the application for funding all those years ago in 1985 it was to enable me to put on a play I wanted to do passionately. I never thought that this might be the foundation for a proud, "facety little but tallawah" theatre company. One thing led to another and the first few years were undiluted fantastic fun. I was able to choose what I wanted, cast it how I wanted, present it where I wanted. Funding seemed to follow as the night the day. The thing was on a roll.

'With recognition from the Arts Council my wings were clipped somewhat, as I had to formalise the company and have an administrator when, before, great friends like Mary Lauder, Jo Beddoe and Nick Owen would help whenever they could. So I had to have a proper administrator and a proper office, whereas before we got by in the back bedroom at home. Dame Jocelyn Barrow was persuaded to lend us timely and wise support as our original Patron.

'This is quite correct procedure, I am sure – after all it was public money – but you tend to get what you pay for. The money allocated by the Arts Council for administration couldn't pay for the calibre of person who before had helped because they wanted to and believed in the work. We had a different level of help. That made it so much harder.

'During those dark days of administrative hell there was one particularly bright beacon in the generous shape of David Hoare. As I said, the money wasn't great so his dinner jacket was always hanging on the back of the door in our minute office in the Africa Centre in Covent Garden. He had to supplement his income and did this by serving in the American Bar at the Savoy, which he carried off with consummate style.

'On occasion I would sit in the Palm Court atmosphere of the American Bar's tinkling piano, nursing a tonic water masquerading as a G and T and devouring the tasty Brazil nuts, olives and other upmarket snacks. We, David and I, would snatch moments when he might pretend to be serving me, but was really finishing the Talawa day's business. Great guy. It was he who made our *Antony and Cleopatra* a hot ticket among many of London's posh public schools, arranging a deal with the

British Museum of a tour and talk of the Egyptian room, a packed lunch and then a matinee just up the road at the Bloomsbury Theatre.

'David and I also pasted up the artwork for the poster and we put together the pitch which netted us, Talawa, the money for the refurbishment of the then Jeanetta Cochrane Theatre. I always remember him with great admiration. And gratitude. And a smile.'

'How much money did you raise?'

'In those days it was a lot. It had to do with bottle, with imagination, and with sheer cheek. There was a massive project in London also funded by the Greater London Council to redevelop an old train terminus building in Chalk Farm called the Roundhouse. The idea was to turn this remarkable building, which had been used for innovative theatre for many years, into a grandiose Arts Centre for Black Arts. Suffice it to say that many millions later the Roundhouse is not a grandiose Arts Centre for Black Arts. A white elephant into a black elephant.

'A sum of money remained, however, some three hundred thousand pounds, which had been earmarked for the Roundhouse by the Arts Council before the project collapsed in a pile of recrimination. The Arts Council decided to offer ten black cultural organisations the opportunity of bidding for a tenth of the money. Each company would be given the chance to make a five-minute presentation in the boardroom at the Council to a committee which might include the then Chairman, Lord Palumbo. David and I thought we might like *all* the money.'

I spluttered at the cheek of it all.

Yvonne winked at me and continued, 'I appreciate this is not the perfect way to endear oneself to one's colleagues but . . . Mummy, will you stop grinning? OK, we thought five minutes in which to make one's case was a bit arbitrary but those were the rules. We therefore set about creating a presentation so utterly compelling that we should, if there was any justice, win the day. The plan was not to talk our way through the five minutes. No. Knowing me, the five minutes would have been used up in saying hello. We would produce a five-minute video which would make the case for us. It would be highly ironic, amusing and daring.

'A Victorian pamphlet written by a West Indian actor called Robert Adams entitled *Why Not a Negro Theatre?* had come our way. Adams used similar arguments to those in current use, self-determination, no art can flourish with out a greenhouse home in which to experiment. The official answer to Adams was: "Yes, you may have it when conditions permit."

'The message was pretty clear. One was left in no doubt that conditions would *never* permit.

'In the video we repeated the catchphrase "When conditions permit" over and over again to provide the irony. In David's upper-class plummy accent, the voiceover was quite amusing. Ben Thomas filmed me entering the old rundown Jeanetta Cochrane Theatre and spouting some lyrics about what Black Theatre practitioners in Britain would gain if such a place was available for them to call their own, that the time had to be right sometime, then rounded this off with David's white arm and hand wearing a pinstriped shirt of the sort the Chairman of the Arts Council of Great Britain might wear, adorned with a pair of his cufflinks previously coaxed out of one of his assistants, filmed about to sign a blank Arts Council cheque for the entire amount of three hundred thousand pounds to Talawa.

'The video did its job. It was received with hoots of laughter – apparently the only time anyone laughed that day – and bingo! We got over a quarter of a million pounds.'

'You raised so much money?' I had to remember to close my mouth.

'Yes, Mummy. This did not endear us to everybody, understandably, but a girl's gotta do what a girl's gotta do. This kind of single-mindedness is not too well admired, especially if it gets the results others would have liked for themselves, so the bitching began and hasn't stopped really. I always sing Bob Marley's "No Woman No Cry", when it gets too much. The important thing is that Talawa is still going strong and is, under the astute chairmanship of gracious Lady Howells, the lovely supportive Baroness of St Davids, about to embark on building its own home in Central London. Finally the time is right. Conditions finally permit.'

'Tell me something about this Cochrane Theatre,' I suggested. 'You seem to have a fondness for the place.'

'It wasn't all plain sailing, Mummy. Back then in 1990 negotiating with the London Institute, who own the Cochrane Theatre, for the right to occupy it, when refurbished, for a specified number of weeks per year was a little stressful. It involved working out a peaceful co-existence plan with this large educational monolith. I think it found us more of a nuisance, a tick in its elephantine backside, than anything else, Finally, imperially, the London Institute collaborated with us and in February 1992 we opened the doors of the Cochrane Theatre, newly re-modelled to the design of two brilliant young architects, Abe Odedina and Alex Allardyce.

'During our three years of residence, Talawa produced twelve plays. From Wole Soyinka, Ntozake Shange, John Ford, Sylvia Wynter, Biyi Bandele, Trevor Rhone, Carmen Tipling, Tariq Ali, Pearl Cleage, William Shakespeare to Endesha Ida Mae Holland. The range was all-embracing. Most schools of theatre were addressed. It was a time of trying to be all things to all

230

black audiences.' My daughter sighed but not too deeply, 'On reflection it was of course an impossible task. Worth trying though, Mummy.

'In England there had been a leap in the audience for the light-hearted and sexually explicit *Bups* or *Blue Mountain* farcical Jamaican theatre imports which played at weekends only in large municipal halls. These productions satisfied the entertainment need for a large part of the black population, which enjoyed seeing itself represented on the stage, even if it was in unchallenging stereotypical "plays", very risqué, brimful of innuendo and Jamaican dialectic niceties. These productions didn't set out to challenge, the scripts could hardly be called literature, the objective was entertainment. Still, they certainly made the people laugh a lot, and feel good enough to face the world on Monday morning.'

While I tried to look wise, my daughter went on to inform me: 'This phenomenon is not exclusive to Britain, by the way. In the United States it exists under the name of the Chitlin circuit, Sunday afternoon theatre which provides rigorous competition for the more serious African-American work of people like August Wilson.

'Talawa as a nationally subsidised company was funded to do more challenging work. The real uphill task was to convince the target audience that there was room for both types of theatre in their diaries. The company had to constantly remind itself that although we were being very serious about glorifying and edifying the black audience we should also entertain it. The audience figures climbed steadily during our time in residence at the Cochrane. The tragedy was that we were only allowed to stay there for three years.'

'How you mean, "allowed?"' Had I missed something here?

'Oh, you know how it is. In England they don't

confront you, they use the subtlety of the language, they lobby, they derail, debunk, defuse, and before you know it you've had it. Most debilitating are the series of unrelenting meetings, duly recorded by the powers-that-be, which in the end wear you down no matter how strong you may think you are.

'Our then Chair was Dr Marie Stewart – an elegant, bejewelled, six-footer on whom there are no flies. I used to watch the reaction when she made a telling point in board meetings with the Institute. It was not a gracious relationship except with Don Gratton, who always tried to do the best for us.

'Well, Mother, we had to face the facts. When the lease came up for renewal it was time for us to leave. We had been offered fewer weeks there, and most of these were in the doldrum months of the year for fringe theatre in London such as August and December. There was also a question about whether we really needed an office in the building.'

For one split second, I could swear that my own child looked older that I do – and as we all know, the milestone of ninety years awaits. My old heart burned for her.

'I can only say,' she went on slowly, 'one never quite gets over this kind of thing. It's a good lesson in caution, of course, but if caution is to be the ruling emotion in a creative endeavour, that endeavour gets tamer and tamer. I wasn't interested in tame touring of acceptable work to pragmatic venues who wanted to produce their five per cent of black work in order to keep their grant.'

My daughter looked me straight in the eye. 'The truth is I wanted out of Talawa a couple of years after we left the Cochrane.

'That wasn't as easy as you might think. I have never been sentimental about Talawa. People go on about it being my baby and all that stuff ad nauseam. When I insist that this is *not* the only thing I have done in my life, that I have done things *before* and that I intend to do others *after*, I am invariably met with a patronising pat on the back and a nod and a wink that say, "We know better, you'll never be able to give up the reins." Huh!' Yvonne's eyes are sparkling again, but with a different sort of passion, this time.

'That really upsets me, you know, Mummy. To think I am seen as so boring, so lacking in adventure, as to want to continue going round in ever-diminishing circles, doing something I know needs a different kind of person, a younger person, to get excited about it. My motto is: "Been there, done that. What's next?"

'My horizon always has to be slightly impossible to see, just always that much out of normal reach. This is what keeps me alive. The person behind the scenes is usually an unknown quantity and that's me. Anyway, she who laughs last, nuh so?'

'So colloquial!'

'I'll ignore that. It took an age to find the right person for the job of Artistic Director of Talawa, not because it's so hard but because the Board didn't really have much of a clue what I did, what the job was. This is a problem which can arise when someone who founds an organisation from scratch is in post and has formulated policy and product around a singular personal vision. So much is in the shorthand that develops over the years.

'After a number of "succession" false starts with really talented younger people like Topher Campbell, Michael Buffong and Bonnie Greer, Talawa now has a one-time student of mine, Paulette Randall, in charge. Good luck to her.'

'Didn't I meet her when she visited Jamaica along with her twin sister, Beverley?' This tired old brain still functions sometimes.

'That's right! Paulette is always talking about when

233

she met you. Bev is her slightly older sister, just in passing.'

'You love to split hairs, don't you?' I grumble. 'Let's get one thing straight: running Talawa hasn't made you a millionaire, has it? In fact, you will get a big round zero when you leave, so what are you going to do with yourself?'

'You are on the button as usual, Mrs Clarke. I really will get nothing from Talawa – no pension, probably not even a thank you – so you are right to ask. As long as I have my health I will work. People all over the place offer me stuff to do, which I sift and sort, and I only agree to get involved with those I am excited by. It doesn't much matter if it's a big and prestigious project which will get the cognoscenti excited and sharpening their knives, or a one-person show in a tiny theatre. It's got to have something to make my head go *zing* at the thought. So it's basically back to my basics. That is how I have always been.'

My daughter leans forward and taps me on the knee. 'I don't suppose I'll starve!'

'Disgrace you are,' I laugh. 'You know there's Starr to bail you out. And then I'm always here as a very last resort, aren't I?' This was not the right thing and she is escaping. 'Come back here, darling. Surely, you know I was only joking? My goodness, don't you people ever laugh in England? That's better. Tell me about one-person shows. That was the sort of thing you cooked up with Trevor, wasn't it?'

'Got it in one. And by the way, yes, we do laugh in England but only when it's subtle and witty. OK? Yes, Trevor's *Bellas Gate Boy* was a one-person show.

'He emailed me some pages of his autobiography, which he had read at the annual in-thing literary festival on the South Coast called Calabash. Kwame Dawes, one of the founders of the festival, had emailed me in

London to say what a success the reading had been. I know Kwame – he is not one of your "What can I say?" types, he comes straight to the point. I listened.

'Trevor wanted to stage the thing. Trevor wanted it done at the Barn. Trevor also wanted to act in it. Now, this last item required some thought on my part. It had been years since he had done any serious acting. Yes, he'd done a bit in this film, and a cameo role in that one, but this was going to be one of the most difficult assignments an actor can take on. One and a half hours with no one to hide behind, no one to blame, no one to shift the emphasis on to in moments of stress.

'Did Trevor know what he was getting himself into? With hindsight, that twenty-twenty vision facility, I don't believe he did fully at the beginning. This was surely a challenge but I decided to go with it. As sentimental old fools, it felt right that we should be working together at the Barn for the first time since I directed the first production of *School's Out* so many decades ago.'

'Oh yes, I remember *School's Out*. That was one of the last productions at the Barn when we still lived at Oxford Road. You know how much I miss that old house. Of course, I love living in smart Queensway, but Oxford Road will always hold my heart.' I had to pull myself together. I was in danger of getting emotional. I encouraged Yvonne to continue, with a bright look on my face.

She did. 'I saw immediately that an editor from hell (me) would have to take the text, which after all was in novel format, and turn it into a play. And so the long months of exchanging emails and phone calls, even handwritten letters began. I must say I enjoyed it.

'From the beginning the parameters were set. It would be a professional arrangement. I would need my friend and colleague Ellen Cairns to design the piece, which she did brilliantly – even bringing snow to the tiny tropical stage of the Barn, if you recall. Didn't that go down well? We would rehearse during the day, not at night, we would have a stage manager at all times in the rehearsal room to notate the highs and lows of every day. We would have a proper lighting person and, most importantly, there would be two actors learning the part. Trevor suggested Alwyn Scott. Wonderful.

'You see, I remembered Alwyn as a young actor whom director Paul Stone, then head of BBC Children's TV, cast to play the lead role in *My Father Son Son Johnson*, which was filmed in Jamaica in the 1970s. Great little actor he was then. Even better one now.

'The trials and tribulations are for another day but in the end Trevor did it. He did it. Whee-ew! I remember the absorption with which he approached the role. I also think we should give a prize to Nicole Brown for learning her role as stage manager so swiftly and so well. This is one of the most ungrateful jobs in theatre. You work just as hard as the actor, director, designer, but the audience only knows you are there when things go wrong. You, Mrs Clarke, never said what you thought of it?'

Trevor mentioned my name too often in the play. I know I helped them set up the Barn in the beginning, but there was no need for him to go telling the world. But I only sighed and replied, 'What can I say?' I learn quickly.

'I think it was a bit off the beaten track of theatre in Jamaica today, and of course did not attract the size of crowds that other more traditional Jamaican Christmas offerings enjoyed, but what the audience lacked in quantity it certainly made up for in quality! Every name in the galaxy of Jamaican theatre made sure to see the show, taking their houseguests from "foreign". As a result the life of the *Bellas Gate Boy* after the Barn has been rather encouraging internationally. For instance,

Harvard loved it.' My daughter grinned at me. Storm over, sun shinning through.

'It amazes me that you have managed to work your way to so many interesting places doing crazy things while I have been here burying the dead.' I patted my brow: it was hot today. Then I told her, 'To share a secret with you, your father and I at first thought you might, at best, end up in a radio studio reading the news.'

'Nothing wrong with that if you do it right.'

'Yes, yes, yes. Don't preach at me, child.'

'Well, I did do some good work in radio which wasn't only playing records and reading the news. When Wycliffe Bennett was General Manager of the JBC he did many things, but not everybody remembers that under his lion grip the station produced, I think it was four, LPs called *Voices from the Caribbean* in which he got the people he considered to have sufficiently clear voice production – Greta Lyons, Eddie Baugh, Leonie Forbes, Trevor Rhone and Yvonne Jones (me) – to read an anthology of poems and short stories from around the Caribbean.

'The quality of production and performance matched the excellent content. In fact, JBC Radio *Sunday Afternoon*, the radio programme which these recordings spawned, ran for many moons and was voted in a listener poll as the most popular programme. I am fond of my copies but they were showing signs of age and not long ago a kind friend Delroy Murray (guess where he's from with that name?) made them into CDs for me. They certainly stand the test of time.

'He, Wycliffe, also made some similar recordings under the title of *Music and Youth* which were directed by Ouida Tomlinson, now Mrs Hugh Dumphy, and these are equally valuable.

'Then I got to meet fascinating people whom I was sent to interview – Errol John, Eartha Kitt, to name a couple – and learned to write news reports under the tutelage of experts like JC Proute. I did quite a few radio plays for the BBC when ages ago I first started working in London – radio has not lost its edge as was predicted when television became everyday. It has, in fact, become more popular – maybe because it allows you to make up your own mind and use your imagination, a precious jewel in a television world where it is almost impossible to escape reality TV, which is anything but in touch with reality.

'And guess what? I am acting in a new series of half-hour BBC Radio Four comedy programmes called *Do Nothing till You Hear from Me*. I really enjoyed getting back to radio, even if it meant recording the show with a live audience, something I had never done before.'

'Old dog new tricks,' I commented, then: 'Don't look at me like that! I could have said "old bitch". And talking of new tricks, before I give up and go to bed, I would really like you to tell me how you fit in with your Italian connection. I mean, you barely understand a word when it's spoken rapidly and you by your own admission only use nouns and gestures to get around.'

'Enough, no more, 'tis not so sweet now.'

'Your grandfather has a lot to answer for! Have you really been here twelve days?' I ask, surprised at how quickly the time is speeding away.

'And twelve nights, too. I promise I'll tell you all about Italy on the morrow. Come on, no need to sulk! Now it's time to enjoy the moon and the sweet cool breeze. Go on, sing.'

I did, and she hummed along. What a wonderful world.

Chapter 26

Behind the Scenes

A few days later I was able to beard the lioness, and being in an expansive mood she brought me up to date about her real life in England as, she says, "an immigrant from the visible minorities".

'Mummy, England is a mysterious place to try and fathom. The secrecy which hides under the cloak of the stiff upper lip contains answers to the deep-text understanding of the culture. Attempting to decode the culture is often a bitter task.

'I spent many years of my life in England, sitting on boards and committees. Plenty minutes to read! You must understand that Great Britain plc operates on an almost underground network of boards and committees. These are for the most part grace and favour appointments, and materialise through the "who you know" system of recommendation. It's worked like this for centuries. People are expected to give freely of their time, expertise and knowledge so that public institutions may have access to the best brains outside the civil service. It's seen as an honour to be asked to be on these boards and committees – and in fact I think it is. To serve the country in which you live and have your being is something you should feel a sense of pride in doing.

'Over the years I have notched up some heavy hours of this kind of work, in the Arts and in Health. While the Health work was more satisfying, the work in the

Arts was more high profile. For instance, I sat on the London Arts Board for eight years and during that time the system of funding changed radically. Essentially for the better, I believe, as the route to funding is now less hedged around with precipices and pitfalls – less biased towards the usual suspects continuing to dominate the system.

'In fact, change was on every agenda. However, change needs time to bed down, to be tested. Change needs to be the result of real not perceived need. Change for the sake of change can just make certain people fool themselves into thinking they are helping others, when in reality they are polishing their individual halos.

'What is more, the volatile nature of some of the artists and their hysterical reaction to change often obstructs appreciation of their real worth. Unfortunately, the loudest often manage most successfully to catch the ear of the funders and end up getting the dosh. It's an imperfect system but at least there is a system. Look at Jamaica, where there is absolutely no provision for the furtherance of the Arts within the country.'

I timidly suggest, 'Maybe subsidy is not the answer. Think of the number of international artists who are/ were of Jamaican origin. Bob Marley is the perfect example. How much state subsidy did *he* get?'

'One swallow does not a summer make, as you, Mrs Clarke, have said many times. You think Willard White would have arrived at his place of international distinction without publicly subsidised companies and buildings outside of Jamaica in which to perform? Anyway, too many years sitting on the London Arts Board, the British Council Drama and Dance Committee, the Arts Council's BRIT (British Regional Initiative for Theatre), the Black Theatre Forum and countless others have now rendered me committee-ed out. I can't do this any more. I can tell you it's extremely easy to become yesterday's woman. But that's OK. It's my choice.

'The Health work was very much harder as it required greater attention to detail rather than desire. I was approached on a few occasions to join one of many National Health Trusts, but was really interested in working with a Mental Health Trust.

'I had seen at first hand how many young black men were diagnosed as mentally ill. When one visited the secure wards in mental-health hospitals, especially in the inner-city areas of Britain, one was always shocked to see what a large percentage of the patients were young black men. This was not a new observation. Figures that point to this phenomenon have existed for some time, but the numbers keep on rising.

'That's why I wanted to join an inner-city Mental Health NHS Trust. My first appointment was to the Riverside Trust, which had jurisdiction over West London provision in this area of medicine. It was eye-opening to realise how much time and effort really busy and important pillars of the community were prepared to spend to ensure that the mentally challenged patients in their care were given access to the best, most up-to-date treatment the Trust could afford, and that the good staff it has employed found working for the Trust attractive.

'Mental Health has a Cinderella role in the National Health Service. It is difficult to compete with other more glamorous parts of the Health hierarchy, like heart and brain surgery. You have to work very hard to keep it on the agenda and it is the selfless efforts of these people which have secured a much better profile for the services for people with mental health complications.

'At first I was somewhat in awe of the big guns around the board table. There were general managers and directors of large national and multinational corporations, professors, QCs, et cetera However, having found myself around the table, I realised that sitting silent just wouldn't work with these guys so I paid close attention and in time I was putting my toe in the water, ending up chairing one or two of the sub-committees.

'I formed a distinct impression that the over-representation of young black men in the Mental Health system was aired more frequently because of my presence, and a little more attention was paid to the causes and their prevention. Slow but, one hopes, sure. Great Britain plc works like that. You have to put back into the system. It's a culture of payback.

'When Riverside Trust was abolished as a result of one of the regular organisational re-thinks of the London Mental Health Service, I was asked to continue as a Director but this time of one of the largest Mental Health NHS Trusts in England, one whose catchment area ranged from Brent to Kensington, Chelsea and Westminster. With some of the busiest rail termini – Victoria and Paddington for starters – this was a mammoth job as each train brought more people from all over the country, Europe and the world in need of care and protection into the arms of the Trust.

'Together with mounting inner-city demands on the service, it's a big job. Once again the commitment of lay persons of note in various fields of endeavour brought a taste of reality and release to the Health professionals, who sometimes were distressed by the sheer volume of work and the public's negative reaction to the sterling things they do with people whom society finds it easier to ignore or to fear in the abstract.

'The job of the Non-Executive Director, for this was what we were called, extended to the legal aspect. To make sure, in an environment where a person can be denied his freedom and can be incarcerated in locked wards if the Health professionals decide he is a risk to himself or others, that a very weather eye is kept on the procedures; to make doubly sure that not only the letter of the law but also its spirit is closely observed.

'Should a patient wish to appeal against a decision, one of the most important duties of the Non-Executive Director is to ensure that this appeal is held as quickly as possible and in an appropriate and fair manner. It is hard, gruelling and very sad work, but that's the job. Unsung but vital.'

Silence reigned for a moment. Then I said, 'How serious you've become. That's a side you don't show too often.'

'Not everything good fi know good fi tell. What I want *you* to tell *me* is how you would like your birthday party to be? Food? Guests? What?'

'Nothing, thank you.'

'OK, that's fine by me. I will continue to plan the menu and invite the guests for a special party on the twenty-third. Don't you dare complain if you don't like what happens. "Nothing" is not an option. I am inviting you now, so please put it in your diary.'

Lord, give me strength.

Jimmy Cliff's 'Many Rivers to Cross' is blaring out and Yvonne is singing along. She never gets the words quite right but this is her theme tune. Says it's one of the finest Jamaican poems. And she continues to sing. Looks like she is in a good mood – must be the thought of that dratted party.

'So you don't know any other song?' I snap. 'One which you might be able to sing in tune, maybe?'

'Can't you let me enjoy myself? Being in Jamaica I can do things I wouldn't dream of doing anywhere else on earth. Like singing Jimmy Cliff at the top of my voice, knowing that it's OK to do this. Like going out to Lime Cay on a rusty old boat which looks like it will never make it across the few miles of water to that most special of places. Remember we filmed some of *The Harder They Come* on Lime Cay at night? Like going out to Port Royal and eating fish and lobster at tables set up in the middle of the street where the cars have to ask permission to sneak through, seeing "peenie wallies" flash their evening glow in the logwood forest around Newcastle, swimming at the University Beach in St Thomas when you are almost sure to have the most beautiful beach in Jamaica all to yourself. Yes, and singing "Many Rivers to Cross". I'll have you know I've sung on the stage. Badly.'

'You said you have gone back to acting on the telly since running away from Talawa. Are we going to get any of these things out here?'

'I doubt it. I did nearly fourteen months in a new series of half-hour programmes called, very imaginatively, *Doctors* and yes, it was set in a medical practice of four or five doctors and two nurses – and yes, I was a nurse. I swore once never to play a nurse ever again, as earlier in my career I had notched up dozens of them. I am supposed to look how the English public think a nice jolly Jamaican nurse should. Little do they know that I almost faint at the sight of blood, and hospitals, waiting rooms, X-rays, injections – they all bring me out in a sweat.

'However, I got the part of Ruth the practice nurse in *Doctors* and stayed with it for two series. Fourteen months doing three episodes a week was hard work, especially as they were filmed at the BBC Pebble Mill Studios in Birmingham. This meant a lot of commuting during one of the worst spells of transport failures in Britain. Sometimes the journey from King's Cross to Birmingham, which should take one hour forty-five minutes, would last four hours. But travel woes aside, it was fun. The regular cast of nine including Yours Truly got on really well together and partied a lot as well as working really very hard indeed.

'Often the schedule would demand that twenty-five pages be filmed in one day. Not much time to muck around, as you got a couple of goes at a rehearsal and then it was record – and in a couple of takes if at all possible. It was quite amazing, the quality of the work produced, when I think back to just how quickly everything was done.

'I was probably the only person in the cast except Christopher Timothy, who played the lead, who could remember the halcyon days of television when one had five days' rehearsal at North Acton, with the producer's run on Thursday, Saturday off and record on Sunday at BBC White City Studios – and this for only one episode of forty-five minutes! Now it's three episodes in five days.

'Of course technology has allowed the technical aspects to be so much more flexible and immediate. Unfortunately the human element, the poor old actor as a species, can't evolve as quickly as machines. As a result the process of acting on television has required a very quick study of the lines and less time than is really necessary for depth of character portrayal. The younger ones, however, cope remarkably well as they have never known anything else and have been trained at drama school to expect to act with people they have sometimes met for the first time minutes before being called on set. The old actors have to put up or shut up. Adjust or die, as they say.

'But *Doctors* as a series got a big following and is still going strong although very few of the original cast are in it now.'

My daughter thought for a minute and said, 'Telly . . . I did a number of episodes on a soap opera, *Family Affairs*, as a mother-in-law from hell. That made a welcome change from a sweet-natured nurse. I could show my true nature, Mummy! I've whipped through *East*

Enders although no one who wasn't looking very carefully would have seen me. I am in a couple of episodes of *Rose and Maloney* and so on. I am cool with being a sort of performing glowworm. No star I. I'm doing other things, too, which I had to put on the back burner during the Talawa years.'

'Like?' I interrupted. This might be interesting. What secrets would be revealed? Unfortunately, visitors arrived at that moment, putting my new career as investigative journalist on hold till tomorrow.

Chapter 27

Ice Cream and Cake

—•⊙•—

'So, young lady: what are you planning to do, now that Talawa is safe?' It was the next day and we were tidying up the plants on the patio.

'Writing. Living. Learning Italian properly. Directing for fun again.'

'That reminds me, exactly where are you living at the moment? London? Italy?'

'In a Ryan Air plane, I think.'

'Come again?'

'Because the Irish airline Ryan Air offers such good deals in flights from Pisa to Stansted, Starr and I almost commute between Florence and London. He still has a lot to do, tidying up things since his father died, and I like Italy so I'm not making a fuss. But Mummy, if I am to enjoy the country properly I really must learn to speak the language. The palaver to get myself understood must be quite comic to watch, as I point to things, mime their use, then throw in the odd noun. I manage quite well buying onions but beyond this it's really impossible.

'You might well wonder how I could have been going to Italy for over thirty years and still can't speak in sentences. I was always around those who spoke English, you see, and this is a disaster, as you don't have to try to make yourself understood. Even those Italians with less English than my Italian insist on speaking English. I

247

found my nouns very helpful in crises as together with *buon giorno, buona sera, bellissima, pane integrale* and *vino rosso* I managed to survive for the few days per year I was there.

'Now it's different as I'm expending more effort. We'll see how I get on. It's quite easy for me to slip into the Italian way of life as it's the closest to the Jamaican anywhere.

'In Africa it may be laidback but there is always the unknown quotient which keeps me from being completely comfortable. I suppose it goes back to my days as a student at Rose Bruford when I was told by Janet Badjan, a Ghanaian who had become a student during my time there, who felt she was being starved of parts because they gave them all to me (quite the opposite was true, but there you go): "OK, Yvonne Clarke, you may think you are the bee's knees here, but in Ghana I am a Princess and you, you are nothing but a mongrel." This enlisted the pathetic response from me: 'Janet Badjan, I would rather be a mongrel and look like me than a Princess and look like you.' Not the most elegant of rejoinders. She did ask for it, I feel.'

'Too damn right she did. Facety woman, calling my daughter a mongrel!'

'Chill out, Mrs Clarke. Like it or not, I find an underlying attitude of arrogant superiority, even dislike, from many of our African brothers and sisters towards their relatives from the Caribbean. Something about their purity of origin always manages to make itself felt. This has improved considerably over the last half a century or so, but it sometimes still rears its ugly head.

'Discussions with some of my great Nigerian friends, especially Femi Euba, lead me to believe it may have something to do with the generation of Caribbean people who were taught that there was nothing of interest or worth in Africa, having difficulty, understandably, in relating to the generation of Africans who regard the descendants of those who survived the Middle Passage as damaged goods who have no culture of their own. So for me, much as I enjoy visits to Africa, I still feel I need to know more to be comfortable.

'In Italy I feel no threat at all, as there is nothing that I am supposed to understand instinctively by nature of my race. I am totally foreign and as such I can be totally Jamaican – which I must tell you is quite a good thing to be there. Ask Merlene Ottey.

'Not long ago there was an open-air concert in the central square of Pisa. On the bill were the I threes, Linton Kwesi Johnson, the Dennis Bovell Band and Jean Binta Breeze. For this line-up the square was crammed full. More than twenty thousand people rocked the night away. They sure love Jamaicans just as they are, in Tuscany anyway. Suits me. Then there is the essential style which accompanies every store-front display – every bottle of wine, bit of stationery, slice of foccacia, T-shirt, hand basin and cup of espresso. Makes you enjoy making the effort to celebrate the scenery, the weather, the latest Armani, the latest scandal with such energy.'

Whoops! Here comes nostalgia. 'Your father loved Italy,' I remind her, 'probably because they often mistook him for a Neapolitan. Remember you telling me how he responded to the Italians who spoke to him by giving them his best flowery Spanish. Lovely old fool. So while we are on to Italy, tell me how you really feel about spending so much time in San Francesco?'

'The first time I went to San Francesco with Starr, who had not mentioned one word about the existence of this marvellous place in Florence, is etched in my memory. We got a taxi from the station and in a few minutes we were set down in front of some massive green gates with a large *Passo caribile* (No parking) sign emblazoned

249

on them. In answer to Starr's ring the gates flew open and there stood three or four Italians who I was soon to learn were members of the Ceri family who have lived in San Francesco and looked after its inhabitants for a number of generations. The eldest Ceri, Piero, kept repeating what sounded to me like Stalin, but was really the diminutive of Starr, Starling.

'Many salutations and kisses and bravos later, Starr and I were in a splendid bedroom with frescos of some very active nymphs frolicking naked on the walls, and looming larger than life in the middle of the room an enormous fourposter bed. I was just a little non-plussed. Who exactly were these people, and where exactly did this marvellous house fit into the scheme of things?

'"Oh, Cloclo my aunt and Harry live here, amongst others." Full stop. That's all I got. The old monastery was spectacular enough, but nothing prepared me for the gardens. Acres of gently tamed parkland filled with cypress, ilex, olive and fig trees and pulsating with wild mint, laurel, rosemary and sage. Sounds almost Shake-spearean, doesn't it? And in fact, it's the perfect set for *As You Like It*.

'From the top of the hill the view over all Florence is nothing short of magnificent. It is peace personified and where, if I find I have to prepare for a job – especially directing a big show– I can retire for a week or two and find the answers. Also, writing comes very easy in this heavenly place.'

'You mentioned writing as something you intend to do now. Coming from you, who have always said you couldn't even write a letter – and I have many to prove it – what kind of turnaround is this?'

'I have always written stuff but never shown it to anybody. I don't write to be an author, I write to think.'

'I have one of the stories you thought no one has ever

seen. Remember this? Written when you were but a
child. Listen up, girl.

A Light in the Dark by Yvonne Clarke

The frosted glass in the staffroom door shook. Miss
Harris had made another of her dramatic entrances
and the members of staff obligingly paused mid-
sentence, yoghurt crispy apple mouths half-
opened, waiting for the outburst.

'If that girl crosses my path once more this week
I shall murder her!'

'Which one is it this time?'

'I give you ten guesses.'

'Not necessary. Lovely Lady Light.'

'Light's her name. Dark's her brain.'

'Witty.'

Much laughter.

'What's another word for inept? Eight letters
dash dash s u dash . . . ' and crunchtime continued
as before.

Jasmine Light is thirteen years old. A tall, striking girl with a proud cropped head and very long
athletic legs. Her mother came to London so long
ago she remembers only the good things about
Jamaica and gets very uptight when you ask her
why she left in the first place if it was so lovely.

'Chile, no badder me nuh. Pay attention to you
Bible and yuh lesson dem, and lef'me alone. Choh.'

The end of the third year at school is very
important because there are tests to decide which
subjects you will continue doing in the fourth
year. It is those subjects which will determine
what you are fit for when you leave school. Jasmine Light wanted to be a Lab Technician chiefly
because when the Careers Officer talked to the
girls once, it sounded exciting. For days afterwards

Jasmine told everyone that she would be a Lab Technician.

'So you want to be a Lab Technician, do you, Jasmine? Have you any idea in your tiny mind what the requirements are for the job?'

'No, Miss, I thought you could find out for me.'

'Very well, Miss Light, you need Biology, Physics, Maths and English. I suggest you now stop thinking about such ridiculous things and get on with your work.'

The work at that moment was Cookery.

Jasmine decided that Biology, Physics, Maths and English were going to receive a lot of her attention.

'Jasmine, what kind of caper you going on with?' This from her best friend Brigit. 'Lab Technician? I just want to get out of here as quickly as possible. You should really try and get up your typing speed because you're quite good at that and it will help you. Come on, Jasmine, they weren't talking to you about those fancy jobs, you know.'

'They won't take me seriously, Mum. I'm typing material and that's it. Couldn't you write a letter to the Head, Mum, and tell her what I want to do? It's not too late. *Please*, Mum.'

'Now anybody ever see my dying trial dis day, Lawd? I mus' write to Headmissis. What I must write, ehn? You tell me dat? After I doan even know what Lab Technician is. You just better mind dem doan trow you outta de school with all you foolishness. You doan have no homework?'

'Read any good plasma lately?' was the one halfway decent joke Andy, Jasmine's boyfriend, could manage as he combed his wild and wonderful Afro and regretted the watermarks on his brand new three and a half inch heels. 'Blimey, Jasmine, you don't half look terrible these days. Too much Biology.' Only half joking, menacing. Andy was a catch.

Exams came. Jasmine swotted. Jasmine failed Typing, Cookery, Biology, Physics, Maths and English. Everything.

'So you gaan an' fail all the exams dem! Jesus in Heaven. I did tell you to listen to de teacher.'

Silence.

'Who you tink goin' look afer you wen you caan get no job?'

Silence

'You just come outta de place, mek I do my work you hear.'

That evening when the school stood alone, Jasmine climbed the fence, finished breaking a pane of glass and unlawfully entered GLC property. First she paid the staffroom a visit, then the cookery room, the typewriters were heavy and finally the Lab where every tinkle of broken glass spurred her on.

She knew they were there long before the lights went on. She was exhausted anyway . . .

This story always shocks me. Gently I said, 'Yvonne, there is a deep anger here.'

'Maybe. Wherever did you find that?'

'I stole it. Good thing you didn't give up the day job.'

'It was outrageous of you to root around and steal my things. This was never meant to see the light of day and all you can say instead of apologising is "Don't give up the day job." Kathleen Clarke, you are incorrigible. You listen up, now. The birthday party is all arranged and the only thing missing is your dress. I don't see anything vaguely suitable in your wardrobe. So come along – we're going shopping.'

And I go. It might be fun. But before I go, did I tell you that she tried this birthday party business on me ten years ago when she swooped down from on high and arranged what turned out to be my eightieth birthday celebration? In four days she arranged a sit-down four-course meal for eighty people. Eight tables seating ten people each. White tiny fairy-lights in the garden up every tree and hedge and bush. Every eighty-year-old fogey she could find seemed to be there, with a sprinkling of younger folks.

Apparently transportation was the most taxing aspect of this operation as all the old dears had to be collected from near and far and ferried gently into my garden. Hence the younger folk – for their cars, of course. I was supposed to be in the dark about these plans, and like the good sport I am, I went along with it. Did, however, take my ancient Schiaparelli dress down to the office and changed there to enable my entrance. Surprised I duly was. Wow!

What *did* surprise me was this beautiful black man dressed for all the world like Liberace. He was called Burroace. Can't think why, as he did not resemble a donkey at all. However, there he was on my entrance, playing my very favourite Nat King Cole: 'Dinner for One, Please, James' on Valerie's baby grand, dangerously topped by candelabra. Dramatic. I was impressed and moved to see so many people I thought had died and not been brought to Sam Isaacs for their funerals.

Back to the ninetieth-birthday-party shopping spree. When I was in my youth I loved Schiaparelli pink and I still love it. They say you always imagine yourself still looking as you did when you were in your pink. It's true in my case and how fantastic when there, on show in the most expensive boutique in Kingston, was a dream of a dress, my size, not too mutton-dressed-as-lamb and in Schiaparelli pink. Caution thrown to the wind, Yvonne's plastic was bent. Good for her, but I have always paid for everything in cash. Doesn't feel the same to hand over a piece of plastic.

During the shopping trip I finally came clean. I told her what I really wanted the party to be, and blow me down, she actually listened. And I got it. I didn't want lots of people milling around with me having to make small talk, which I dislike intensely. I wanted to have every member of the family, from Great-grandson Shane to Mervys, my faithful housekeeper, to be there on the patio, and we would all have homemade ice cream and cake. Second childhood, know what I mean? And thus it came to pass and it was wonderful. The heavens opened at exactly six o'clock and everyone had to rush inside with ice cream melting and cake crumbling and laughter and song and love. Lovely. Happy Birthday, after all.

Y's ticket is up. She must go back to her unforgiving city. And I must bid farewell.

'So you're living, writing, learning more than nouns in Italian, and directing and acting for fun. You are blessed, you know, being able to do what you want to do. In fact, you have really done what you wanted to do all your life.'

'For that, Mother, I give thanks.' And she's gone.

Afterword

You need a fair amount of confidence, tenacity and straightforward balls to succeed in the life my daughter chose. That's why I get so het up when a visit from her looms. You see, I'm not sure I will live up to her expectations. Truth is, I knew the birthday party would be just great in the end, but I couldn't seem to let on what I wanted until the eleventh hour. It is chronic with me, this inability to show emotion. In fact, it's my nerves which have made me write all this down. Kept me busy.

There is a clever young woman, a talented sister of Barbara Gloudon named Lorna Goodison, who wrote the poem 'I Am Becoming My Mother'. Very clever, very good. Yvonne sent it to me once. I certainly never became *my* mother. Hilda's influence was negative in most respects and I managed to put her and them out of my mind quite successfully.

But I begin to see Yvonne becoming me and there is nothing I can do about it. The nervousness I am prey to these days comes from being able to second-guess her, pretending I can't but all the while knowing for sure she knows I can and I do.

You see, I have always had to keep my own counsel, and with this love of privacy found a welcome role in the masquerade as a sort of pontificator, the One Who Knows. I have never been able to drop the mask. It is frightening now to see it very much in place on my child's face. I like looking at photographs. Change is the enemy of memory and they don't change. I have a likeness of Claude staring down at me from the wall, fixed for ever in a knowing smile. Among my gallery of likenesses are many of Y.

A recent arrival is one in her yellow and blue robes receiving her Honorary Doctorate from the Open University, which goes right beside the one with the gong from Her Majesty. Takes me back to the time when she was regarded as the not-so-bright sister, the ugly duckling, the troublesome one from the Rose Bruford days who was never expected to succeed but who is now a Patron and Fellow of that august institution, and here she is in her doctoral robes. What a turn-up for the books. Perhaps if they had liked her more, given her an easier ride, she would have settled for seductive safety. Thank God she didn't. Hasn't. I wonder if she knows I am really a little proud of her resilience?

Go, girl. There's more to do.

Walk good.